JUST DRIVE

ANCHOR POINT, BOOK 1

L.A. WITT

Copyright Information

Just Drive, Anchor Point Book 1

Second edition

Copyright © 2016, 2022 L.A. Witt

First edition published by Riptide Publishing.

Cover Art by L.C. Chase

ISBN: 978-1-64230-921-8

Print ISBN: 979-8-36290-994-9

❦ Created with Vellum

ABOUT JUST DRIVE

For Sean Wright, driving a cab in the tiny Navy town of Anchor Point isn't an exciting job . . . until he picks up just-dumped Paul Richards. A drive turns into a walk on the pier, which turns into the hottest hookup Sean's had in ages.

After a long overdue breakup, Paul can't believe his luck. Of all the drivers, he's picked up by the gorgeous, gay, and very willing Sean. Younger guys aren't usually his thing, but Paul can't resist.

One taste and neither man can get enough . . . right up until they realize that Paul is Sean's father's commanding officer and the last man Sean should be involved with.

With two careers on the line, their only option is to back off. It's not easy, though; the sex and the emotional connection are exactly what both men have been craving for a long time. But Paul has devoted twenty-four years to his career and his dream of making admiral. If he's caught with Sean, that's all over. He has to choose—stay the course, or trade it all for the man who drove off with his heart.

This book was previously published.

CHAPTER 1

SEAN

"JUST DRIVE."

The voice from the backseat was quiet and flat. Not rude, not demanding, but not all that friendly either. Which was fine—people called the company for a cab, not conversation.

I didn't move, though. Tapping my thumbs on the wheel, I looked in the rearview. I couldn't see him very well; he'd taken the seat directly behind mine, and he was staring out the window toward the strip mall across the street. What little of his face made it to the mirror was heavily shadowed thanks to the bright lights from the hotel's reception area.

"Um." I cleared my throat. "I need an address. Or the name of a place." I glanced at the screen with the message from dispatch. My passenger had specifically requested someone with base access. "Do you want to go to the base?"

He released a long breath, and clothes and upholstery rustled as he shifted behind me. "You get paid by time or distance?"

Dude, what the hell? You want to go somewhere or not?

"Distance. Unless I'm waiting for you."

He turned toward me. Shadows slipped far enough off his face to give me a glimpse of tired eyes and prominent, angular features. "Whatever the meter says at the end of the night, I'll double it." He faced the window again. "Just drive."

I bit back my frustration. "Where?"

"Anywhere." He seemed to be focused on something outside. All I could see was the outline of the back of his head and neck, and the top of his jacket collar. In a voice so low I wondered if he was speaking to me or himself, he added, "I'm not ready to go home, and I sure as fuck can't stay here."

I glanced at the hotel he'd come out of. Message received. I put the car in drive, pulled out of the reception area, and turned onto the road. Maybe he'd be more willing to cough up a destination once this place had disappeared into the rearview.

Suit yourself, dude. I'm holding you to that double fare.

Admittedly, I was curious. If this was a walk of shame, he wouldn't be the first. I'd picked up plenty of people who were slinking out after a one-night stand they obviously regretted, and a few who needed to make a quick exit before they were busted by a partner who wouldn't be pleased. Then there were the people who'd obviously had an amazing night—maybe with a stranger, maybe not—and grinned all the way back to their own places. Hotel pickups in this town were nothing if not interesting.

This guy hadn't been carrying a bag when he'd come out. Eyes down, hands in his jacket pockets, he'd walked like he was on autopilot. Maybe he'd been kicked out by someone who was still in a room with his luggage? Or he and someone else had rented a room for a short time, and things hadn't gone as planned?

I wasn't clairvoyant, so I wasn't going to figure it out.

For a solid ten minutes, the only sounds in my car were the AC and the road noise as I followed the gritty highway toward town. I didn't even have the radio on—I never did when I had a passenger—but I was tempted right then to find some music. With my luck, though, I'd probably put on some song that would annoy him, or would strike some nerve. Like the time a guy had gotten into my car and, when a particularly sad country song came on, started bawling about the woman who'd just dumped him. That had been one long, awkward ride.

So yeah. Radio *off*.

I subtly tapped my thumbs on the wheel, keeping the beat of the song that had been stuck in my head all night. It was something to do, anyway.

From time to time, I caught a glimpse of pale light hinting at his features. He must've been doing something on his phone. Maybe a few texts to get in the last word with whoever he'd left in that hotel room or something. I had no idea. He stayed silent, which most passengers did, but for some reason, that silence made me twitch. Probably because I still had no idea where the hell he wanted to go.

We were getting close to downtown now. There weren't a lot of options for directions, but if I got on the highway and headed north or south, there were some stretches where we could go five or ten miles with no place to turn around.

"So, um." I hesitated. I sucked at small talk, and it didn't seem welcome anyway, but I did need some more information from him. "Any, uh, particular direction?"

My passenger was silent for about half a block. "Maybe down by the water."

I bit back an impatient sigh. This was a Navy town, hugging the strip of land between a national forest and the Pacific Ocean. There was no such thing as *not* down by the water.

Dude, where *down by the water?*

Well, whatever. As long as he didn't get annoyed with me for lacking the psychic abilities to know where he wanted to go.

I made a left and headed toward the pier at the south edge of town, and hoped that would satisfy him. Most of the shops and restaurants on the pier and the boardwalk would be closed this time of night, but if he didn't like it, he could give me something more specific.

Then, he broke the silence. "You get a lot of business in a small town like this?"

"That depends." I glanced in the rearview. "You looking to become a driver?"

He laughed quietly, and I caught a hint of smoke in his voice as he said, "No. No. Just making conversation."

"Oh." I hadn't expected him to want conversation, but okay. "Business is all right. It's only a part-time gig for me. During the week is kind of quiet, but the weekends, I scrape up all the Sailors stumbling out of bars."

Another laugh. I decided I liked the way he laughed. Probably because it was better than uncomfortable silence.

"Somebody's got to do it, right?" he mused.

"Yeah." I wasn't sure what else to say, and silence fell again.

The pier was coming up fast, and I was ready for this ride to be over, but then he leaned forward and gestured up ahead. "There's a 7-Eleven on the left. Could you stop there?"

"Yeah. Sure." I pulled into the parking lot.

"I'll be right back." He unbuckled his seat belt and opened the door, but paused. "Do you want anything?"

I looked at him in the rearview. "What?"

His reflection's eyes met mine. Wow, they were blue. "I was going to get something to drink. You want anything?"

"Um." I glanced down at the water bottle that had been empty in my cup holder for a while now. "You don't... you don't have to—"

"I'll feel less guilty about making you drive me all over town."

Oh hell. Why not? "I could go for some water. Thanks."

He smiled, crinkling the corners of his eyes, and yeah, I needed some water. Something cold, anyway. Jesus.

"All right. I'll be back."

With that, he was out of the car, and I exhaled hard, sagging against my seat. I didn't dislike the guy, and he'd been perfectly polite since I'd picked him up, but I had to admit it was nice to have a short break from that weird silence. I also turned on the radio, but kept the volume way, way down. It was loud enough I'd be able to hear it, but soft enough that, if he noticed it at all, he might believe it had been on the entire time. Why did I care, anyway? We were in my car. We weren't talking. Let me listen to some goddamned music.

Through the 7-Eleven's windows, I finally got a good look at him as he paid the cashier. He was vaguely familiar too, but the fact that he needed to get on base explained that —I drove people on and off post all the time, and I went there myself because my dad was stationed there. It was entirely possible I'd seen this guy at the commissary, in a parking lot, at the gym. The base wasn't as big as Norfolk or San Diego—not by a long shot—so paths crossed on a regular basis.

He didn't have a high-and-tight like the NCOs on the base. His light-brown hair was still short and neat, if not as severe as it was in the younger guys under my dad's command. Even though his fatigue was visible from here— tired eyes, slightly downturned shoulders—he still carried himself like someone who'd worn a uniform for the better part of his life. He stood straight, and if he walked that fast when he was obviously exhausted, he must've been impossible to keep up with the rest of the time. Obviously military, but that was no shock in this town.

After he'd paid, he came back to the car, and he sat on the passenger side of the backseat this time. When I twisted around to take the water bottle he'd brought for me, we made real eye contact for the first time. He also held that eye contact like someone who flinched away from nobody.

"Here you go." He handed a water bottle over the seat.

"Thanks." I glanced at the one he was uncapping. It was the same brand of water as mine. "I figured you were getting a *drink*."

He glanced at the bottle in his hand and shrugged. "Nah. I'm going to feel shitty enough tomorrow. No point in adding to it."

"Fair enough."

He took a deep swallow and leaned back against the seat. I drank a bit too. I was still watching him the whole time, which was much easier now that he wasn't directly behind me. And, God, the light spilling out from the 7-Eleven made him much easier to see too, and up close, he was smoking hot. He was definitely older than me—he had a few lines, and I could make out a few grays too. That didn't necessarily mean much. The military had a habit of aging people prematurely. All the guys I knew looked at least five years older than they were. Ten if they'd been to combat.

So I couldn't tell how old he was, only that he definitely wasn't twenty anymore. Older guys weren't really my thing, but time had been kind to him, and I hoped my heart wasn't beating as loudly as it seemed to be. Of course he wouldn't be able to hear it, but rational thought had gone MIA right then.

When he'd spoken earlier, there'd been a distinctive hint of gravel in his voice, and he had the same creases at the edges of his mouth that both my parents did. If he wasn't a smoker now, he had been at one point in his life. Considering he hadn't stopped outside the 7-Eleven for a smoke, and I couldn't smell any on him, he must've quit.

And why was I so interested in him? Half the time I forgot what my passengers looked like five minutes after they left my car, but this guy needed to be memorized for some reason.

He took another drink, drawing my attention to his slim lips, his jaw, his neck...

I turned back around, nearly unloading my own drink into my lap before I managed to swallow a gulp. Meeting his gaze again—this time in the safety of the rearview—I said, "So, you want to keep driving around?"

He nodded. "Yeah. I still don't know where I want to go."

"Okay."

So I drove. With the road to hold my attention, at least I wasn't staring at him anymore. Even with the radio playing softly in the background, the lack of conversation was more unnerving now that I'd let myself shamelessly check him out. It was one thing to have a weirdly silent passenger. It was another to have a smoking-hot one, especially when I was a few months into the dry spell from hell.

Note to self—don't check out passengers if you haven't gotten laid recently.

I fidgeted as subtly as I could. Thank God for the darkness, so my very attractive and very quiet passenger couldn't see me surreptitiously adjusting myself. Not that he'd have noticed—he was playing on his phone again.

Out of nowhere, he broke the silence. "Christ, I'm such an idiot."

I tapped the wheel. What was I supposed to say to that?

He let his head fall back against the headrest. "You ever wonder why perfectly functional adults turn into utter morons when they're in relationships?"

"Um." I cleared my throat. "Happens to all of us, I think."

"Yeah." He laughed bitterly. "Maybe one of these days I'll learn."

"You'd be the first."

"Probably." He scrubbed a hand over his face and exhaled. "I just... I mean, the worst part is when you invest so much time and energy into a relationship even when you know it's over, and then feel like a moron when it *is* over."

Oh, that explained it. A hotel room breakup. I wondered if he'd gone there expecting to spend a more pleasant evening with his girlfriend, and then found himself single and in the back of my car. Poor dude.

"Sorry to hear it," I said.

"My own damn fault for not putting on the brakes months ago." He muttered something I didn't understand, and shook his head as he looked out the window again. "Didn't have the balls I guess. Can't even be mad that—" He paused and cleared his throat. "Well, I wasn't going to do it. Guess I should be grateful someone finally dropped the hammer."

He went on, mostly rambling about breakups and doomed relationships that seem to go on forever until someone finally works up the courage to call it off. I wasn't sure exactly what he was trying to rationalize, but God knew I'd been there—searching every angle of a breakup to find silver linings and explanations so it wouldn't hurt quite as much.

As he talked, I listened. It was usually my drunk passengers who did this—talking to the window like they didn't even need to be heard as much as they needed to get it out of their system—but he seemed pretty sober. Sober enough to know he was in a car with a stranger. I couldn't help feeling bad for him. This town wasn't huge, but the only person he could find to unload all this shit on was me?

Jesus, man. How lonely are *you?*

Though it was a Navy town. People came and went. Loneliness was par for the course. Didn't I know it?

"Anyway." He blew out a breath. "I'm sorry. You probably didn't get this job to listen to people whine about their boyfriends."

"It's okay. I've been—" *Wait, did he say* boyfriends? I muffled a cough. "I've been there, believe me."

"Sorry to hear it."

"Likewise."

For a few seconds, silence. Then, "Well, that's what I get for trying to maintain a relationship in the military. All it takes is a change of assignment, and..."

I sighed. "The Navy giveth, and the Navy taketh away."

"Yes. Yes, it does." He ran a hand through his hair. "It most definitely does."

And for the hundredth time tonight, I had no idea what to say. He didn't speak either, and I kept driving.

A sign caught my eye. Somehow, I'd circled back toward the pier where we'd been heading earlier.

"Why don't you go ahead and park up there?" he said. "I could stand to get some fresh air, I think."

"Sure." I parked in front of the weathered driftwood fence at the end of the pier.

"I think I might go walk for a while." He unbuckled his seat belt. "You don't have to wait. I can, um, call another driver."

"It's all right. I'm already here." I paused. "I can turn off the meter too."

His eyebrows rose. "You don't have to do that."

I shrugged. "Seems like you could use a little time to clear your head." I switched off the meter. "Won't do you any good if it's costing you by the minute."

My passenger exhaled slowly. "That's... I really appreciate that. Are you sure, though?"

I nodded. "It's fine."

"Okay. Uh, thanks." He opened the door, then paused again. "You want to join me?"

Yes. Yes, I do. I have no idea why, but I do.

I shook my head, though, and killed the engine. "I'll stay here. Take as much time as you need."

He hesitated again, holding my gaze in the mirror. I thought he might say something else, but all he did was mutter something about being back in a little while, and got out.

The door shut, and it was just me, the barely audible radio, and my thumping heart. Sweaty hands on the wheel, I watched him walk toward the pier, then out onto it. He stopped a short ways down, at the far edge of a streetlight's wide circle, and rested his forearms on the railing. He gazed out at something, and I gazed out at him.

He was impossible to read, especially from this far away, but I could empathize. I knew what overdue breakups were like. Even if they were a long time coming, they still sucked, and there were still pieces to pick up.

My stomach tightened. I'd been there. God, I'd been there. And the worst part of my last breakup had been being alone. Completely alone. Dad had been deployed. It was back before we'd moved in with his girlfriend, so I'd been holding down the fort by myself. We'd only been in this town a few months by then, and everyone I could talk to had been scattered all over both coasts and various places overseas. I could text, call, email, but at the end of the day I'd been alone, and stayed that way, and I'd hated it.

I watched my passenger, who still watched something in the distance. Maybe that was why he'd asked me to just drive him around instead of taking him straight home. Maybe it was why he'd invited me to join him while he walked around out there.

Maybe he knew as well as I did how lonely a guy could be in a town of forty thousand.

To hell with it.

I got out of the car, locked it, and started after him.

CHAPTER 2

PAUL

FROM WHERE I stood on that empty wooden pier, the glow of the base was more than visible—it was unavoidable. This part of town was fairly dark, but a few miles up the coast, warm light swelled from behind the hills. Before the base, Anchor Point had probably been one of those places that would get so dark, you could see stars people in major cities didn't know existed. Not anymore.

A peninsula stuck out far enough to block any view of the actual base or the brightly lit pier. Fine. I knew it all by heart. The razor-wire-topped fences. The armed sentries patrolling under spotlights that belonged over a prison yard. The ships with their white hull numbers lit up. Rows of drab utilitarian buildings. Slate-gray metal and white painted stripes and stern Restricted Area signs everywhere. All the places where dock workers and Sailors took their smoke breaks. That one stretch between the aircraft carrier and the supply ship where the seagulls were so aggressive, nobody dared walk through with a visible bag from Subway or Burger King. I couldn't see any of it from here, but it was clear as day in my mind. Six months in that place and I already knew it like the back of my hand.

Tonight, NAS Adams was the last place I wanted to be. Well, second to last. The Sand Dollar Motel definitely topped the list, at least until Jayson checked out tomorrow and left town, probably never to return.

Releasing a breath, I shifted my gaze to the water below me. It was barely visible—only a few flecks of light picked out the gently rolling waves as the tide lapped at the pylons —but it was something to look at besides the glow of the base.

Bases like NAS Adams had been my life for the last twenty-four years. They would be for the next... well, until I retired. And for the most part, I was okay with that. I loved the Navy. I loved my job. I'd worked my ass off, and I was proud of where I was.

But my relationship with Jayson wasn't the first casualty of my career. An instructor at the Academy had once told me that I was married to the Navy, and anyone else who came along would be one more in a string of mistresses who'd be gone as soon as the novelty wore off. Back then, he'd sounded so cynical and jaded, especially to a cocky teenager with stars in his eyes. Specifically, the embroidered stars on an admiral's shoulders.

Twenty-four years, two wedding rings, and too many breakups later, as yet another "mistress" disappeared over the horizon, I decided that instructor might've been onto something after all.

I probably had as much to do with it as the Navy, too. Looking at my track record, a happy, lasting relationship seemed about as attainable as my next rank—I couldn't make things work with a partner any more than I could apparently persuade the Navy to put me in command of a ship, and without commanding a ship, I could kiss that promotion to admiral good-bye.

I really am a fucking shipwreck, aren't I?

And I decided that walking out of the 7-Eleven without that pack of Marlboros had been a really bad idea. I hadn't smoked in eight years, but God, I wanted to start again tonight. Just one cigarette. Maybe two. *Something* to settle my goddamned nerves. Something in my mouth, damn it.

I could always have the driver take me to Flatstick. Good a time as any to check out the local scenery.

From what I'd heard, Flatstick had several gay bars, and even though this was a Wednesday night, the places would be packed with single men. Probably wouldn't take much to find some horny guy to help get my mind off Jayson. Maybe it wasn't the healthiest outlet, but it was probably better than giving in to that latent nicotine craving. It'd keep my mouth busy too.

Scrubbing a hand over my face, I sighed. God, I was pathetic.

Well, at least it was over. Jayson and I weren't playing chicken anymore. After too many months, he'd finally blinked, and after a short, painful conversation, we'd wished each other the best, shared a long hug—I hadn't dared kiss him or I'd never have made it out the door—and now we could get on with our lives. God knew I had enough practice at moving on after shit like this. I should've been good at it by now.

And I supposed I was. Especially since I'd seen this coming a mile away. If anything, I was just getting used to the idea that the inevitable had finally happened, and after months of anticipating, obsessing, losing sleep, I wasn't quite sure what to do with myself.

All I needed to do was suck it up, maybe go out and get laid, and get over it. Then I could get on—

Footsteps snapped me out of my thoughts.

I turned my head as the streetlight illuminated my cab driver. My pulse jumped. "Oh. Hey." I glanced at my watch. "Did you need to—"

"I decided to take you up on the offer." He slipped his hands into his pockets and avoided my eyes. "If it's still open, I mean. To join you."

Pretending my heart hadn't shifted into overdrive, I nodded. "Yeah. Sure." I cleared my throat and mirrored him, putting my hands in my own pockets as I faced him. "You don't mind wandering around with a stranger?"

He chuckled, which did weird things to my blood pressure. "I like walking on the wild side sometimes."

"Can't promise it'll be all that wild, hanging around with an old guy who needs some fresh air."

He gave me a quick and almost subtle down-up. With a shrug, he said, "More exciting than letting the radio put me to sleep in the car."

I laughed. "Fair enough."

We stood in silence for a moment. Then I gestured toward the end of the pier, and we started walking.

It was kind of weird to be out here with no one else in sight. During the day, especially during the summer, this pier would be teeming with people. It reminded me a little of Santa Monica. Or at least, a place that desperately wanted to be Santa Monica. It was half carnival, half beach, with people fishing, boating, playing fairway games, drinking. The smell of seawater would be almost completely masked by the heavy scents of funnel cakes, popcorn, and elephant ears.

Tonight, though, it was just us. Just me and this cab

driver who didn't seem to mind strolling along a deserted pier with some idiot he'd picked up from a hotel. Up ahead, I thought I saw the vague shadow of someone fishing over the railing. There were some muffled voices in the distance too, though I couldn't tell if they were coming from farther down the pier or back on land. But for the most part, it was us, the smell of the ocean, and the gentle sloshing of the tide.

We moved between light and shadow, in and out of the milky beams of overhead streetlights. In some places, I couldn't even see the boards beneath our feet. A few steps later, everything was visible, from the rusty bolts holding it all together to the spackle of seagull shit and petrified chewing gum that foot traffic had pounded down into the aging wood.

About halfway down the pier, the driver slowed a little and took in a deep breath through his nose. "Man, I love it down here. Especially when it's practically empty."

"Yeah, it's nice." No Sailors, no ships—what wasn't to love? "You come here a lot?"

"Yeah." He stared up ahead at the light-shadow-light of the empty pier. "My ex loved this place." He paused, swallowed, and added in a barely audible whisper, "This was always his favorite spot to fish."

He turned slightly, as if glancing at me to see if I'd caught that pronoun.

Oh, yes. I caught it. Don't you worry.

Blood pounded in my ears. Maybe he didn't need to drive me down to Flatstick after all.

I shook myself and shoved that thought out of my mind. He was probably half my age, and even if he had taken me up on my offer to join me out here, that didn't mean he wanted to hook up. I was being an idiot. A desperate, freshly dumped idiot who couldn't tell a nicotine craving from a hard-on, and would probably be better off picking up a pack of Marlboros before going home to feel sorry for myself while I let him get on with his shift.

Though as we strolled down the pier and I stole a few glances at him, I had to admit he was walking temptation if I'd ever seen it. His jaw had a fine dusting of five-o'clock shadow, and every time his dark eyes darted my way, my whole body tingled. As soon as I'd snapped out of my haze in the car and actually looked at him, I'd noticed his dyed-black hair, but now the streetlights picked out some cobalt highlights. Why did that make my body temperature rise? Wild colors didn't usually do it for me, but something about the blue and black was perfect on him.

He was a little shorter than me, and from his straight back and set shoulders, he was no stranger to the gym. The thought of him lifting made my knees weak.

Anytime you need a spotter, do give me a call.

I shook myself again. What the hell? He was a kid, for god's sake. He couldn't have been older than twenty-five, and I doubted he was even that old. Unbearably hot? Absolutely. Someone I had any business checking out? Not even a little.

And I knew damn well it wasn't him screwing with my senses. He was gorgeous, but I knew me, and I knew why I was looking at him this way. I had half a mind to go back to the car and tell him to take me to Flatstick. Grieving a relationship happened in very predictable stages for me, and I was already past the first stage: berating myself for whatever I'd done to screw things up. Not an hour later, I was well into stage two: needing to get screwed until I couldn't think and couldn't walk. Hell, I'd already reinstalled Grindr while in the backseat of the cab. A little effort and a few messages, and I could be on my way into another man's bed before too long.

But I stayed out here on this pier with the cute young cab driver who'd declined, then accepted, my offer to join me.

That didn't mean it was his bed I should be trying to get into, though. He was working, not clubbing or prowling around in search of another desperate, horny guy like I was.

He slowed his gait again and glanced at me. "So, um. I didn't catch your name."

"Paul. Yours?"

"Sean." Silence tried to work its way in again, but he cleared his throat. "I guess there are worse places to hang out when you're having a rough night, right?" He cringed, grimacing like the words had sounded better in his head than in the air.

"Well, it's either this or a bar." I shrugged. "And I didn't really feel like drinking tonight."

"Yeah, that's what you said. About not wanting to feel like shit tomorrow."

"No shittier than I already do," I muttered.

"Sorry to hear it."

"Eh, it is what it is." I fixed my gaze on the water. What I could see of it, anyway. "Long-distance relationships are hard. You spend most of your time wishing you were together, and then when you *are* together, you spend the whole time dreading the day he has to leave. Without any light at the end of the tunnel, knowing you might have to move and end up even farther apart makes it really hard." I paused, realizing a little too late that I'd been running off at the mouth. "I'm sorry. You... probably didn't come out here to—"

"It's okay." He glanced at me, and his shy smile settled my nerves. "I've been there. I get it."

"Really?"

Sean nodded. "Yeah. I was dating a guy when I moved here last year." Sighing, he looked out at the water. "*That* was over in a hurry."

"Ouch."

"Yeah. But like you said—it is what it is." He rolled his shoulders beneath his jacket. "Probably wouldn't have lasted much longer anyway." He didn't sound bitter or angry. A little resigned, maybe, but not like it was a raw nerve or an open wound. "Long-distance relationships can work, but they're fucking hard."

"They really are." I paused. "It's a shame yours didn't work out."

"Nah." He gestured dismissively and kept his gaze fixed on the dark water. "It probably sped up the inevitable. Me coming out here, I mean."

I nodded. "Sometimes it does." I exhaled. "I, uh... Sorry to be a bit of a downer."

"No, it's okay." He turned toward me, and his faint, shy smile made my breath catch. "Seemed like you could use some company. So..."

I swallowed, facing forward again. "Much appreciated. Kind of, um, seems like going above and beyond for your customers. I hope I'm not asking too—"

"No, not at all. Not, um... not at all."

We exchanged glances, then kept walking in silence.

After a while, we stopped by the railing. I wasn't even sure why. Or who initiated it. We just... stopped. For a minute or two, neither of us said anything. I couldn't think of anything that wouldn't sound weird, stupid, or plain old desperate, and I was somewhat afraid that if I opened my mouth, something really awkward would tumble out. Something to the effect of *I could definitely use some company* or *I'm pretty sure that motel still has rooms available.* I didn't even know if it was him, or if it was my near-desperate need to fuck Jayson out of my system.

As subtly as I could, I looked him up and down in the blanched light. Yeah, he would definitely be on my radar even if I hadn't been dumped tonight. A little young for anything more than a roll in the hay—what the hell would a good-looking twentysomething want with a cynical burnt-out bastard in his forties?—but attractive as fuck, especially now that I knew we played for the same team.

Seemingly oblivious to how much work it was taking for me to *not* hit on him, Sean folded his arms on the railing and leaned over them. "By the way, I hope I wasn't out of line earlier. Thinking you'd gone in for a drink instead of..."

I laughed. "No, it's okay. I thought about it, actually."

"Okay. I..." He sighed, shaking his head. "Sometimes the mouth moves before the brain does."

"I'd like to tell you that gets better with age, but if I'm any indication, it doesn't."

Sean chuckled and turned to me, the overhead light catching his eyes and sending a tingle up my spine. "So if I don't have an internal censor now, I don't have to have one?"

"Well, I don't know if I'd advise against *trying* to develop one, but don't hold your breath."

He laughed again. "I'll keep that in mind." He held my gaze, and I wasn't sure I could've looked away if I'd wanted to. Mostly because I didn't want to, so it was kind of a moot point. Jesus, he had beautiful eyes. And humor had quirked his lips in a way that made me wonder—

I cleared my throat and looked out at the water. Beside

me, he shifted, but I didn't dare glance at him because those comments about company and motel vacancies were back at the tip of my tongue.

Sean drummed his fingers on the railing. "So have—"

"Excuse me, gentlemen."

We spun around, and my heart dropped into my feet. The glint of light off a badge sent that all too familiar panic through me—getting caught out with a man was bad, bad, career-threatening bad.

Except we weren't doing anything. Literally just walking and talking.

"Can we, uh, help you, Officer?" I asked.

The cop gestured over his shoulder with his thumb. "You're on private property. I'm gonna need you to leave."

"Oh." I cleared my throat. "Sorry. I... didn't realize..."

"It's all right." The cop smiled, but motioned again for us to get out. "A lot of people make that mistake."

Sean and I exchanged glances, then headed back toward his car. The cop continued down the pier, probably searching for other trespassers.

While we walked, my pulse slowly returned to normal.

As subtly as I could, I took a few deep breaths to calm myself the rest of the way down. It had been a long time since being gay, or having someone suspect I was gay, could hurt my career. Hell, I'd been fully out since two years after DADT was lifted. The paranoia was still there, though. I knew damn well I was no longer in danger of losing my career if someone caught me with a man, but it was a habit as ingrained as saluting superiors and taking off my cover when I went indoors. Apparently it was deep-seated enough that merely being alone with a good-looking man could trigger it.

Especially when I was horny as hell and wouldn't have

said no to being more than just alone with this particular good-looking man.

I quickly tamped down that thought. Sean was being polite, not flirting. He was working, and probably not even aware he was being leered at by the much older stranger he most likely wanted to butter up for a better tip.

As we passed the entrance to the pier, Sean glanced over his shoulder, then shook his head. "You'd think they would *mark* this as private property if they wanted people to keep off."

I glanced back too. "I'm sure they did. Somewhere."

"In size ten font, right?"

I laughed. "Wouldn't surprise me in the least." I slid my hands back into my pockets. "Well, it was nice while it lasted."

"Yeah, it was." He turned toward me, and his shy smile nearly made me trip over my own feet. "Thanks again for inviting me out with you. It was a nice switch from sitting in the car."

"Don't mention it. Thanks for the company."

We held each other's gaze for a moment, then kept walking toward the car. It was a sedan of some sort. Not an actual marked cab, but I hadn't expected one. The company he worked for was Anchor Point's local competition for Uber, so most of the drivers used their personal cars.

He paused at the driver's side. "You can, uh, sit up here if you want to."

"You sure?"

"Yeah." He laughed. "Unless you like talking to the back of my head."

I blinked. *Did he just go there?* "Talking to the—"

From the backseat, idiot.

Heat rushed into my cheeks. "Right. Sure. Front seat."

He unlocked the doors, and we both took our seats. Sean drove us about a block from the pier, so we were well away from the private property we'd apparently been trespassing on. At a stoplight, he put both hands on the wheel and turned toward me. "So. Where to?"

Oh, I could think of a few places. Especially after that comment about talking to the back of your head.

Christ. Maybe I did need a drink tonight. And a cigarette.

I drummed my fingers on the armrest. "I suppose I should have you drop me off at home. I'm sure you need to pick up other people and..."

A faint smile formed on Sean's lips. "I'm not in a big hurry, to be honest."

"But you're working."

"I know. But I..." He paused, and if I wasn't mistaken, his eyes flicked toward my lips. "I really don't mind."

We locked eyes, and I wondered if I was imagining the glint in his. My heart sped up. Wishful thinking. Had to be wishful thinking. I needed to get my mind off Jayson, and I was in a car with an attractive—*hello, understatement*—guy.

Sean tilted his head slightly. "*Should* I be in a hurry to drop you off?"

Probably, yes. "Depends."

"On?"

I swallowed. "What you think will happen if you don't drop me off."

"Maybe I'm curious."

"Isn't much to be curious about." I hoped I didn't sound as nervous as I suddenly felt. "You're in a car with a guy who just broke up with someone."

"Uh-huh." He didn't break eye contact.

"Now might be a good time for you to know you're in a

car with a guy who thinks the best way to get over a breakup is to dive headlong into bed with someone new."

Sean gulped, but still didn't look away. "Good to know."

I swept my tongue across my lips. "You're here to do your job, though. I don't... I don't want to take advantage of that. The customer isn't always right."

Sean reached for the dashboard and pressed a button. The timer on the meter froze. "Now I'm off the clock." In the turquoise glow of the car's gauges, he met my eyes again. "Your move."

Well, if you're gonna put it like that...

I unbuckled my seat belt. When I inched closer to him, he tensed. One hand came off the wheel, disappeared into the shadows, and materialized on my thigh.

I closed my eyes and pulled in a sharp breath. No amount of nicotine or alcohol would satisfy this craving. And no strangers from gay bars in Flatstick. As he slid his hand a little higher, stopping just shy of my growing erection, I met his gaze. Oh yes, this particular stranger was exactly what I needed tonight.

I put a hand on his leg and leaned in a little closer, anticipation tingling along every nerve ending as my heart thumped against my ribs. Sean mirrored me, leaning in as much as the console between us allowed, and tilted his head, and—

The goddamned car behind us honked.

CHAPTER 3

SEAN

"SON OF A BITCH!" I jumped back into my seat and hit the gas hard, throwing Paul and me back as the tires squealed beneath the car. How long that light had been green, I had no idea—I'd been way too focused on the green light I was getting from Paul.

"Jesus." Paul shifted beside me, and I glanced over in time to see him adjusting the front of his pants. *Yeah. Know the feeling.*

The car behind us turned after a couple of blocks. Once again, it was just us on the mostly darkened street. I exhaled. "There's like five cars out at this time of night in Anchor Point, and lucky us, one of them ends up behind us."

"Cockblocking fuckers," Paul muttered, and the growl in his voice went straight to my balls. If he was as frustrated as I was, there was going to be nothing left of my car's upholstery once I found a place to stop. Which meant I really, *really* needed to find a place to stop.

"There's a back road up ahead." I pressed a little harder on the accelerator. "Unless you have any objections to—"

"None at all." He sounded out of breath. And now that I thought about it, *I* was out of breath. It was probably a good thing that car had interrupted us, or we'd still be sitting at that green light, and *I would be kissing him right fucking now you fucking bastard...*

I fidgeted, gripping the wheel tighter. That back road *was* right up ahead, wasn't it? I hadn't mentally compressed twenty miles of highway into twelve feet because I was in that much of a hurry to pull over and pick up where we'd left off?

Please let it be right where I remember it. Please let me get there before Paul comes to his senses and changes his mind.

I didn't know why, but I was convinced he was going to do exactly that. If he had enough time, or if I said something dumb, he'd realize what he'd been about to do, and tell me to turn around and take him back to the base like I'd expected to do in the first place. So the sooner I made it to that dark, barely paved road; stopped this car; and closed some of this space between us, the less likely he was to figure out it was a bad idea.

I put some more pressure on the gas pedal. Just in case.

Beside me, Paul fidgeted, but he didn't say anything. Up ahead, the turnoff came into view, and I slowed down. When I put on my blinker, he shifted again. Then again. As I braked and started to take the turn, I swore he murmured something to the effect of, "Fucking finally."

My sentiments exactly.

I drove far enough that Officer Friendly wouldn't see us if he happened to go cruising by, and nosed off the road onto the soft shoulder. I put the car in park, but didn't even have a chance to shut off the engine before Paul lunged across the console, grabbed the back of my neck, and kissed me.

Oh God. Whoa.

Either I'd forgotten how to breathe, Paul had pulled the air out of my lungs, or both, but whatever. If I passed out, I passed out. I combed my fingers through his hair and slid my other hand up his thigh, tracing his inseam like I had right before we'd been startled apart earlier. This time, we weren't interrupted, and I cupped his cock and balls through his pants. He groaned, gripping my hair tighter —*when the hell did he put his hand in my hair?*—and pressed into my palm. This was not how I'd expected tonight to play out when I'd clocked in earlier, but I wasn't complaining.

I inched closer to him. As close as the stupid console would allow, anyway. It had been way too long since I'd even made it this far with a guy, and Paul was one hell of a kisser. Not only did his lips and tongue tease mine exactly right to make my toes curl, but he kissed with his hands as much as his mouth—running his fingers through my hair, cradling my neck, kneading my thigh with his other hand. I loved it. I didn't even care if we went farther than this, but I was pretty sure we would. As rock-hard and needy as we both were, I didn't see us coming up for air until some orgasms had happened.

He tugged my hair, and when I tilted my head back, his lips went right to my neck. Fuck, he was good at this. He must have shaved recently—his chin wasn't nearly as rough as I'd expected, but it was coarse enough to give me goose bumps. Nothing hotter in the world than a guy with stubble kissing my neck.

I tried to move even closer to him, but the damn console bit into my hip and refused to move. I swore under my breath. Then, "Think we should move to the backseat?"

"No." His hand slid over the front of my pants. "Front seat is plausible deniability. In case that cop shows up."

"P-plausible..." I closed my eyes, tilting my head even farther as he kissed up and down my neck. "How can you even... remember words like that when you're this..." I squeezed his cock.

Paul hissed sharply, then kissed under my jaw.

"Backseat wouldn't make a difference," I said, slurring a little. "Anyone comes by, they're gonna know exactly what we're doing."

He paused, then pulled back enough to meet my gaze in the faint light.

Wait, why are the dashboard lights still on?

Oh right. The engine was still running.

I turned the key. The engine shuddered, and then the world outside the car went dark and—aside from my crazy pounding heart—silent.

I licked my lips. "Backseat?"

"Backseat."

We separated, got out of the car, and met again in the backseat. This time there was nothing between us except clothes, and nothing—not wild horses, not Anchor Point PD —was going to stop us. In the middle of the bench seat, we kissed and groped, tugging shirts free in between sliding hands over way-too-covered erections.

I was practically in his lap now, my leg hooked over his and my torso twisted in a way that wasn't going to be comfortable for much longer. I pushed him back against the seat and—careful not to hit my head against the low roof— straddled him.

He stroked my cock through my jeans and damn near turned me inside out. I couldn't help rocking against him, riding him like we were fucking instead of just making out, and despite the thick layer between his skin and mine, he had my head spinning and my spine tingling.

"You're gonna make me come in my pants," I murmured.

"Can't have that," he said, barely breaking the kiss, and suddenly he was drawing my zipper down. "But I do plan to make you come."

I let my head fall beside Paul's as he undid my belt.

"Of all the drivers they could've sent tonight," he panted, "I am so fucking glad they sent you."

"Y-yeah. Me... me too. I'm—"

Then his fingers were around my cock. Nothing separating them. Skin on skin. Stroking slowly. Squeezing gently. Words? What words? Fuck words.

Paul murmured something I didn't understand. I lifted my head a little, and he found my lips with his, and then we were kissing again. With one hand in my hair, he stroked me with the other while we kissed, and every cop in Anchor Point could've surrounded us right then, lights and sirens and everything, and I wouldn't have noticed.

Go ahead and arrest me, but for the love of God, let him finish with me first.

"Pity I didn't bring any condoms with me tonight," he said between kisses. "Those might've come in handy."

I shivered and kissed him again. Yeah, they might've come in handy, but I wasn't going to think about what we couldn't do. Only what we could, which was making out and groping and whatever else two guys could do in close confines.

Paul nudged me gently, and somehow that translated to *change positions*, and somehow, even in those cramped quarters, we managed to untangle and shift around without too much effort. I had barely leaned back against the seat on the driver's side before Paul turned onto his knees and—

Oh.

Shit.

Yes.

His lips were around my cock. His tongue was... my God. How did he *do* that?

Back arching off the seat, I combed my fingers through his hair, careful not to push on his head. Especially since he was already deep-throating me now and then, taking my cock all the way down... teasing with his tongue and... did he even *have* a gag reflex?

"Oh shit," I breathed. "Oh... fuck..."

He moaned. The vibration of his voice drove me insane. It was probably a good thing I couldn't move much in this position—the temptation to thrust my hips and fuck his mouth was almost irresistible. As quickly as he bobbed his head on my dick, and as far as he took me into his throat, he probably wouldn't have even minded. Hell, maybe he would've liked it. Maybe he was the kind of guy who liked when the dude he was blowing took over and—

And just like that, just thinking about Paul on his knees and loving it while I fucked his mouth, I came. I didn't make a sound. I couldn't. I couldn't breathe in or out. I fucking came, shuddering and jerking as Paul kept my orgasm going, and going, and going...

"S-stop." I released his hair, wondering when I'd grabbed on to it so tightly, and sank back against the seat. "Fuck..."

Paul sat up. I couldn't really see him—it was way too dark out here on this back road—but I'd already memorized his features. He leaned in but hesitated, like he wasn't sure if I'd be willing to kiss him, so I pulled him in and made sure he knew without a doubt that yes, I would absolutely kiss a man after he'd sucked me off.

We were both panting, gripping clothes and hair in between pawing at each other and leaning to one side, then the other, like we couldn't decide if I was going to push him onto his back or if he was going to pin me against the seat. Somehow, we stayed right there in the middle, upright and kissing while my head still spun from that orgasm.

I traced his inner thigh with my fingertips, and when I cupped his dick, he broke the kiss with a gasp.

"*Fuck.*" He pressed into my hand.

I grinned. "Turned on, are we?"

"Of course I am." He ground his fully erect cock against my palm. "Jesus fucking Christ..."

"Maybe I should return the favor, hmm?" I didn't wait for a response, and started unzipping his pants. He fumbled with his belt, and between the two of us, it was only a matter of seconds before we'd freed his very impressive cock.

I couldn't wait. Shifting around as much as the backseat allowed, I leaned down and took him between my lips. God, it was just as well he'd already gotten me off, or I'd have needed one hand on my own cock. Probably because it had been too long since I'd sucked dick, but the instant I tasted the salt of his skin, I started getting dizzy and turned on all over again.

Paul exhaled hard, kneading my shoulder almost like a cat as he squirmed against the seat. It had definitely been too long since I'd done this, and way too long since I'd been with someone who enjoyed it as much as he apparently did. I loved the sounds he made, and the subtle little responses—his breath hitching whenever I changed what I was doing, how he moaned and swore when I ran my tongue around the head, how his whole body tensed when I added a slight twist to my strokes.

And I loved the way he ran his fingers through my hair. Maybe other guys had done it before and I hadn't noticed, but I noticed it now, and it turned my insides to liquid.

He'd deep-throated me a lot, so I did the same to him and was rewarded with a full-body shudder.

"Jesus," he moaned. "That's..." I did it again, and he gasped. "Oh God." Another low groan escaped from his lips, and it fell to a soft whimper as his hand tightened in my hair. "Oh, that's good," he breathed, fingers twitching against my scalp. "Just... just like that."

I kept doing exactly what I'd been doing—stroking him, teasing him, deep-throating him—and his cock got even harder between my lips. He whispered curses, each a little less formed than the last, and then he gasped, and ground out *"Shit!"* a split second before hot semen flooded my tongue. I kept going until he stopped me, then lifted my head. I couldn't help grinning as he ground out, "Jesus..."

I sat up, ready to fire back a comment about my name being Sean and not Jesus, but Paul immediately grabbed me and kissed me. Forget snark. I wrapped my arms around him and melted against him.

Was this really happening? This was really happening. Maybe an hour ago, I'd picked up an all-too-quiet guy who'd apparently just broken up with someone. Now we were kissing in the backseat of my car, pants undone and belts jingling every time we moved.

How the...?

Hell. I wasn't looking this gift horse in the very, very talented mouth.

At some point, we pulled apart enough to fix our

clothes. Or at least make a half-assed attempt. Then we were back to kissing lazily.

Eventually, though, Paul sighed and glanced at his watch. "Damn it. I should probably get home." He brushed his lips across mine. "Early meetings and shit tomorrow."

Disappointment tugged at my gut, but I nodded. It wasn't like this was an evening that could last forever. I'd had hurried backseat quickies with strangers before—I knew this game.

"Okay. And, uh, don't let me leave without giving you my card."

He kissed me again. "I won't. Believe me."

I drove Paul onto the base, and he directed me to the Navy Exchange. The shopping center parking lot was deserted, of course, so it seemed like an odd place for me to let him out, but it was where he wanted me to stop. Base housing was just on the other side of the building, so maybe he didn't want his neighbors seeing us.

Or his wife?

I cringed. He'd split up with a boyfriend tonight, but that didn't mean... did it?

I shook myself. It was none of my business.

Paul faced me in the bleached glow of headlights ricocheting off one of the concrete barriers lined up in front of the sidewalk. "I'm... not even sure what we're supposed to say at this point. 'Thanks for the ride' seems a bit crass, but, uh, thanks for the ride."

I laughed. "Likewise."

Our eyes met. Then he cleared his throat and gestured at the meter. "So how much do I owe you?"

"Um." Right. This was a paid cab ride, wasn't it? "Let me see..."

I pulled up the total, and as promised, he paid twice what the meter showed. Technically, he was probably still coming out ahead since the meter hadn't been on the whole time, but it was a good payout for me, so I called it even.

"For the record," he said as he tucked his wallet into his back pocket, "that's for the drive and the time. Not... um..."

I held up the bills he'd given me. "If you were paying me for that, there'd be at least a couple more twenties in here."

Paul stared at me incredulously, but when I grinned, he laughed. "Right. Right. Well, I..." His humor faded a bit. "I didn't want you thinking I thought you were..."

"A whore?"

"Yeah. That."

"It's okay." I waved a hand. "I prefer 'slut.'"

Paul laughed again, and I was pretty sure some red appeared in his cheeks. "Well, even if you were getting paid, you'd get a hell of a lot more than a couple of twenties for that."

"I don't see why." I winked. "You did as much of the work as I did."

"I wouldn't go that far." He put his hand on my thigh. "Anyway, thanks. Tonight was definitely what I needed."

Me too, but you don't need to know that.

He reached for the door. Hesitated. Drew his hand back. "I... meant to get one of your cards."

"Oh. Right." I dug around in the change tray where I kept the stack and pulled one out. It wasn't a good idea, giving him a way to contact me again. I had absolutely no business getting anywhere near him, but I could still feel the aftershocks of that orgasm too much to care.

"Here." I held it out to him. "Anytime you need a lift, give me a call."

He held my gaze and plucked the card from between my fingers. "I'll do that." He paused, and this time when he reached for the door, he opened it, and the change in air pressure was like a spell being broken. "Have a good night."

"Yeah. You too."

One last smile, and then he was gone.

CHAPTER 4

PAUL

IT HAD BEEN days since I'd watched Sean's taillights disappear out of the Navy Exchange parking lot. Tempting as it had been to have him drop me off at home, I'd resisted. One, I'd already taken him away from his job for too long. Two, I lived on Admiral's Row, and really didn't need to fuel the gossip mill by bringing a young, hot man to my house in the middle of the night.

So, I'd gotten out at the Exchange and walked home, slept like the dead, and now I *still* couldn't get him out of my mind.

I'd had plenty of one-night stands in my life, and none of them had been as hard to forget as Sean. I couldn't even put my finger on why. Because he hadn't minded letting me vent after Jayson had kicked me out? Because he'd been nothing like Jayson and he'd been the nearest warm body and had therefore been the best possible person to distract me that night? Because he was *that* good with his mouth?

I had no idea. All I knew was I needed to let him go. And now that it was Friday night, I was bound and determined to forget him and Jayson so I could get on with my life.

Which was why I'd taken a cab—one from a company Sean *didn't* work for—down to Flatstick to check out the alleged abundance of thriving gay bars.

I wasn't disappointed by the number of places down here. On the outskirts of town where they wouldn't offend the sensibilities of children, tourists, and upstanding citizens, there was a row of old warehouses and such that had been covertly transformed into bars and clubs. Most looked more or less unassuming from the outside, but a rainbow flag in a window or a suggestive name like Ok Lumberjack or Backdoor Bob gave them away. One place—a drag bar called LeeAnn's—had given up all subtlety and had giant garish signs out front to let people know about the Tuesday and Thursday night drag shows.

I wasn't big on country-western bars, so Ok Lumberjack wasn't really my style, and LeeAnn's was crawling with what must've been bachelorette parties. I even thought I recognized some wives I'd met at officer functions, and although it was no secret I was gay, I didn't really want to cross paths with people from the base in this kind of setting.

Backdoor Bob seemed like a decent place, but it was pretty dead tonight. Everyone there seemed more interested in drinking than anything else, and my days of drinking myself senseless were long over. I wasn't the hothead pilot who could drink half a paycheck in a weekend anymore. And for that matter, in those days I might've gotten away with being hauled back to the base by civilian cops for drunk and disorderly, but doing that now would not bode well for making admiral.

I finally settled on the Four-Leaf, which was busy but not horrible. At the bar, I ordered a gin and tonic, and as I sipped it, surveyed the room. It amazed me there was even one gay nightclub out here, never mind several, and that they were as populated as they were. Small as this town was, I suspected most of the people here had come from Anchor Point or one of the other towns along this strip of the Oregon coast. Maybe even one of the inland cities like Salem or Eugene; they might have come here after tiring of Portland's thriving gay scene. There couldn't really be this many gay men in a town of fifty thousand, could there?

Well, wherever they'd come from, they were here now. Some were already making eyes at each other or leaning in close to talk over the music. Others were heading toward the crowded dance floor. I'd seen at least two or three pairs slip out the back, either toward the men's room or the alley behind the club. Maybe heading toward the nearby shore to live out a sex-on-the-beach fantasy. Hopefully they were wiser about it than I'd been that night in Hawaii ten or fifteen years ago. There were some places a man did *not* need to get sand.

I shuddered at the memory and took another drink. No point in focusing on that experience. I was looking to have a newer—and less gritty—experience tonight. All I needed was a willing partner to share it with me.

I fidgeted on my barstool, looking from one man to the next. Every so often, I scanned the crowd in search of familiar faces. It was no crime for me to be caught here, just like it was no crime for any of my subordinates to be here, but I was cautious nonetheless. Part of it was old habit. Scouring clubs under the looming shadow of DADT made a man wary as hell.

But there'd also been some less than scrupulous Sailors who'd caught members of their command engaging in flat-out inappropriate public behavior in gay bars. Sometimes the activity itself was the problem, not the gender. I knew of at least one chief who'd been spotted by a group of E4s with his hands down a man's pants at a club near Yokosuka. Both had been enthusiastically consenting adults, but word made it back up his chain of command, and he'd been encouraged to quickly and quietly retire unless he really wanted to face adultery charges. It didn't matter that his wife not only knew about her husband's activities, she encouraged them; he'd been busted in flagrante with someone not his wife, and his career was over.

Of course, I was unmarried, so no one could throw the book at me for adultery. There were, however, some who believed a man could be nailed with conduct unbecoming an officer and a gentleman for picking up men in a gay bar. Never mind that I hadn't ever heard of a single straight officer being court-martialed for picking up women, but such was the reality of the post-DADT Navy.

I sipped my gin and tonic. I could not relax in this place.

It wasn't just that I couldn't relax. Here I was, knee-deep in good booze and surrounded by hot men, and none of them did a damn thing for me.

Not when that cab driver's face was still fresh in my mind. Or when I could convince myself I still tasted his kiss or his cum.

I took a deep swallow, nearly finishing my gin and tonic. I gestured to the bartender for another, and held on to the glass for something cold.

I had Sean's number. His card was in my wallet, and all I had to do was call him or shoot him a text, and maybe there could be a rematch tonight.

No. I was crazy. Clearly. Yeah, he'd been game for a blowjob in his backseat, but what kid wouldn't take advantage of getting his dick sucked instead of working? I'd have done the same thing in my twenties. Hell, I *had* done the same thing. More than once. Didn't mean I ever wanted to see their faces or cocks again.

On the other hand, Sean had given me his card. Had it really been so he could get another fare out of me?

I scanned the room again, searching for a promising glance or an attractive face. There were plenty—this club was definitely the jackpot compared to the others—but every single one of them was getting mentally stacked up against the black-and-blue-haired cab driver. It annoyed me, but somehow didn't surprise me. I'd come all the way down here in the backseat of another cab when I really should've saved myself the fifty bucks and called him.

The bartender handed me my drink, and when I took out the ten to pay him, the edge of Sean's card caught my eye.

Sometimes, I convinced myself my hothead young pilot days were over. I was no longer the guy who'd drink anything—in any quantity—if the stakes were high enough. I didn't get tattoos on bets anymore. I no longer had to stand at attention and try not to smirk while being screamed at by a higher-up for some midair stunt that had *totally* been worth it.

But that Maverick-wannabe idiot still existed somewhere in my mind. Fact was, the only thing separating me from him tonight was that ten-years-ago Paul would've had Sean's dick down his throat by now. Present-day Paul was hesitating, still eyeballing that card and trying to talk himself out of it, but I was and always would be *me*—the guy who saw something, went for it, and worried about the consequences later.

I pulled the card out of my wallet and my phone out of my pocket, and texted him.

Down in Flatstick—could use a lift. You available?

And then I sat there staring at my phone like an idiot. A minute passed. Then two. I put the phone on the bar and took another drink. Three minutes. Four. Awesome.

After ten minutes, I hadn't heard anything, so I sighed and put my phone in my pocket. Disappointing, but probably for the best. As I worked my way to the bottom of my gin and tonic, it occurred to me that there were a lot of reasons I really had no business getting in touch with him.

I'd had a moment of panic at the gate when I'd realized he had base access. Was he a dependent of someone under my command? He'd produced one of the passes issued to cab drivers, and I'd let out my breath, but the fact I hadn't even considered the possibility before then made me question my judgment.

He was also way too young for me. Probably half my age, if that. He was in his twenties, I was coming down off a breakup. Getting involved with anyone right now was a bad idea.

On the other hand, bad ideas *were* kind of the story of my life, and I had some scars and a couple of tattoos to prove it.

Well, not that it mattered in this case. Sean had probably only wanted anything to do with me because I was there and horny. What twentysomething guy turned down readily available sex? And that was enough. A fling in the dark on a back road was one thing. I wasn't so sure I wanted him to see me in the daylight, especially with clothes off. I took damn good care of myself, but I was *not* twenty-five anymore.

So it was better that he hadn't responded. There were other cabs who could get me back to Anchor Point tonight or, if I found someone to share a bed with, tomorrow morning. I didn't need to wait for—

My phone vibrated against my leg. I pulled it out of my pocket so quickly I damn near dropped it, and—*Yes!*—he'd responded.

Sorry, was on a run. Can be there, but it'll take a while. Still in A. Point.

My pulse pounded in time with the bass. *No problem. Not in a hurry.*

But, my brain added, *the sooner you get here, the better.*

And whichever part of my brain wasn't governed by my dick threw in, *Uh, Paul? Hello? Younger dude? You aren't quite the guy you were twenty years ago? Any of that ringing a bell?*

I cringed. Shit.

The phone vibrated again: *Am I coming as a cab driver or something else?*

Well wasn't that a complicated question? And I had no way to know if he was asking it while weighing whether or not to slip a few condoms in his pocket, or while balking at the door and thinking twice about getting in the car.

I gnawed my lip. Regardless of why he was asking, there it was—my opportunity to man up and back out before I did something really, really stupid. Except that part of my brain was uncharacteristically silent, while the other part obeyed my dick and typed out, *Happy to see you either way.*

I'd put the ball in his court. I wasn't sure if I had done it because I was a coward, or if I was giving him an out if he wanted one. Probably both.

Whatever the case, he responded with, *See you in forty-five*, and so much for not doing something really stupid tonight.

I set my phone on the bar, wondering when my palms

had gotten so damp. Idly wiping them on my jeans, I read and reread his message, wondering which option he'd decided on. Was he putting the ball back in my court? Was he undecided?

Guess I'll find out when he gets here.

———

Not quite forty-five minutes later, my phone buzzed.

Outside.

One word had me on my feet and halfway to the door. As soon as I stepped out, sure enough, I saw Sean's car idling on the curb.

As I approached, I hesitated, not sure if I was supposed to ride in the front or the back. I gestured back and forth between the two options, eyebrows up.

The passenger-side window came down.

"Depends," Sean said. "Am I here to drive you? Or do you want a ride?"

I gulped.

He grinned.

And I got in the front seat.

As he pulled away from the club, he tapped his thumbs on the wheel and glanced at me. "So where are we going?"

"Anywhere we can be alone."

He met my gaze. Held it. Swallowed.

"I mean..." I cleared my throat. "Unless you don't—"

"No, I do. I definitely do." He faced the road again. "And I think I know a place."

My pulse shot upward. That settled that, didn't it?

He made a few turns, taking us closer to the seashore via progressively darker and less paved roads. Then he pulled into a gravel parking lot. I caught a glimpse of a hand-painted sign—something about a beach and a boat launch—before the headlights focused on trees and a small fence.

"I think this'll work," he said as gravel crunched beneath the tires.

I unbuckled my seat belt. "You seem to know a lot of places to park without someone finding you."

"Mm-hmm." He threw the car in park and shut off the engine. "I do." Sean leaned across the console and grabbed my shirt. "Good thing one of us does, right?"

And sweet Mother of God, I finally had him in my arms again. Despite the obnoxious console keeping our hips apart, we kissed each other, groped each other, dragged fingers through hair and grabbed handfuls of clothes—obviously we were very much on the same page tonight. A very pornographic page.

"So glad you texted," he said. "Been thinking... since the other..."

"Me too."

He ran a hand up my leg and cupped my erection, murmuring something I didn't understand.

"Went out looking to get fucked tonight," I slurred between kisses, "and get my mind off my ex, but all I could think of was you."

Sean met my gaze in the dashboard glow. "Yeah?"

"Yeah. Especially since I know what you're packing."

He groaned softly. "What do you want to do with it?"

"Do I have to spell it out?" I fished a condom out of my pocket and held it up. "Or are you going to—"

"Get out of the car."

Panic shot through me. "What?"

"C'mon." He pulled away and opened his own door. "Out."

The panic vanished when I realized he was getting out too, and I fumbled with the handle before getting my own door open.

We scrambled out and onto our feet, and met around the back of the car. Suddenly we had room that we'd never had before. I could kiss him and run my hands all over him at the same time. God, he was so responsive too. When I curved my hand over his ass, he moaned into my kiss as he arched against me.

He took advantage of all the space too. He pushed me up against the back of the car and held me there with his hips. He explored my neck and jaw with his mouth, pausing now and then to nip my earlobe and send me out of my fucking mind.

"Like that?" he murmured.

"Very much."

He laughed softly, then did it again, pressing his teeth in just enough to sting.

"Fuck," I breathed, holding on to him as a shudder almost dropped me to my knees.

"That's a good idea. You still have that condom?"

"Of course. Think we should—"

"Yes." Sean plucked it from my hand and tore the wrapper with his teeth.

I blinked. "Right here?"

He nodded, looking me in the eyes. "Right here."

This is insane. This is—

So hot.

Clumsily, I undid the front of his pants, and then grabbed him and kissed him. The car kept us upright, which was good since the extent of my multitasking was kissing Sean and rolling the condom onto his cock. Even as I felt around in my pockets for that little packet of lube, I didn't want to stop kissing him. We really needed to do this in a place where we could make out and fuck at the same time. Though I supposed the backseat would do, even if it would be a bit cramped. No, we needed space. Privacy. A bed.

"You've got lube, right?" he asked between breathless kisses.

"Mm-hmm. Got it some... here!" I found the packet and held it up.

He took the lube from me. "Turn around."

I licked my lips as I unbuckled my belt. While Sean lubed himself up, I turned around and rested my forearms on the trunk, hoping he didn't notice that I was practically vibrating with excitement. Or hell, let him notice. Just get that lube on and fuck me before I come unglued.

He shoved my jeans and boxers down over my hips, and the weight of my belt, wallet, and phone dropped it all to the ground with a quiet *clink* of the buckle hitting gravel. He nudged my knees apart with his, and I adjusted my stance as much as I could. Then the head of his cock pressed against my ass, and I closed my eyes, gripping the edge of the trunk lid as anticipation turned my knees to liquid. I didn't know why I was this desperate for sex tonight—this desperate for sex with him in particular—only that I was.

As Sean pushed himself into me, the night air was cool against my bare skin, reminding me how exposed I was. If anyone happened by, there was no talking ourselves out of this. There was no denying what we were doing when he had me bent over his car with our pants around our ankles.

Any other night, that would've had me panicking, but not tonight. Tonight, the thought of someone showing up and seeing me taking Sean's dick was erotic as hell. Maybe that meant I was losing my mind. I didn't know. Didn't really care either. All I wanted was for Sean to keep working that thick cock into me, and I didn't care who knew about it.

He took his time, easing in every inch until he was taking long, smooth strokes.

"After this," he murmured in my ear, "let's... go someplace else. So I can fuck you again." As if for emphasis, he thrust into me hard enough to make the shocks creak.

"Yes. Please." I almost choked on the words. "We can go... we can go to..." We'd figure it out later. Right now, the only thing that mattered was how good his dick felt inside me.

We'd barely started, and already, I was getting close. What the hell? I could go for-fucking-ever, but now that I was bent over his car and taking his cock, Sean had me right on the edge.

He put his hands on the trunk lid on either side of mine and rocked his hips faster, and that didn't help at all. I closed my eyes and held my breath, but even that wasn't enough to let me regain any semblance of control.

"Gonna..." I shivered. "Gonna make you think I'm a minuteman."

"Why's that?" He slammed into me so hard he knocked me off-balance, but the car was already doing most of the work of holding me up. "Kinda seems like... a compliment." Another hard, violent thrust. "Love it when a guy loses it while I'm fucking him."

"Oh Jesus." I gripped the trunk lid and pressed my knees against the bumper so they didn't drop all the way out from under me. "H-hard as you... as you can."

Sean groaned, and God bless him, he fucked me *hard*. The shocks creaked. The gravel beneath our feet crunched. Skin slapped against skin.

And I was coming. I blinked, and the next thing I knew, I was in the middle of a can't-breathe, can't-moan, can't-fucking-move orgasm.

Sean's hands moved to my hips, and his fingers bit in. He held his breath as he relentlessly pounded my ass, and when he came, he wasn't nearly as mute as I was.

"Fuck!" he roared, and forced himself all the way in. My kneecap smarted against the bumper, but it was well worth it to feel him and hear him as his thick cock pulsed inside me. His hips jerked as the roar fell to a soft moan, and then he released a ragged breath as he slumped over me.

For a moment, neither of us moved. In the distance, waves rolled and crashed, and somewhere, a logging truck or something rumbled down the highway. Here, though, the only sound was the two of us panting in unison.

Sean pulled out, and suddenly the idea of going somewhere else so we could fuck again took on a whole new sense of urgency. I *needed* more of this. More of him.

"Stay there." He paused to kiss the side of my neck. Then he was gone. Well, not really. Still right there, but he was no longer touching me. Clothes rustled and his belt buckle jingled.

While I fixed my own clothes, he stepped away to toss the condom in one of the trash cans by the fence. Had we really done that? Fucked right here out in the open like it didn't matter if we got caught?

Yes. Yes, we had. And I wanted him to fuck me again as soon as humanly possible.

He grinned as he came back to where I was standing. "You really do make the drive to Flatstick worth it, you know that?"

Laughing, I hooked my fingers in his belt and pulled him toward me. "Glad you didn't come all the way down here for nothing." I wrapped my arms around him and casually leaned against the car. "We should definitely go someplace else."

He nodded. "Any ideas?"

"Well, there are plenty of motels nearby." I paused. "Quicker than trying to get back to your place or mine."

"Probably not my place anyway. Motel sounds good to me."

I didn't push the issue. Maybe he had roommates. Maybe less than presentable housekeeping. Maybe, like me, he didn't want his neighbors to see him bringing guys home.

Whatever—I didn't care about who he lived with or how he lived as long as we found a place with a flat surface that wouldn't collapse when he fucked me that hard.

"So..." I raised my eyebrows. "Motel?"

Sean grinned. "Motel."

CHAPTER 5

SEAN

PAUL CHECKED us in while I waited in the car.

I still couldn't believe I was even here. I'd assumed he'd just needed the nearest warm body to get over the one who'd left him cold in his motel, so I hadn't expected to hear from him again.

And yet, I had. And then I'd driven clear down to Flatstick, picked him up, and fucked him over the back of my car in a public place where we could have been caught. It wasn't likely—I'd had plenty of sex in that parking lot and never seen heads or tails of a cop—but it was possible.

Why was I being so stupid? I wasn't even working tonight. When Paul had texted, I hadn't been out on a run like I'd told him. Even though it was a Friday night, I'd been hunched over my desk in my bedroom, studying for next week's English midterm. The message had come through, and at first, I'd ignored it. Rematches had a habit of turning into... well... habits. And I was no man's rebound.

But then, while I'd tried to return my attention to studying, memories of the other night had started trickling back in. Paul's kiss alone was enough to kill any hope I'd had of concentrating on *King Lear* or *A Midsummer Night's Dream.*

And then my brain had helpfully reminded me that I'd jerked off no fewer than four times to thoughts of Paul—what we'd done and what I *wished* we'd done. He wasn't going to get any less distracting if I didn't pick him up in Flatstick tonight, and the more I'd tried to talk myself out of it, the more I'd thought of what could happen if I went to get him.

So I'd texted him back, pretending the delay had been a result of driving another passenger somewhere, and suddenly we were arranging to meet up. I'd marked my page, closed my book, tucked a couple of condoms and some packets of lube in my back pocket, and grabbed my keys.

I'd felt a little guilty walking through the living room past Dad and his girlfriend, Julie, on the way out to the car. Like I was still a teenager who would be grounded for decades for sneaking out to get laid. Old habits died hard, apparently.

I wasn't a kid anymore, though, so they didn't question me when I came and went. They never did. Thank God for that too—I was constitutionally incapable of lying to my father except by omission. I could withhold anything from him forever, but if he asked me point-blank? I was screwed.

But he didn't ask, so I didn't tell him I was heading down to Flatstick to pick up a horny older man from a gay bar.

And now Paul was checking us into a hotel room while I tried to ignore this increasingly uncomfortable hard-on. Jesus—how long did it take to process a credit card and sign a form?

Finally, though, he came out, holding up a key and grinning, which did nothing to help with that hard-on but definitely brought a smile to my face.

We hurried into the room, and... yes. As soon as we were through the door, Paul turned around, hooked his fingers in my front pockets, pulled me to him, and kissed me.

I wrapped my arms around him and leaned into him. Sliding my hands down over his ass, I tilted my head and deepened the kiss. Oh God, yes. *This* was why I'd blown off studying and good sense—nobody kissed like Paul. Something about the way his lips moved with mine, and the way he ran his fingers through my hair and took his sweet time, made the rest of the world disappear. In the car, we'd been frantic and needy to the point that fucking right there over the trunk hadn't seemed insane. Now, with time and privacy on our side and two orgasms already out of the way, we weren't in such a hurry.

I wasn't in any hurry to let him go either. Whatever doubts I'd had still grumbled in the back of my mind, but I ignored them all because holy *shit*, this man could kiss.

He pushed me back a step, and my back hit the wall. Barely breaking the kiss, he murmured, "I've been fantasizing about this since the last time I saw you."

"Have you?"

"Mm-hmm." He curved his hands over my ass, pulling me closer and making sure I felt every inch of his erection through our clothes. "For the record..." He started kissing his way down my neck, turning me inside out with soft lips and lightly abrasive stubble. "I don't usually go looking for younger guys. But you've had my attention since the other night."

I dragged my nails up his back. "Well, for the record, I'm not that young. I *am* legal."

He laughed, which sent a rush of hot breath past my neck. "You're younger than I am."

"Doesn't bother me if it doesn't bother you."

"Does it seem like it bothers me?"

"Not even a little." I rubbed my clothed erection against his. "Only thing that bothers me is all these damn clothes."

"They're a problem, aren't they?" He nipped the side of my neck, and when I gasped and shivered, he grinned against my skin.

We inched closer to the bed. Shoes came off and were kicked out of the way. He made no move to turn off the light. Good. After all, he'd given me two orgasms—hell, we'd sucked each other's dicks and I'd fucked him—and I *still* hadn't seen him completely naked. That was changing tonight.

I kissed him hard. He gripped my hair and kept his other arm tight around my waist, and he gave as good as he got—Christ, I didn't even care if we fucked again tonight. I could've done this till dawn.

I tugged at his shirt, but Paul stiffened.

I looked up at him. "What's wrong?"

"I..." He glanced down and swallowed, then shook his head. "Nothing."

"You sure?"

His cheeks colored. "Just, uh, haven't... I'm not as young as I used to—"

I kissed him and wrapped my arms around him again. "We wouldn't have made it this far if I didn't think you were attractive."

"To be fair, this is the first time you've seen me in the light."

I grinned at him. "The pier wasn't exactly pitch-black."

Sliding a hand over his groin, I added, "I like what I've seen so far."

Paul bit his lip, sucking in a breath through his nose. "Well, uh, keep your expectations reasonable, okay? I'm not twenty-five."

"If you were twenty-five, we probably would've annoyed each other to death by now." I paused. "Look, I don't want you to be self-conscious or anything. We've been mostly dressed every time so far—we can keep some clothes on if you want."

He studied me for a few seconds. Long enough for disappointment to sink in my gut. I really was cool with making sure he was comfortable, but I also really, *really* wanted to see him naked.

And right then he shrugged and pulled off his shirt. As he dropped it on the floor, he put his arms out and laughed shyly. "There you go."

I didn't want to make him even more self-conscious by staring, but... holy fuck. I could only imagine what he'd looked like at twenty-five if he thought this was going to put me off. Maybe he'd had a six-pack back then or something. Whatever. His smooth, flat stomach and narrow waist were begging to have my hands all over them. He had a few tattoos—one on his upper arm, one on the side of his rib cage, a third peeking up from the waistband of his low-slung jeans—and I'd look at them in detail eventually, but the whole picture? Christ.

So glad I made the drive tonight.

I licked my lips again. "You have tattoos."

He smiled sheepishly. "Don't tell my mom, okay?"

"Promise." I laughed, running my fingers over the intricate lines on his ribs. "This one must've hurt."

"You better believe it." He claimed a deep kiss, and

when I pressed my nails into the tattoo, he groaned softly, shivering against me.

"Doesn't sound like you minded a little pain, hmm?"

He arched and shivered again. "A little pain is... is good. That one was a bit much."

"It looks great, though."

"Thanks." He smiled, a hint of shyness lingering in his expression. "And, um..." He cleared his throat, gesturing at my shirt. "I showed you mine."

"You did." I peeled off my shirt and dropped it on top of his. "Better?"

"Much."

"Good. And by the way, I don't know what you were so worried about." Meeting his gaze, I ran my hands up his chest. "I like what I see."

Paul grinned, and some tension in his shoulders eased. "Well in that case—" he brushed his lips across mine "—guess we can leave the lights on."

Damn right we can.

I cradled the back of his head and kissed him full-on. His skin was hot against mine, and when his hands drifted up my back, they gave me goose bumps.

"I didn't get a chance to look at you," he said between kisses.

"You want to look?" I dragged my nails up his back. "Or touch?"

He groaned, tilting his head back and shivering. "That is... quite the dilemma. I'm going to say both."

"Yeah? How you going to manage that?"

Paul hooked his fingers in my belt loops and led me toward the king-sized bed. He lay back on it, gesturing for me to come down with him. I started to, but paused. Oh, wasn't that a sight—a hot, fit man wearing nothing but a pair of jeans, with an impressive hard-on straining the seams.

"Come on," he whispered. "Can't touch you when you're all the way over there."

"That is kind of a problem, isn't it?" I joined him on the bed and straddled him. He cupped the back of my neck, pulled me down, and kissed me again.

So much for looking at each other. Oh well—this was perfect. I loved the way Paul's arms felt around me, especially with no shirts in the way. Eventually, we'd get rid of the rest of our clothes, but for now we were too busy kissing and touching above the belt.

And my God, I loved that he was as content as I was to make out like this. The best part? His addictive kiss. He wasn't lazy or passive, just... not aggressive. Or not *too* aggressive. Not pushy. He explored my mouth like I explored his, all without ramming his tongue down my throat or pinching lips between teeth. And teeth didn't crack against teeth—I fucking hated that. The way Paul kissed, I was tempted to take him back out to my car and head to a movie theater or a drive-in if we could find one, just so we could ignore the movie and make out; he kissed like someone who could happily keep this going until the credits rolled. We didn't even need to have sex as long as he kept kissing me like this while a film flickered in the background.

My arm was getting tired, so I nudged him onto his back and put my weight on my other arm. Then I dipped my head and kissed his neck. As I worked my way down, Paul rested his hands on my sides, then my shoulders, and whispered curses as I kissed his neck, collarbone, chest, abs.

"Fuck," he breathed, combing his fingers through my hair. "You do know how to turn a guy on, don't you?"

I grinned and pressed another kiss to his skin. There was something insanely hot about an older guy complimenting my technique. Like he wasn't just some inexperienced kid who didn't know good from *good*.

I flicked my tongue right above his navel. He squirmed, and the motion drew my attention to that tattoo by his hip. It must've been a dragon or something—only the tail was visible right now, following the contour of his hip bone before disappearing under his waistband. I wanted to see it. And more than that, I wanted to see the thick cock that was obviously straining to get out of his snug pants.

Paul swore softly and helped me, and between us, we managed to get his pants out of the way.

Once he'd wriggled out of them, I tossed them off the bed and let him pull me down into his arms. I thought he'd turned me on when we'd been mostly dressed in the car. Completely naked and tangled up on his bed? Fuck yes.

I glanced down, and finally got a look at the tattoo that had been partially hidden. It was a dragon—Japanese style, I thought—extending from beside his navel to just above his groin. I traced a finger over it. "That looks like it stung too."

"Mm-hmm." He teased my nipple with his thumbnail. "It was worth it. Now why the hell do you still have pants on?"

I arched an eyebrow. "You tell me."

Paul grinned. Then he grabbed me, kissed me, and got the rest of my clothes off in short order. All that unhurried kissing was a distant memory now. We were both as hungry and demanding as we'd been in the car—panting hard, clawing at skin, rubbing two very erect dicks against each other.

"I don't want to rush," he whispered breathlessly, "but I want you to fuck me again."

I shuddered right down to my toes. "Gimme a condom. Now."

"Don't have to tell me twice."

He broke the kiss and leaned away, reaching for his pants on the floor, and I took advantage of the moment to look him up and down.

Oh God. He's got a lot of ink.

There was another tattoo between his shoulders. Some emblem I kind of recognized but couldn't place. And there was yet another tattoo on his ass. I thought I'd caught a glimpse of one in that dark parking lot, but had brushed it off as shadows playing tricks on my eyes. No, it was really there, clear as day, and I had to know the story behind it.

That could wait, though, because right now, I had to have him, and anyway, I didn't get a chance to really look before he came back to me, condom and lube in hand.

Yeah, screw the whole "not being in a hurry" thing. Suddenly it seemed like days since I'd fucked him over the car, and if I didn't get this condom on and this man on his hands and knees in the next thirty seconds...

Paul tore the wrapper, and a jolt of panic shot through me—*he did say he wanted* me *to fuck* him, *right?*—but then he rolled the rubber onto my cock, and I relaxed. Well, as much as any man could relax when he was about to have someone as hot and horny as Paul.

Hand over the lube and let's do this.

"Get on your back," I whispered as I took the lube from him.

"Not my hands and—"

"Changed my mind."

"Fine by me." He got on his back. Slowly stroking himself, he watched me put on the lube, and when I positioned myself between his legs, he bit his lip.

"If I didn't know any better," I said, guiding my cock to him, "I'd think you were a little turned on."

"A little?" He spread his legs wider. "Doesn't begin to describe it."

I met his gaze, and we both grinned. As I pressed the head of my cock against him, he closed his eyes and exhaled. Yeah. A little turned on? That wasn't even the half of it. Good thing I'd already come once, or I would've as I pushed into him.

I took my time even though this wasn't our first round tonight. I eased myself in, partly to tease him and partly because I wasn't in a hurry. Even after he'd relaxed completely, and I was moving in fluid, easy strokes, I didn't speed up. I couldn't help myself—this was too damn hot to do anything except savor every second.

Paul pulled me down to him. I couldn't move much like this, but I didn't mind. I was inside him, and I was against him, and I was kissing him. God, yes. This was perfect. A half-dressed quickie in the dark was fine and good. This was how I liked it, though—naked, lights on, skin touching skin and no reason to rush and a man who loved, loved, *loved* to kiss.

My head was spinning now. I was so fucking turned on, and probably wasn't even remembering to breathe between kisses, but... oh well. Maybe I would pass out. Kind of hard to imagine feeling this good and not passing out. Or waking up from a dream and realizing I was home alone in my own bed with my hand on my dick.

Just don't wake me up yet. Let me enjoy this for a while.

"Sit up," Paul whispered, sounding out of breath. "Do it... a little harder."

I did as he asked, and as soon as I picked up speed, he squeezed his eyes shut and moaned. He kept a hand on my arm, maybe to brace himself, and with his other, he pumped his cock.

"Fuck..." He groaned and arched his back, clenching around me as I thrust into him. "Gonna... gonna come. Do it just like that."

Nope, wasn't dreaming. This was one hundred percent real. Paul was under me, legs apart, stroking his cock while he took mine, skin flushed and gleaming and inked...

I kept my rhythm as steady as possible, ignoring the burning in my hips and thighs, and gritted my teeth to keep myself from coming. Just the sight of him jerking himself off while he took my dick was enough to put me right on the brink, and every time his breath hitched or his abs contracted, I was sure we were both about to lose it.

Then his eyes flew open. His lips parted. A shudder brought his shoulders up off the bed, and he whispered, "Oh God," right as semen shot across his tense abs.

And like I knew I would, I came too. I fucked him, and he stroked himself, and rhythm went completely out the window and who the hell cared when I was coming inside him while he swore and shuddered.

His hand stopped. He relaxed onto the bed with a blissed-out sigh, and I took a few more jerky, uneven thrusts before I also relaxed. I leaned over him, resting my weight on my shaking arms.

Paul lifted his head and kissed me lightly, and as he sank back to the bed, drew me down with him. I stayed there for a moment, enjoying some lazy kisses before I sat up again and pulled out.

We both got up to clean ourselves off.

"Be right back." I stepped into the bathroom and took care of the condom. After I'd washed my hands, I came back to bed, where Paul had collapsed onto his back. As I joined him, I cautiously slid toward him, wondering if he was the type who didn't like to be touched after sex.

And that was another point in his favor—he didn't push me away. We were both wrung out and shaking, but he gathered me in his arms and, while we caught our breath, stole light kisses here and there. After the last couple of guys I'd dated, the affection was more novel than it should've been, but whatever. I liked it.

After a while, as he reached up to smooth my hair, the tattoo on his arm caught my eye.

"Oh hey." I propped myself up on my elbow. "Now I can finally look at your tattoos."

"Mm-hmm." He lay back so I could see them better. "You really like ink?"

"A lot."

"But none of your own?"

"Not yet." I traced the curve of the dragon on his hip. "These have stories behind them?"

"Every one of them."

I was curious about the story behind the elaborate sailing ship on the left side of his ribs, but it was the slightly faded and incredibly intricate fighter jet on his upper arm that kept drawing my focus. "Okay, tell me about that one."

He glanced at it. "It's a Super Hornet." He grinned, tracing his fingers over the lines. "I used to fly them."

An image of him in a flight suit flickered through my mind.

Oh, Paul, you have no idea how much hotter you just became.

"I didn't realize you were a fighter pilot." I snickered. "Maybe we should have 'Danger Zone' playing next time we fuck."

"Oh my God, no." He laughed. "Besides, they fucked to 'Take My Breath Away,' not 'Danger Zone.'"

I waved a hand. "Yeah well, I wasn't jerking off to the scenes with that song."

"Don't tell me you jerked off to the dog fights."

My face burned. "Come on—hot guys in flight suits being badass at Mach 1? Wouldn't you jerk off to that?"

"Well, yeah. That's why I became a fighter pilot."

I snorted. "You're joking."

Paul chuckled. "Yeah, I am. Sort of. It was mostly because I liked the idea of flying, especially at that speed."

I traced the edge of the jet's wing. "So was it actually as fun as you thought it would be?"

"It... Most of the time, yes." He paused, and his eyes lost focus for a split second. Then he shook himself and cleared his throat as he met my gaze again. "It had its moments that made me think twice, but for the most part, it was pretty amazing."

I was about to ask what it was like, but he trailed his fingers down my side, and when I gasped, he asked, "You in any hurry to get going?"

"Depends." I grinned, running with the subject change. "What happens if I stay?"

"Only one way to find out."

"Well, as long as you're not sick of me..."

He slid closer and kissed me. "Not a chance."

"Then no, I'm not in a hurry."

"Good." He kissed me again, and didn't stop.

I decided I could get seriously hooked on hooking up with him. Paul was something else in bed. He was like a checklist of everything I always hoped for when I slept with someone new.

Attentive? Check.

Loves kissing? Check.

Enjoys being on the bottom? Check.

God knew if we had anything in common outside the bedroom, and maybe we'd eventually realize we were incompatible for anything that didn't involve orgasms.

Until then, I had every intention of staying in this bed until neither of us could walk.

CHAPTER 6

PAUL

IT WAS SUNDAY, so the office was mostly deserted. That was the beauty of a base so small and quiet—unless there was a major crisis or a base-wide training exercise, a lot of departments worked Monday through Friday, nine to five. There wasn't the usual constant stream of chaos that generally came with being the CO, and for that, I was thankful. Before coming here, I'd been executive officer of a base where we all got nervous when shit *stopped* hitting the fan. NAS Adams was a nice change of pace.

Sometimes my phone rang on the weekends, but it was rare that I had to come into the office outside my normal working hours. Most of the time, if I came in on a weekend, it was because I chose to, and that usually happened on days like this when it was pouring down rain and I couldn't go golfing. Might as well take advantage of the empty office to get some paperwork done and answer a few hundred emails. Of course my golf clubs were in my trunk in case the weather broke, but as shitty as it was out there now, I wasn't holding my breath.

If that additional squadron moved here, the base would

be busier. More people meant more potential for bullshit that I'd have to deal with. If a ship moved in, even more. From the sound of it, the ship wouldn't be docking here for another three years or so, and I'd probably transfer out before then anyway, so I wasn't worried. My cushy-ass job would most likely stay that way.

Assuming, of course, I could focus on that cushy-ass job and didn't get myself fired.

Sitting here on a Sunday afternoon and staring off into space wasn't all that risky, but I'd been doing this all week. That was why I had emails and crap to catch up on in the first place. I'd even zoned out while I was on a conference call with the senators who were coming to town next week, but thank God I hadn't missed anything important. At least I hoped I hadn't. I'd find out when the senators showed up.

I pulled my gaze away from the hypnotic gray rain and turned back to the stack of papers on my desk. Then to my screen, where there were dozens of emails still marked as unread. Most of it should have been done by Friday. Some of it, Saturday. But where had my brain been? Not here. Nowhere near here. All I'd been able to think about was the blue-and-black-haired guy who'd still been dozing in the motel bed when I'd left. I'd spent every long, dull meeting thinking about all the racy sexts we'd been exchanging.

Tonight, I was meeting up with Sean after he finished his shift in the car. So there probably wasn't much point in my being here, and if the weather had been nice, my golf game would have been shit.

I shook myself. Whether or not there was a hot guy spending time in my bed, I did have a job—cushy-ass or otherwise—that needed my attention. For one thing, I had two Sailors coming in for Captain's Mast this week, and I needed to have my head screwed on for that. They were facing potentially serious charges, and it was up to me to determine whether they would be punished at my level or advanced to court-martial. Whether or not they'd fucked up, they deserved a fair hearing and a resolution from someone who wasn't busy daydreaming about a cab driver with a fantastic mouth and an amazing cock.

Everything kept circling right back to Sean. Of course it did. He was shiny and new. He was something that didn't hurt like Jayson or our breakup. So maybe I needed to—

No. I was stupid if I thought I could get him out of my system. That never worked. Especially not with someone like me who'd only needed two drags to develop a nicotine habit that had taken twenty years to kick. Trying to get him out of my system would only get me hopelessly hooked on him, but I was pretty sure the USS *Hooked On Sean* had already disappeared over the horizon.

Some footsteps in the hall pulled me out of my thoughts. I could tell who it was even before I saw him; Travis Wilson, a colleague and buddy of mine, walked with a slight limp, so his footsteps were pretty distinct.

Sure enough, he appeared in the doorway. "Hey. Thought I heard you rustling around."

"And here I thought I was being quiet."

"You? Pfft. That'll be the day, my friend." He came into the office, tossed his cover on one chair, and eased himself gingerly into the other. Wincing slightly, he added, "Let me guess—tee time got rained out?"

"Yep. How are you?"

He gave a slight shrug. "Held together by stubbornness and Motrin. The usual. You?"

"About the same." I pushed my chair back and stood. "In fact, I think I could use some coffee."

"Yeah, me too. I was heading that way when I realized you were here."

We headed down the hall to the break room. On the way, I walked a little bit slower than usual, and not just because my hips were pleasantly sore. Travis would never ask someone to slow down, not even when he was obviously struggling to keep up, so I tried not to make him rush. How the hell he managed to run for his physical readiness tests, I had no idea, but the man wasn't kidding about being held together by stubbornness and Motrin. Probably more stubbornness than anything. Like me, he hated letting on that he still felt any of his old injuries. I sometimes wondered if he had the same nagging fear in the back of his mind that if he let the pain show, the Navy would reconsider their decision not to medically retire him. I sure as fuck worried about it every time I had a twinge in my neck.

The break room, like the rest of the building, was empty. We each went through the motions of making ourselves some coffee—thank God for a Keurig so we didn't have to wait for the pot to brew. Once he'd finished polluting his with creamers and sweeteners, we headed back to my office.

As we stepped into my office and gingerly took our seats, creaking and groaning like eighty-year-olds, it was hard to imagine there'd been a time when we were two feisty young guys who didn't believe in our own mortality. We'd been stationed together on and off throughout our careers. We'd known each other since he was a freshman and I was a senior at the Academy. Even slept together a handful of times over the years, though it never went anywhere. Now we were here, both moving a little slower than we had in our younger days. He'd been at NAS Adams a few months longer than I had.

"No surprise to see you here," he'd said when we'd run into each other. "I think this is where all dented and damaged pilots end up sooner or later."

I was starting to think he was right. The CO before me had been grounded after his second ejection, and retired after the stress fractures in his spine got too painful to ignore. Travis's limp was thanks to an accident that had nearly killed him and paralyzed his radar intercept officer. The last two XOs had been, as Travis called them, gimpy flyboys—one had barely walked away after his helo was shot down in Afghanistan, and the other fucked himself up landing a cargo jet, though I never got the whole story about that incident.

And of course I'd had to hang up my wings earlier than I'd planned, and still had the neck and back problems to remind me why.

But today, my bad landing wasn't the reason I was walking uncomfortably. At least these aches and pains were from something fun.

Travis leaned back in his chair, resting his foot against the edge of my desk, and eyed me as he sipped his coffee. "What's on your mind? You seem like you're"—he gestured at the window—"out there."

"Nothing. Nothing." I rubbed my stiffening neck. "Just, uh..."

"Let me guess." He arched his eyebrow. "Your Friday night was a hell of a lot more exciting than your Sunday?"

I laughed. "You could say that."

He tilted his head. "So does that mean you're doing all right since Jayson took off?"

Jayson? Oh. Right. That guy I was in love with—sort of—for the last... however long that disaster had dragged on.

"Yeah. Yeah. I'm doing good." I exhaled. "It needed to happen."

"Breakups that need to happen can still suck."

"I think this one was past that point." *And it didn't hurt that I waited all of fifteen minutes before I had another guy's dick down my throat.* I shifted in my chair. "Hell, I've already got someone else to keep my mind off him."

Travis's eyes widened. "Already?"

"Already."

He raised his eyebrows, silently asking for details, but I didn't volunteer any. After a brief silence, he shook his head and chuckled. "Well, it's good to see you getting back on the horse. I kind of thought you'd face-plant after this one finally broke down."

I eyed him. "You're not disappointed that you won't get your usual dose of schadenfreude?"

"What?" He put a hand to his chest. "My God, Paul. You make me sound like a sadistic monster."

"Yeah. And?"

"I'm offended."

"No, you're not."

His lips quirked. Then he shrugged. "Okay, I'm not. And yes, I am mildly disappointed that I don't get to enjoy your post-split pain, but I'll get over it."

I laughed, rolling my eyes. "Good. Wouldn't want any lasting trauma over my breakup."

"Right?"

We both chuckled, and shot the shit for a while longer while we drank our coffee. When the clock started creeping up on three thirty, it became clear that I would accomplish precisely nothing today, so I reached for my keys. "All right, Wilson. Don't you have some work to do?"

"Why? You kicking me out?"

"Yes. I am. I need to get my shit done so I can go finish getting over... whatever his name was."

Travis laughed as he stood, which nearly masked the subtle wince. "That's the spirit. All right, I'll get back to work."

As Travis headed back to his office, I tapped my nail on my coffee mug and stared at the chair he'd been occupying. It was weird to hold something back from him. We'd talked about anything and everything over the years, including commiserating over our long strings of broken relationships. A one-night stand wasn't complete without spilling the sordid details to Travis the next day. We were dorks like that. So keeping something back from him felt... off.

On the other hand, he kept some of his cards close to the vest too. Like me, he'd been married twice, and he'd had a number of girlfriends over the years, but he'd never had a lasting relationship with a man that I knew of, and he never said why. For whatever reason, he liked sex with men and relationships with women. The one time he'd let himself get close to a man—he'd never admitted it, but I was pretty sure he'd been in love with him—the end had cut him to the bone. Ten years later, I couldn't imagine he was over it. Maybe that was why he didn't date men. If that was the case, though, he never talked about it. Not even to me.

But that still didn't explain why I couldn't bring myself to mention anything about Sean except generic comments about getting my rocks off. Why was I keeping Sean under wraps?

Oh. Right.

Because he's half my age and this is probably just a fling for him.

Yeah, maybe I should keep this to myself.

CHAPTER 7

SEAN

PAUL and I couldn't see each other all the time, but we sure made use of the time we could spend together. Whatever his job was—undoubtedly *something* involving aircraft, since he was probably still in the same field even if he didn't fly anymore—it sometimes involved long hours and the odd last-minute cancellation. Sometimes all we could manage was a late-night quickie in the backseat on some unmarked side road. Other times, we were luckier.

Tonight, I'd busted my ass to finish a paper for one of my classes so I'd be free when Paul left work. In the space of five minutes, I'd sent the paper to my instructor, and Paul had texted me to let me know he'd checked into a no-tell motel outside of town. Twenty minutes later, we'd been in bed.

It occurred to me more than once that we were spending a lot of money on places to fuck, and there might be a reason he wouldn't take me back to his place. A wife, maybe? I didn't bring it up, though. I wasn't keen on explaining that we couldn't go back to my place because I was embarrassed as fuck about still living with my father.

And he didn't like talking about work, unlike most military guys I'd known. That was fine by me. Apparently we'd instilled our own little Don't Ask, Don't Tell policy.

Whatever. He was getting some rebound sex, and I was getting some amazing sex, so to hell with it. If I went more than two or three days without some of that oh-my-God-addictive sex, I started getting twitchy.

Now, we were exactly where I'd wanted to be all fucking week—under the covers and kissing lazily. My hair was still damp from the shower we'd shared after we'd worked up a hell of a sweat. His was mostly dry because it was shorter than mine, but was still cool between my fingers.

After a while, Paul drew back a bit and tilted his head to one side, then the other, wincing subtly.

"What's wrong?" I asked.

"Oh, just an old injury." He waved a hand. "Comes with age. And a military career."

I grimaced. "Ouch."

"Eh, it's not bad. Was a bit stiff yesterday, but the chiropractor worked some magic on it, so it's better now." He grinned. "Couldn't let it ruin tonight, could I?"

I laughed. "Well, yeah, that helps. But seriously, I really was hoping you felt better."

"I know." He pressed a soft kiss to my forehead. "And I do appreciate it. Unfortunately, this will probably be with me for the rest of my life. Sometimes it's not so bad, sometimes, well..."

"Sounds... pleasant." I was curious what had happened, but he seemed kind of evasive about the subject, so I didn't touch it. "I never did ask you about some of your tattoos." I ran my hand over the Super Hornet. "Besides this one, I mean."

"They all have stories behind them. Ask away."

"Well, what about the one between your shoulders? I swear I've seen that emblem before, but I can't remember what it is."

He glanced over his shoulder as if he could somehow bring the tattoo into his peripheral vision. "Oh, a bunch of us did that after we graduated from the Academy. We were full of ourselves and thought we were gods because we'd been through Annapolis." He rolled his eyes. "So we had the Academy's emblem tattooed on."

"I guess I can see why. I mean, who wouldn't have their Hogwarts—"

"Shut up." He laughed, batting my hand away. "So what about you? Any tattoos in the future?"

I gestured at my unmarked skin. "Maybe when I have some money."

"Just don't do any on a bet. Trust me."

"I'll keep that in mind."

He chuckled again and kissed my cheek.

"So do you still fly?" I asked.

A faint wince flicked across his face, and he shook his head. "No. Those days are, um... behind me."

"Oh." I wasn't sure what to say to that. I was admittedly curious about what it was like to fly, but the subject seemed a bit tender. Maybe that was why he didn't talk about work much. I had no idea what he did now that he wasn't flying, but he wasn't in a hurry to volunteer that or what had grounded him, so I cleared my throat and changed the subject. "So, um... that club where I picked you up the other day. You go there a lot?"

Paul seemed to relax a bit, like he was relieved by the subject change. Settling back against the pillows, he absently ran a hand along my arm. "That was my first time there, actually. You?"

"I've only been there once." I wrinkled my nose. "Wasn't all that impressed."

"Neither was I." His eyes shifted toward me, and he grinned. "But then, I was kind of distracted."

Goose bumps prickled my back, not to mention my forearm where his fingers were trailing back and forth.

"So which of the clubs *do* you like?" he asked. "Any of them?"

"Backdoor Bob is a good one."

"Really?" His fingers stopped, and he eyed me. "That one seemed like kind of a dump."

I shook my head. "It's old and rundown, but it's got a pretty good crowd after about ten."

"I would not have guessed."

"And fair warning—they do not water down the drinks."

"Good to know." He smirked. "Pretty sure they don't pour them as strong as they do in some ports overseas."

"I thought the ports watered them down."

"Some. But not all. Definitely not all. When you order a Long Island Iced Tea, and it's almost completely clear?" Paul laughed. "You better drink it slow or you will be *fucked* up."

"Sounds like my kind of place."

"Really?"

"Well." My cheeks burned. "I don't drink that heavily. But man, if I'm going to fork over twelve bucks for a drink, it better be strong."

"I am completely with you on that." He paused. "Hmm. Now you've got me curious about that club, though."

Weirdly, a pang of jealousy caught me right in the chest.

Why was I jealous? So we'd slept together a few (dozen) times?

Then, with a mischievous grin, he added, "Except that seems like an awful long way to go just to get one drink and then call you." He winked.

I shivered. "You could always save time and money by having me take you down there in the first place."

"What's the point of that?" He reached up and drew me down to him. "By the end of the night, I'm going to be begging you to fuck me whether we're here or in Flatstick." He brushed his lips across mine. "Might as well stay in Anchor Point, you know?"

"I am so not going to argue with that." I kissed him, and suddenly clubs and drinks didn't need to be discussed any further.

Then I remembered how he'd winced and stretched earlier, and I broke the kiss. "Wait. Your neck isn't too—"

"Nope." He slid an arm around my waist. "Absolutely not."

"You sure? We can—"

Paul kissed me. He held me tighter, and I melted against him, blood pounding in my ears as my cock hardened against his thigh. If his neck bothered him at all, he didn't let on.

Well, if he wasn't too sore for another round, I sure as hell wasn't saying no.

So I rolled him onto his back, and made sure neither of us could walk the next day.

CHAPTER 8

PAUL

THANKS to some obnoxious streetlights beyond our window, the motel room was brighter than I would have liked. Not that I was sleeping anyway.

Beside me, Sean had long since dozed off. It was nearly midnight, and we'd had sex twice since we'd checked in, so normally I wouldn't have been far behind him, but there was one problem—my neck was *killing* me.

At home, I would've pulled a bag of peas from the freezer and leaned against that for a while, but since Sean and I were still meeting in motels instead of going back to his place or mine, that wasn't an option. I had to do something, though, or sleep wasn't going to happen. Between my neck, the rock-hard mattress, and the pillows stuffed with magazines or whatever, I was miserable.

Careful not to wake him, I got out of bed and slipped on my boxers. In the bathroom, I dug through my shaving kit to find the ever-present bottle of Motrin—good ol' Vitamin M —and dry-swallowed two.

Then... ice.

There was an ice machine down the hall and a small

bucket on the table. A bunch of ice cubes wrapped up in one of the thirty-grit towels wouldn't be comfortable, but it might help.

I glanced toward the bed. Sean was still asleep, and he wasn't a light sleeper by any means. Still, he might notice if I actually left the room and came back.

Damn. Maybe we needed to give up this motel nonsense and meet at my place. The bored housewives of Admiral's Row would notice, and they'd talk, and the gossip would be swirling around the base until the end of time, but at least we'd be sleeping on a decent bed with easy access to ice packs. As much as my neck hurt tonight, fueling the rumor mill actually seemed like a reasonable trade off.

I sighed, kneading the rigid muscles on the left side of my neck. No, I didn't like putting anyone on that radar unless something was serious. People could talk about me all they wanted—and apparently the sordid love life of the openly gay commanding officer was a hot topic—but I didn't want Sean in the middle of that.

Well, whether I started taking him home or not, I was here now, with no frozen peas for my sore neck. If I could at least put something cold on it, though, it would help. I glanced around the bathroom, then took down one of the bath towels. I rolled it up, ran the faucet over it, wrung it out, and then wrapped it around the back of my neck. The cold drew a hiss out of me. As often as I iced my neck, I should've been used to something like this against—

"Paul?"

I spun around, which made my neck feel *great.*

Sean blinked a few times, shielding his eyes from the bathroom light. "You okay?"

"Yeah. Yeah. Just, uh..." Now I probably looked like an

idiot, standing here with a wet towel on my neck. "Didn't hear you get up."

He smiled sleepily. "Didn't hear *you* get up either."

"Yeah, that was the idea." I smiled back. "I didn't want to disturb you."

"Much appreciated. But..." His brow pinched. "What's wrong with your neck?"

"Hurts a bit. I figured something cold would help, and this was the closest thing."

He pointed at the door. "Isn't there an ice machine out there?"

"Yeah, but... like I said, I didn't want to disturb you."

He rolled his eyes. "Jesus, Paul. If you're hurting enough to be awake, go get some damn ice." He paused. "Actually, stay here. I'll go get some."

Before I could respond, he disappeared. I took off the damp towel and dropped it in the sink, and when I stepped out into the room, he'd pulled on a pair of jeans.

"I'll be back in a second." He took the bucket and room key. "Should I fill it? How much do you need?"

"Eh, half the bucket's probably fine."

"Okay. Be right back."

With that, he was gone.

I blew out a breath and leaned against the wall. I felt bad for waking him up, but God bless him. I'd been with one too many guys who would've either been annoyed at being woken up, or seen it as an opportunity for another orgasm. I should've known Sean was different.

Because he's different in every way. He's not like any guy I've ever known.

You can't really want to be with an old guy whose blood is half Motrin. Can you?

As if on cue, the door opened, and Sean came in with the bucket of ice.

"Sorry it took longer than it should've." He handed me the bucket. "The machine was out of order, so I had to go to the one on the other side of the building."

"The—" I glanced at the ice. I'd been so lost in my own thoughts, I hadn't even realized he'd been gone very long, never mind long enough to go all the way around the building. "Thanks. You're a godsend."

He smiled. "You're welcome. Do you need a hand with it?"

"No, no. I've got it."

There was a plastic bag inside the bucket, so I kept the ice inside that, knotted it, and wrapped the whole thing in a thin, coarse towel. Then I laid it on my neck where the wet towel had been earlier. It was a lot more comfortable against my skin than something wet and cold. I really should have gone and gotten the ice myself. Idiot.

With the comforting chill against my sore muscles, I sighed heavily. "Oh. Much better."

"Good." He smiled faintly, but it faded. "Is that... is that why you don't fly anymore?"

"Yeah. When I—" *Flight deck. There. Gone. Too fast. Pull up! Too late.* I shuddered. Almost ten years, and that memory could still fuck with me.

"Paul?" Sean tilted his head. "You okay?"

"Yeah. Yeah." I adjusted the makeshift ice pack on my neck. "It's from a bad landing. Could've been a lot worse, though."

His lips parted. "Oh. Well, I'd offer to massage it for you, but..." He grimaced. "If there's an actual injury, I don't want to fuck it up more."

"It's okay. The ice helps." I took his hand and squeezed

gently. "Can't promise much more excitement tonight, though."

He ran his thumb along the side of my hand. "I'll live. Glad you're okay, though."

"Yeah, yeah. I'm fine. It's just an age-old injury and compounded by old age. Word to the wise—don't get old."

Sean laughed. "I'll keep that in mind." He watched me for a moment as I pressed the pack of ice against the stiff muscles. "So, if you don't mind me asking... what exactly happened when you..." He gestured at my neck. "I mean, you don't have to. If it's... you know..."

"It's okay." I took a deep breath. "The short version is I crashed when I was landing on an aircraft carrier."

His whole body stiffened. "Whoa. Are you serious?"

"Yep." The ache in my neck intensified from the memory, and I dug the ice in a little harder. "We were doing carrier quals. Practicing takeoffs and landing. Which you have to do—a lot—because you're aiming for something the size of a floating leaf that's bouncing around and going thirty knots or so."

"Jesus..."

"Yeah. So that day, the seas were horrendous. In theory, flight ops could've been canceled, and probably should've, but we need experience in rough seas. We can't only fly when the seas are calm. Problem was, no one realized how much worse the weather was going to get that day until we were already in the air."

"How much you wanna bet this landing's gonna be shit?" my RIO had mused on our approach.

"Long as we don't end up in the water, right?"

"No pressure, man."

My mouth went dry, and I kneaded the ice pack to occupy my fingers. "So we were coming back in, and right before I came down, the deck pitched harder than I antici-pated. We missed the arresting wire because it wasn't there anymore because the damn deck had dropped out from under the tail hook, but my landing gear hit one side and not the other. Not just with the force of the plane coming down, but the deck coming up. Destroyed the landing gear, and then—"

My stomach turned, and not because I'd thrown back some Motrin without food. To this day, I could feel the spin-ning-falling-weightlessness of my bird losing control. I had been absolutely certain we were going to die, and I'd prayed it would be quick instead of slow and fiery.

"Anyway. It... Everything after that's kind of a blur." Everything except broken glass, and shouts, and pain, and the sight of my unconscious RIO with blood all over one side of his face... I cleared my throat as I adjusted the ice pack. "We both made it out, thank God, but that was the end of flying for both of us."

"I can see why. That sounds terrifying."

"You are not kidding." I lowered the ice pack and rolled my shoulders. "It could have been so much worse, though. Even without killing us." I stared at the motel room's ugly carpet. "A good friend of mine hit the back of the ship during a night landing in rough seas. Thank God he was high enough that he didn't actually smash into it, or he'd be dead."

"So what happened? He sheer off his landing gear or something?"

"And a good chunk of the bird with it, yeah. Worst part was they had to eject right before the jet went off the edge of the deck into the water. Had to send search and rescue in after them."

"In bad seas?"

I nodded. "One of the SAR swimmers got hurt, but by some miracle, they got my buddy and his RIO out."

"Were *they* all right?"

"Sort of. Both were unconscious, and it was a good forty-eight hours before anyone knew for sure if they'd make it. Travis has some nasty chronic back problems now, but he got lucky as hell." I grimaced. "His RIO wound up paralyzed—he broke his back in the crash, and they jostled his spinal cord pulling him out of the water."

Sean blinked. "Oh my God."

"He survived, though. After a crash like that, having both of them make it out alive was a miracle enough."

"No kidding."

I chuckled. "Though, if you knew Travis, you wouldn't be surprised he got out. He's a stubborn motherfucker."

Sean's eyebrow rose. "Birds of a feather?"

"Something like that, yeah." I tilted my head to one side, then the other, stretching the muscles that were slowly relaxing. "Pilots are all crazy. That's why we all get along."

He laughed. "Is that why *we* get along?"

I laughed too, glad he couldn't see the way my stomach somersaulted. "Well, we do more than fly together, so..."

"That's true." He came closer and put his hands on my waist. "I kind of like our brand of crazy, though."

My heart fluttered. God, that playful gleam in his eyes —if my neck didn't hurt to the point of distraction...

"Too bad we can't have any more of that tonight." I grimaced apologetically and touched the towel-wrapped ice. "Sorry."

"Sorry?" Sean grinned. He kissed me softly, and when our eyes met again, his smile was gentle. "I'm not going to suggest we go another round when you're hurting enough to put a wet towel on your skin." He squeezed my arm. "Don't worry about it. I'm not going to be walking straight tomorrow anyway."

"You're welcome." I winked, relieved beyond words that he seemed genuinely okay with no more fooling around tonight. "We, um..." I glanced at the ancient clock radio on the bedside table and cleared my throat. "We probably should get some sleep."

His brow creased. "You might want to ice that a little longer."

"I know, but—"

"I'm sure we can find a movie or something to watch." He nodded toward the TV. "There's got to be some stupid late-night programming or something."

I stared at him. "You... Don't you have class tomorrow?"

"At noon, yeah."

"But you—"

He kissed me again. "Relax. We can watch something until we start to fall asleep. By then, hopefully your neck won't hurt so much."

"Oh. I... Yeah. That sounds good. I think the remote is by the TV."

While I got comfortable—sort of—on the bed, Sean scrolled through the channels until we found some old good cop/bad cop movie from like the 1970s. Once I was situated, he sat beside me, and we both leaned against the headboard while I continued icing my neck.

Of all the outcomes I'd pictured if I woke him up while getting myself some pain relief, this hadn't even occurred to me. Even though I knew damn well Sean wasn't a jackass, past experience had me expecting opportunistic attempts at sex. Or a grumbled "turn off the fucking light." Or bitching about how little sleep *he'd* gotten because of me.

I shouldn't have been surprised when none of those

things happened. Sean wasn't like that. As soon as he'd real-ized why I was awake, he'd gone out and found some ice, and now he was perfectly content to watch a stupid movie until I was comfortable enough to go to sleep. He took everything in stride. He was so easygoing and chill. About this. About everything.

And as we sat there and watched the ridiculous movie, all I could think was...

Where the hell have you been all my life?

Leaning back in my office chair, I stared up at the ceiling. Wasn't like I was getting anything done except wondering what was going on with Sean. There was a pile of paper-work on my desk, and several dozen unanswered emails in my inbox, but today... wasn't happening. The major crises had been handled, of course, but the more tedious shit would have to wait until coffee or a run or *something* shook me out of this space-cadet mode.

The day had started in the best way any day could—with lazy, sleepy sex. He'd had to take off shortly after so he could finish a paper before class, but I'd been in an amazing mood ever since. Now if I could combine that mood with the ability to concentrate, I'd be in good shape.

Instead, I'd been thinking about him all day. This wasn't a rare occurrence, either. The more time I spent with Sean in bed, the more space he took up in my brain.

But was I deluding myself? After all, Sean was half my age, give or take a year. Sure, he was always enthusi-astic in the bedroom, and he'd never once balked when he'd seen my this-is-what-over-the-hill-looks-like body. But at the end of the day, I couldn't imagine anything could really be happening here beyond sex and a little afterglow banter.

Except it sure as fuck felt that way. More so every time I saw him.

What are you getting yourself into this time, Richards?

Someone knocked at my door, startling me back into reality.

"It's open."

Travis leaned into my office. "Hey, you busy?"

"Not really. Come on in."

He stepped in and toed the door shut behind him. As he crossed my office, his limp was slightly more pronounced than usual. I wasn't surprised—he'd been out on the flight line all day yesterday overseeing a quality-control inspection. Technically that wasn't his job, but after the disastrous inspection last year, he wasn't taking any chances. Unfortunately, that meant being on his feet longer than he probably should have.

I rubbed some stiffness out of my neck. "How's your back?"

He grimaced and offered a tight shrug. "Stubbornness and Motrin, man. Stubbornness and Motrin."

"You'd probably feel a bit better if you didn't push yourself quite so hard."

"Uh-huh. And after relaxing this weekend, I'll be fine, and neither of us will be explaining to Admiral Cruz why we failed the inspection."

"Okay, fair. But don't be a martyr for a damn inspection." I smirked. "Because no, I am not putting you in for a Purple Heart because you were on your feet too long."

He flipped me the bird, and we both chuckled.

Travis sat back, slouching in the chair and leaning on his elbow—the very picture of military bearing. He was probably also trying to hide the fact that his back hurt. I did the same thing—better to adopt a slightly sloppy posture than let anyone catch on that it hurt to breathe. Dumb flyboys and their dumb pride, as my first wife would've joked.

I rolled some stiffness out of my shoulders. This time, it was less from my injury and more from being on my hands and knees for a while last night. My hips had a similar ache, and I was pretty sure there was a bruise right under where my wallet sat in my front pocket. Couldn't really complain about that, though.

Suppressing a grin, I said, "So, you come in here to shoot the shit, or you got something work-related to discuss?"

"On a weekend?" He snorted. "Please."

"Eh. Yeah. Good point. Why are you even at work, then?"

He waved a hand in the general direction of his office. "Needed to get caught up on some emails, and there's a big stack of chits on my desk that I don't want to see on Monday."

"Same here." I nodded toward my inbox, which had magically accumulated about five hundred chits after I swore it was empty yesterday afternoon. "But what brings you into my office?"

"Taking a state-mandated break, obviously."

We both burst out laughing. State-mandated breaks. In the military. *Right.*

"Actually, as long as we're both being unproductive, I'm curious about something," he said.

"Yeah?"

"Yeah. What's going on with you lately?" He tilted his

head and narrowed his eyes. "You've been on another planet recently."

"Nothing. I'm—"

"With all due respect, Captain"—he winked—"I'm gonna have to call bullshit."

I avoided his eyes.

"I knew it." He tapped his knuckle on the edge of my desk. "Come on—out with it."

There was no point in trying to get anything past him. The CIA, the Spanish Inquisition, and my second wife had nothing on Travis Wilson's ability to drag information out of me.

So I took a breath. "I've, uh, been seeing someone."

"Okay. Tell me something I don't know. I know when you're getting laid and when you're not. I *asked* what's going on with you."

"Okay, well." I cleared my throat. "Remember when I said I already had somebody to take my mind off Jayson? It's still that same guy. We kind of jumped into things. Like, it was maybe an hour between walking out of Jayson's room and hooking up with this guy, and somehow we keep hooking up."

"Wow." Travis's eyes widened. "An hour? That's impressive."

I chuckled. "It sure changed the tone of that evening, I'll tell you that."

"I believe it. Where the hell'd you meet him? Because I've been down to those clubs in Flatstick, but haven't had any luck recently."

"I kind of stumbled across him."

"Lucky bastard," he muttered. "Maybe I need to get back on Grindr or something. There wasn't a lot of selection a year ago."

"Worth a shot, right?"

"Says the man who doesn't have to troll the internet for cock at the moment." He studied me. "So what's the problem, then? You wiped out from all the sex with Dickus Maximus, or is there something else going on?"

"Well..."

His eyebrow arched.

"The thing is..." I tapped my fingers on the armrest. "Okay. I've got a question for you."

"Sure. Shoot."

"What do you think about dating people with huge age gaps?"

Travis shrugged. "Guess it depends on how much of an age gap we're talking about."

"Well..." I hesitated. "I mean, what if Kimber brought home a guy like me?"

He laughed. "If she brought home a guy like you, I'd get her head checked, but not because of your age."

"Fuck you." I rolled my eyes. "Seriously, though—it wouldn't bother you?"

"Well." His eyes lost focus for a moment. "I guess it would depend on the guy. I mean, I'm honestly surprised whenever Kimber *doesn't* date someone older than her."

"Why's that?"

"You know her. She's always been a few years ahead of her peers when it comes to maturity. If she started seeing someone older, I'm going to say something if he's a complete creep, but if he seems like a decent guy, I'll trust her judgment."

"Even if he's, say, twice her age?"

Travis's eyebrows rose. "Don't tell me you've got an eighty-year-old oil tycoon on the hook or something."

I burst out laughing. "No, no. I'm the older guy."

"Really? You snagged yourself a twentysomething? Nicely done, shipmate."

"Yeah, well. I keep wondering if I'm being an idiot, or if I... I don't know. He's in his twenties. Like, *early* twenties. I'm forty-two. Is that... weird?"

"Well, I mean..." He paused. "Look, you've been in the Navy since Jesus was an ensign. This kid doesn't remember presidents you voted for. But if you've still got enough common ground to even think about dating, then... well, who's to say it can't work? It depends on the people."

I kept my gaze down. Truth was, the only common ground I knew I had with Sean was in the bedroom. We hadn't gone much farther than that. And if we did, we'd probably find out that the twenty-some-odd years between us were a bigger problem than I wanted to think about right now.

"Obviously you've got something in common with him," Travis went on. "Somehow I don't think it's just that you're having a good time with him in bed and the novelty hasn't worn off."

I laughed, heat rushing into my cheeks. "No, it definitely hasn't worn off." I glanced past him, as if I might see anyone who'd stealthily materialized in the hall outside my office. Irrational paranoia. "But we do seem to have a lot to talk about. He's young, but I... I mean, I kind of forget he is, if that makes sense."

"It does." Travis absently thumbed his jaw. "Are you worried he's a gold digger or something?"

I mulled that over, then shook my head. "He doesn't seem like the type, no. For one thing, he always insists on paying his own way whenever we order out or something."

"Definitely not a gold digger, then."

"No, I don't think so."

"Hmm. Well." He shrugged again. "Like I said, if Kimber started seeing someone older, I'd guess it was because she found someone who can keep her interest. People her own age aren't very good at that. So, maybe this kid likes you because you hit some notes that other guys in their twenties don't."

"That makes sense. He doesn't really seem like guys his own age."

"So maybe he doesn't *like* guys his own age."

"Fair point. But I guess..."

"What are you worried about? If you click with him, go with it."

"Doesn't really seem that simple."

"Why not? What's the worst that could happen?" Travis inclined his head. "You have some horrible breakup? Same thing that's happened with people your own age?"

"I don't know." I sighed. "I think I'm just worried he'll realize he can do better."

"So what if he does?"

I blinked. "What?"

"Look, you've got two choices. You can either date him and see what happens, or you can dump him preemptively because he might hypothetically decide he's too good for you. One of those guarantees things fall apart. The other... well, there's a possibility things don't."

"You really think something like this could work out in the long run?"

"Why not?"

"I don't know." I pinched the bridge of my nose and exhaled. "I want to be realistic and not get my hopes up, but I do want to see where this goes. There's something about him that's..." I dropped my hand. "He's something else."

I expected a typically snide response, but he just watched me silently for a moment before he spoke.

"Paul, thanks to the Navy, we've both learned more than most civilians ever will that life is short and it can change on a dime. Shit, look at us—I can barely walk most of the time, and you're fucked up too."

I nodded, the tension in the back of my neck underscoring his point.

He went on. "Maybe ten years ago, I'd have told you something like this was a bad idea that would probably blow up in your face. But now, I mean, trust your gut. If you've got a good thing going, and the only thing stopping you is his age, go for it." Travis held my gaze with an uncharacteristically serious expression. "Even if it does blow up in your face, it's better than looking back and wondering what might have been."

I swallowed. From anyone else, that would've sounded like something off a stupid inspirational poster. From Travis, it resonated. In all the years I'd known him, he'd only pursued one man for something more than sex, but he'd held back. He'd been afraid of rejection, of damaging both their careers because of DADT, of losing his daughter, and he'd let the guy slip through his fingers. By the time he'd realized what he'd lost, it was too late to go back—I could only imagine how much that regret weighed on him to this day, because *I* was still haunted by the pain in Travis's eyes when he'd watched them lower the casket.

Clearing my throat, I fidgeted in my chair. "I hadn't thought of it that way." I paused. "I'm not even sure this will go anywhere. Maybe I'm getting ahead of myself."

"Maybe. But don't kill it if you think something could come of it. If it doesn't work out, it doesn't work out. If it does..." He smiled. "Then obviously it does."

I released a breath. "You make a good point."

His smile inched toward a grin. "And somehow you're still surprised whenever that happens."

"Hey, considering the source..."

He rolled his eyes and gave me the finger. "On that note, some of us have work to do." Gingerly, he pushed himself up out of his chair. "So I'll go play Solitaire while you do your work."

"I assume Solitaire is a euphemism for Grindr?"

"Shut up."

He left my office, and I was once again leaning back in my chair and staring upward.

Well, Paul. Now what?

It was way too soon to have half a clue about where this thing with Sean could go. Even Jayson and I had still liked each other this early in our relationship. A few months down the line might see me and Sean cruising along happily or fighting at every opportunity. But after talking to Travis, I felt a lot better about taking a chance.

I had no idea where things were headed, but I was sure as hell going to stick around to find out.

CHAPTER 9

SEAN

ON SATURDAY, there was a big festival out on the pier, which meant every driver in town was on duty. Fine by me —lots of rides meant lots of money. And since I could get on base, that meant I was taking sober Sailors to the festival and drunk Sailors home. The drunk ones sometimes forgot to tip, but most of them were entertaining, and so far no one had puked in my car.

The best part? Every time I stopped, I had a new text.

Golfed my worst game in years today, his latest message read. *Your fault. ;)*

I laughed and wrote back, *Too sore or too distracted?*

Almost immediately, he responded, *Yes.*

I put my phone in the cupholder without sending anything—Paul knew I was driving, so he expected my responses to be sporadic.

This afternoon is crawling by. Would go much faster with you.

Oh. *Oh.* He was killing me.

I adjusted the front of my pants, hoping no one on the

sidewalk noticed, and wrote back, *I'll make it up to you tonight.*

I grinned like an idiot. Tonight was going to be hot, especially if we kept flirting and teasing each other all damned day.

Some guys about my age flagged me down, so I put my phone back in the cupholder and pulled up to the curb.

"Can you take us to the base?" one asked.

"Can do. Which gate?"

"Gate one."

"Got it."

I took them to the base, trying not to visibly fidget in my seat as my phone buzzed with what was probably a message from Paul. When I dropped them off, there were some other guys looking for a lift to the pier, so while they climbed in, I quickly read and replied to his message.

I'm looking forward to it. You're always worth the wait.

You're making it impossible to work. You know that, right? ;)

Then I headed back to the pier to drop the new guys off and find some more day-drunk passengers. As expected, there were a couple of Sailors needing a lift, so I pulled up and let them pour themselves into the back of my car. I took them back to the base. Checked my texts. Picked up some more passengers. Took them to the pier. Texted Paul. Picked people up. Dropped them off. Texted. Over and over and over. Not a bad way to spend a shift.

Shortly after I'd stopped for a quick bite, another text came through, but it was from my dad: *You coming to the gym w/me tomorrow?*

I groaned and rolled my eyes. He'd been after me for the last couple of weeks, and experience told me he wasn't going to let up anytime soon. He knew I hit up the base gym on a sporadic but somewhat frequent basis, and that I kicked my own ass without his help. Just... not as often as I should, which was why he was nagging me.

But I had a free evening with Paul tomorrow night, and if I spent the morning at the gym with my dad, I'd be hurting. Which was good—he knew how far to push me with weight lifting—but not terribly appealing. Especially since my muscles already ached thanks to some recent... cardio.

So I wrote back, *Probably not. Have to study.*

At least studying was a bulletproof excuse. God help me when the semester was over.

Toward late afternoon, after I'd dropped off a group of Sailors at the pier, I checked my phone like I'd been doing all day. There was a message, but this time, it wasn't Paul. It was an email notification.

And the email was from medical.

Test results.

Not surprisingly, they were negative. I'd only been with one other guy since the last time I'd had a test. I felt like an idiot for being slightly nervous whenever I checked my results, but it kind of made sense. It wasn't that I was worried about a positive result. If anything, it was leftover nerves from the first few times I'd gone in for testing and convinced myself my dad would have a fit. He'd never given me crap for being gay, but what if he had confirmation that I was sexually active? Back then, I'd been convinced he'd ground me for the rest of my life, though obviously that wasn't an issue now.

And anyway I'd let go of that worry after a corpsman had let it slip to my dad that I'd come in for an HIV/STI test. Apparently he'd thought he was being responsible by breaking protocol and notifying him that his underage son was engaging in "risky behavior."

Dad wasn't having it. He'd read him the riot act, then dragged him into the hospital command master chief's office to let her do the same.

"My son is being responsible for his health," he'd shouted loud enough for the whole office, including me, to hear. "What are you trying to do? Embarrass him? Make him afraid or ashamed to come in down the road? When you have a sexually active teenager coming in here to stay on top of his goddamn health, you test him, give him the results, and keep your bullshit comments to yourself, or I will make sure you're in front of a disciplinary board explaining the meaning of HIPAA. Got it?"

In the car on the way home, he'd apologized, assured me I would never get in trouble for going in for tests, and made me promise I was using—and would continue to use —condoms.

And that was the end of it, but an echo of that nervous "am I about to be busted?" feeling *still* showed up every damn time I did this.

I closed the email and put my phone in the cupholder again. Now a new feeling made my stomach flutter. Paul had agreed to go in for a routine "nope, no bugs" test too, and his had come back a few days ago with the all clear. With the negative results across the board, was there any reason we couldn't go bareback? I'd never done it with anyone else, but if we both had tests declaring we didn't have anything to transmit... then... maybe?

I squirmed in my seat. It had never occurred to me to go without a condom, but the thought of fucking Paul without one made my skin tingle with excitement. As good as it felt with a condom, I could only imagine how much more intense it would be without.

When my shift finally ended, I couldn't get to the motel

fast enough. With a stomach full of butterflies—excited ones and nervous ones—I pulled up to the address Paul had texted me. He was already checked in, waiting for me, and he opened the door the second I knocked.

We'd barely shut the door behind us before his lips were against mine. His fingers combed through my hair, and his other arm wrapped firmly around my waist, keeping me against him and his very prominent erection.

Gently, he tugged at my hair until I tilted my head back, and then he kissed his way down to my throat.

"Been thinking about this all day," he murmured against my neck.

"Yeah?" I pulled his shirt free. "What have you been thinking about?"

"You fucking me."

"Mmm. Can't wait." I glanced at the bedside table, where a strip of condoms sat beside his wallet and keys. My heart skipped. If I was going to broach the subject, now seemed like a better time than when we were tangled up and naked, so I cleared my throat and drew back enough to meet his eyes. "Listen, uh, before we get to that... I got my test results back. All clear."

Paul smiled. "Great. Not that I was all that concerned."

"Yeah, me neither." I shrugged even though I felt anything but dismissive right then. "But it's always good to know."

"Definitely." He kissed me lightly. "This doesn't mean we have to be exclusive or anything. Just, you know, if you are with anyone else..."

"Say something?"

He nodded, and his eyes flicked toward the bedside table. "And condoms. Of course."

My blood went cold. "What about..." I gestured at him, then me.

"What do you mean?"

"Condoms?"

He shrugged. "I don't really see why we need them at this point."

My heart could not possibly have beat any harder. So we were really going to do this. Condoms with other people if it came to that, but with just the two of us? Bareback. Exactly like I'd fantasized about ever since I'd read that email from medical. Exactly like I'd wanted.

Right?

Fuck.

"Sean?" He touched my face. "What's the matter?"

I chewed my lip. "Look, maybe it's not rational, but I'm..." I took a deep breath, then blurted out, "I'm not sure if I'm ready to go bareback yet." I laughed, shaking my head. "God, this is stupid. We're both negative. But I... I don't know."

"Okay." He shrugged again. "We can still use condoms. It's not a big deal."

I blinked. "You don't mind?"

"Absolutely not. If you change your mind, say so."

"Oh."

He studied me. "Did you think I'd mind?"

Kind of, yeah. Which is dumb, because you're you, and why the hell would I expect you to be a jerk?

I shook my head. "I don't know what I thought."

Paul smiled. "Well, for the record, it's your call. The only time I really feel a difference is if I'm on top, but even then, it's fine. And when I'm bottoming, hell, I'm perfectly happy either way—with or without a condom, it feels almost exactly the same for me."

I hesitated, then smiled too. Wrapping my arms around him, I said, "It feels amazing to me even with the condom."

"So you wouldn't be opposed if I suggested we go get a condom and use one? Like now?"

"Not opposed at all."

"Then let's get out of these clothes."

As we stripped, I was excited as hell, but doubt was creeping in fast. I felt stupid for insisting on condoms. He didn't seem offended, thank God. It wasn't that I distrusted him, and I knew for a fact the Navy tested everyone for HIV on a regular basis. I wasn't sure why two negative tests weren't enough to convince me to go bareback. Or why I'd done such a one-eighty from wanting to skip condoms to feeling way too vulnerable without one.

Was I being an idiot now? Or had that been when I was getting myself all turned on and worked up over fucking him bareback? What the fuck was the matter with me?

Paul reached for me, but hesitated. "Hey, you okay?"

Apparently I was wearing my crazy on my sleeve right then. "Yeah." I avoided his eyes. "I'm... I guess..."

"The condom thing?"

Heat rushed into my cheeks, and I nodded.

"Don't sweat it," he said quietly. "It's not something to take lightly."

"I know. But I..." I lifted my gaze again. "I've never gone bareback with anyone. I guess it's hot to think about, but when the rubber meets the road—"

"So to speak."

I paused, replaying what I'd said. Then I burst out laughing.

Paul laughed too, and gathered me in his arms. "It's okay." His tone and expression turned serious. "You have to remember—I grew up when AIDS was still a horrific death sentence. Living in that era leaves an impression." He kissed me softly. "I wouldn't twist your arm even if I gave you a hundred negative tests in a row."

Slowly, I relaxed, wrapping my arms around his waist. Our earlier conversation echoed in my mind, and my stomach flipped. I drew back and looked up at him. "You said you only notice condoms when you're on top." I paused. "Do you... like being on the bottom? All the time, I mean?"

He shrugged. "I love being fucked, but I'll admit I *do* kind of like being on top once in a while."

"Oh." I swallowed. "I..." Hell, might as well cop to it. "I hate bottoming." I wrinkled my nose. "It's not a power thing or anything; I just... don't like the way it feels. I hate it, actually."

"Painful?"

"No, no. Just didn't do anything for me. I tried it a few times, but really, really don't like it."

He smiled, then brushed a light kiss across my lips. "Not everybody does. It's okay."

"You like it, though, right?"

"Mm-hmm." He dipped his head to kiss my neck. "Fucking love it."

"But you like being on top too?"

"I do."

I bit my lip even as I tilted my head back to give him more access to my throat. "So if I can't... If that's not something..."

"Relax." He kissed his way up to my ear. "I am perfectly happy letting you fuck me." He slid a hand over my dick. "*Perfectly* happy."

"Good. Because I really—" I sucked in a breath and shivered "—really like fucking you."

He laughed. "Thought so." Then he looked in my eyes. "That said, there *is* one thing we can do. So I can... well, sort of be on top, but without actually fucking you, since you don't like that part."

I raised my eyebrows. "What's that?"

He traced the tip of his tongue along his upper lip. "Do you trust me?"

"Yeah." My heart pounded. "What do you have in mind?"

He gestured for me to turn over, but I hesitated.

Paul smiled and kissed me softly. "Trust me."

I did trust him, and I couldn't imagine him trying to do something I'd explicitly said I didn't want, so... I turned onto my side with my back to him.

He molded himself to me, pressing his hard-on against my ass for a second before he reached between us, and pushed his cock between my legs. It was odd, but okay—if this turned him on, I wasn't going to say no.

"This all right?" he asked, rocking his hips a little so his dick slid back and forth.

"Yeah. Kind of different."

"You've never done this?"

"Never." And why the hell not? It was... kind of weird, but I liked it. What wasn't to love about him holding me against him? "What do I do?"

"Stay just like this. Squeeze... your thighs together like— God, yeah. Like that." His hand drifted up my chest, and he hooked his fingers over my shoulder. Using that for leverage, he thrust harder. Jesus, the friction was insane. It wasn't going to make me come, but judging by the way he panted in my ear, it was probably going to make *him* come.

Thighs tightly together, I moved my hips in time with his, and Paul groaned, shuddering against me.

Holy *shit*, this was hot.

I wrapped my fingers around my cock and pumped it, and my eyes rolled back as a low moan escaped my lips.

"Goddamn, that feels good," he breathed.

I couldn't form words and didn't bother trying. The friction was weirdly addictive, and with my own hand on my cock while he made those helpless, breathless sounds beside my ear... hot. So hot.

He burrowed his face against my neck. His groan seemed to reverberate right through me, and suddenly *I* was coming, and Paul was thrusting for all he was worth, and then *he* was coming—shuddering against me, gasping and swearing and digging his fingers into my hip.

We both released our breath, and relaxed.

"What do you know?" he slurred against my neck. "Didn't need condoms after all."

I laughed, heat rushing into my cheeks as our earlier conversation echoed through my mind. "That was... a lot hotter than I thought it would be."

He kissed beneath my ear. "Ditto."

We separated, and I was going to get up and clean myself off, but paused to meet his gaze.

He smiled and touched my face. "See? You don't have to bottom, and I can still kind of top."

"So I see." I lifted my head to kiss him softly. "I'll be right back."

He pressed a tender kiss to my forehead. "I'm not going anywhere."

Please, please, mean that...

CHAPTER 10

PAUL

"I STILL DON'T GET why a guy in the Navy would *want* to have a boat."

"Why's that?" I glanced over my shoulder as I stepped from the dock onto my cabin cruiser. "Seems like the Navy would attract people who like water, don't you think?"

"Well, okay." Sean joined me on the boat. "I guess I thought the novelty of being at sea would wear off."

"Being out on a ship, yeah. But this is my boat. And there's beer onboard." With a wink, I added, "And condoms."

"Oh, I think I'm gonna like this boat."

"I figured you would." I put my hand on the small of his back and kissed his cheek.

It had been weeks since I'd texted him for a lift, and we'd been seeing each other at every available opportunity ever since. Usually we met up to hook up, but we'd both started getting a little cabin fever.

We still had to be kind of discreet. Anchor Point was a small town, and NAS Adams was a small base, and gossip was the local pastime. Openly gay or not, I didn't like my personal life being scrutinized by the base busybodies, so I preferred to fly under the radar as much as possible. Sean didn't seem to mind—he probably didn't feel the need to advertise that he was fucking someone twice his age—so we'd kept it on the down low.

Except all those motel room walls had started closing in, and we'd started noticing we still liked each other when we *weren't* testing the structural integrity of shocks or bed frames, so we'd agreed to go out in public. In broad daylight. Granted we'd only be down at the marina and then out on the water, but this would be a low-key step toward seeing if we were just fuck buddies or stood a chance at more.

So here we were on my boat. I carefully maneuvered us from the marina, and when we were clear of the no-wake zone and in the open water, I gave it some more gas. Under a beautiful blue sky, we cruised along the rolling waves at a nice steady clip. Yeah, this was a perfect day for this.

And as the marina faded behind us and we continued into the Pacific, I started to relax. There weren't any other boats out nearby. On the horizon, a red and black cargo ship inched south. Closer to the base, one of the gray patrol boats cruised around, but we were far from their jurisdiction.

Even with the gentle rocking, Sean moved around on the boat with ease. He did live in a coastal town, so maybe he had experience on the water. That, or he was one of those people who was every Sailor's envy—the kind with natural sea legs. Asshole.

Up ahead, a large swell rose. Fell. Rose again.

"Hang on," I called out.

He put a hand on the railing, and when the boat hit that swell, barely wobbled. "You get a lot of waves like that out here?"

"Open ocean. Anything's possible." I glanced at him

and smirked. "Not that you seem to have any trouble with them."

Chuckling, he came closer, but he did keep a hand on the rail and threw a cautious glance out at the water. "I've been on boats since I was a kid." He shrugged. "Never seemed like a big deal to me."

"You're lucky."

"Had a hard time on a ship?"

"Oh God." I groaned. "My first time at sea, I spent a week heaving."

Sean laughed. "Really?"

I nodded. "My squadron never let me hear the end of it either, the fucking bastards. I kind of deserved it, though."

"Why's that?"

"Because I always gave them shit for getting sick in the air, especially in flight school. I could handle a hell of a lot more than they did. The boat, though? That was my fucking downfall."

"Guess karma is shaped like an aircraft carrier sometimes."

I laughed. "It so is."

"Looks like you've gotten used to it, though."

"Finally," I muttered.

I steered us south, and Anchor Point faded behind us. Off the next few miles of coast, there were some small but deep coves where a boat could slip in and drop anchor without being visible from the open sea. Some of them were even far enough from the highway to be hidden from the view of passing cars if we decided to stop for more than lunch.

As I drove the boat, I stole a few surreptitious glances at Sean. It was hard not to—he was amazingly attractive, and sometimes I couldn't fathom what in the world he saw in me.

His sunglasses covered his eyes, and a hint of sunburn lit up his cheekbones. It was especially noticeable since he'd just dyed his hair again a couple of days ago. The blue had been fading recently, but now it was the same rich cobalt it had been when we'd started dating, and the black was *black*. It was the reason for the faint stains between my fingers—they'd tripped me out the first few times, but eventually, I'd figured out they were a result of running my fingers through Sean's recently dyed hair, especially when it was wet. Which it often was, since we took a lot of showers together.

It wasn't like this was the first time I'd ever been near him, or I'd ever seen him, or he'd ever busted me stealing a glance at him. But every time, my body reacted like it *was* the first time.

No. Not even like it was the first time. Like the effect he had on me was cumulative. Snowballing. Getting more intense every single time our eyes met or our fingers brushed.

And I was staring again.

I cleared my throat. "Hey, um, I could stand to eat. You?"

"Hell yeah." He gestured at the ladder leading down to the cabin. "Want me to get the cooler?"

"Yes, please." While he went down the ladder, I nosed the boat into one of the coves.

Minutes later, we were relaxing on the deck in a pair of deck chairs with a couple of sandwiches and some cold beers.

I *clink*ed my beer can against his. "Cheers."

"Cheers."

As I took a drink, he arched an eyebrow above his sunglasses. "Should you be drinking and boating?"

"I'm in the Navy, Sean." I rolled my eyes. "If one beer is enough to intoxicate me—"

A laugh burst out of him, and he nodded. "Okay, okay. Point taken." He looked around the boat. "So do you fish when you come out here?"

"Not really. Fishing never appealed to me."

"Boring?"

"Boring and not much return. When they start putting precleaned, prebreaded fish down there, we'll talk."

Sean chuckled. "Breaded fish might get a little soggy in the water."

I wrinkled my nose. "Yeah, that does sound pretty gross. So, no fishing."

"No fishing." He took a sip of beer. Balancing the can on his knee, he thumbed the tab. "So I thought you joined the Navy to fly. You seem to like being on the water just fine now. Did you have the change of heart before or after the... that time you talked about?"

"After." I looked out over the water as a familiar prickle wandered up my spine. "Once a pilot, always a pilot, I guess. I told you we're all crazy. We also all need to steer something besides a car once in a while."

Sean grimaced. "You miss it? Flying, I mean—not the landings."

"Sometimes." I gazed up at the sky. "There's really nothing like it." In my mind's eye, I could see clouds whipping past, and maybe it was just the boat gently rocking, but I swore I could feel the G-forces of a barrel roll or a dive. The white-striped black flight deck flashed through my mind, just the way I'd seen it through the windscreen on that last approach.

Shaking myself, I turned to Sean. "I had my fun. I also had some near misses, lost a couple of good friends out there, and *almost* lost several more. So I'm okay with having my feet on the ground from here on out."

"When you put it like that, I can see why." He played with the tab with his thumbnail, punctuating the silence with a *tink-tink-tink*. "Still seems like it'd be hard to quit. After you wanted to do it for so long, I mean."

"In a way, it was." I took a deep swallow of beer, then set the can in the cupholder. "To be honest, I was relieved when they grounded me. No way in hell would I admit it out loud, but after a landing like that, I was afraid to go back up. My confidence was trashed. I'd landed on a carrier hundreds of times, but I was terrified if I tried again, I'd choke and get us both killed. Or even if I didn't choke, the next crash wouldn't be as gentle."

He shuddered. So did I.

Shifting in his chair, he asked, "After something like that, you must have... like..."

"PTSD?"

Sean nodded.

I rolled my shoulders to hide a shiver. "You better believe it."

We didn't say much for a while. I finished my beer and dropped the can in the recycling bag. As I pulled a fresh one from the cooler, I offered him one, but he was still working on his first.

I popped the tab and sat back. Gaze fixed on the horizon, I said, "It's so weird I think there's a lot of people in the military with some form of PTSD. Especially since 2003. Even if they've never been in combat, there's always something to fuck you up. For me, I did two combat tours, got shot at, dropped bombs... and the only flashbacks I ever have are from trying to land during a training exercise."

He was quiet for a moment. "Do you get flashbacks very often?"

"Not so much anymore. Last time it happened was after I had to stop suddenly in the car—apparently a near miss on the road is a trigger." I shifted and willed the queasy feeling in my stomach to go away. "But I can sleep now. I could probably even fly. I'd just... I'd rather not."

Sean nodded again. "Totally makes sense."

I exhaled. "You know, I've never told anyone about this before."

"Really?"

Shaking my head, I looked out at the water. "Not something one pilot's going to admit to another."

More silence. Shit. We'd come out here to enjoy an afternoon on the water, not go down the rabbit hole of why I didn't fly anymore. That line of thought could ruin an entire night of sleep—I didn't dream about it as much as I used to, but it happened sometimes—and I wasn't about to let it ruin today.

"You know, this is one of my favorite parts of being out on a boat like this." I slid my hand up his inner thigh. "Completely out in the open, and completely private at the same time."

"Yeah." He grinned, rolling his shoulders as if relieved by the subject change, and put his hand over my arm. "Out here, we could almost fake it like we're actually dating."

I met his gaze. "Who says we're faking it?"

"*Are* we?"

"I don't know."

He moistened his lips and inched his chair closer to

mine. "Well, maybe we'll just have to sneak off like this a few times until we know for sure."

"I like that plan." I leaned toward him. "Might take more than a few times. You know, since we have a habit of not coming up for air."

Sean laughed, eyes flicking toward my lips before looking right into mine again. "Either way, it sounds like fun."

"Does it?"

He tilted his head, and right before he kissed me, he said, "Sounds like a hell of a good time."

After a couple of orgasms apiece, we'd settled back on the deck chairs again, wearing nothing but swimming trunks and blissed-out grins. Sean was working on his second beer, and I opened a can of Coke for myself—better to go easy on the beer when I was at the helm.

He absently ran his thumb along the side of my hand, oblivious to the invisible sparks he sent crackling along my nerve endings, and we soaked up the sun and the gentle breeze. Neither of us spoke for a long time. I was enjoying the hell out of the afternoon, but then I glanced at him and realized he was... distant. His eyes were fixed on the horizon, but he seemed to be looking right through it. Above his sunglasses, his brow was taut.

"Hey." I squeezed his arm. "Earth to Sean?"

He shook himself, then turned to me, and a faint smile materialized. "Sorry. What?"

The smile seemed forced and made me uneasy. I sat up a little. "You okay?"

"Yeah. Yeah." He sat up too, rolling some tension out of his shoulders before he set his beer can in the cupholder.

My stomach knotted. This was the closest thing to an actual date we'd ever had, and if he was distant and uncomfortable, that didn't bode well for things going forward. Especially since we were two hours from the marina—that could be a long, awkward ride back if things went to shit. "Is, um, everything all right?"

Sean nodded. He took off his sunglasses and met my gaze. "I was thinking about what you said earlier. About the military and PTSD."

"Oh." Hadn't seen that one coming. And I didn't want to be relieved by it—PTSD was fucking brutal—but admittedly, I was, if only because I'd expected things to suddenly go downhill between us. "So, what about it?"

"I guess I was just thinking you're right about everyone involved with the military having it to some extent. Like nobody gets out unscathed anymore, you know?"

I nodded. "Yeah. It's not for the faint of heart."

"No, it isn't." His voice had a weirdly hollow, haunted sound to it.

I studied him. "You sound like you've got some experience."

"Some." He gave a slight nod. "My dad's been kind of fucked up since his last combat tour."

"Damn. Sorry to hear it." *Wait. Your dad is—*

"Kind of comes with the territory, I think," he said sadly. "He's doing better. A lot better. That first year, though..." He swallowed. "It was really bad."

I put a hand on his knee. "It isn't just the veterans who are affected. I know some spouses and kids who are traumatized by... I guess it's secondhand trauma? Trying to live with someone with serious PTSD?"

Gaze once again fixed on something in the distance, Sean nodded. "I don't know if I'd call what happens to us PTSD. Maybe it is. I don't know. But it definitely affected me."

"Of course it did." I squeezed his leg. "If it didn't, I'd say there was something really wrong."

He pursed his lips and nodded.

"He's doing better, though, right?"

"Yeah. Yeah." Sean exhaled. "Way better."

"Good." I gnawed the inside of my cheek. I hadn't realized before that his father was military, and now he had me worried about a few things. "So, your dad—is he still in?"

He nodded and gestured vaguely toward Anchor Point. "That's why we're here. He's stationed on Adams."

My blood turned cold and my spine straightened. "I beg your pardon?"

Sean shrugged. "He's stationed here. Why?"

Oh. Fuck.

Before I could speak, Sean tensed. "Oh God. You don't work with him, do you?"

"Actually..." I grimaced. "I can say with absolute certainty that he works *for* me."

Sean's eyebrows climbed his forehead. "How do you know?"

I shifted my gaze out to the sea. "Because everyone on NAS Adams works for me."

"You— Oh shit. You're joking, right?"

I shook my head and still didn't look at him.

Sean rose. He leaned over his hands on the railing and swore into the wind. "Shit."

"That's about the size of it." I combed my fingers through my hair. What could I even say?

"Damn it!" He smacked his palm on the railing. "So all

the times we've talked, it never once occurred to you to tell me *you're the base CO?*"

I wasn't sure if I was more startled or annoyed. "You never asked. You knew I was Navy and I'm an officer, so—"

"You're..." Sean deflated and looked out at the water again. "Yeah. You're right. I'm sorry."

"It's okay." I started to reach for him, intending to put a hand on the small of his back, but withdrew it. With this new revelation still hanging in the air between us, I was sure if I so much as touched him, we'd suddenly be busted and my career would be done. Less than an hour ago, we'd been below decks, blissfully sixty-nining on the narrow bed, and now I couldn't even bring myself to put a reassuring hand on him.

Drumming my nails on the railing, I said, "You do realize what this means, right?"

Sean flinched, shoulders sagging a little more, and he sighed. "It means we can't keep doing this."

"Yeah. I'm sorry. I—"

"Don't." He put up a hand and shook his head. "It is what it is. Let's..." He glanced over his shoulder toward Anchor Point. "Let's just go back in."

"Good idea."

Minutes later, we were on our way out of the cove.

And I was right about one thing—it was a long, awkward ride back to the marina.

CHAPTER 11

SEAN

I'D NEVER BEEN SO relieved to see the waterfront of Anchor Point. Soon, we'd be back at the marina and I could get off this boat. I was seriously tempted to dive in and fucking swim at this point.

I wasn't angry at Paul, but I'd have been lying if I said I wasn't angry at the situation. How many relationships and friendships had been casualties of my dad's Navy career? Too fucking many. And now this one. Yay.

But it wasn't like Paul and I had been seriously dating or anything. And the cards were pretty well stacked against us. Even if Paul hadn't been my dad's boss, he had twenty-plus years on me. Yet another thing we'd never told each other—our ages. So really, this wasn't even a relationship. Just sex with a few conversations to tide us over until we could get hard again.

Plus, he'd recently split up with somebody. So this was a good thing. We could both move on, and I could find someone my own age. A civilian my own age, too.

I watched him out of the corner of my eye as he drove us toward the marina. My heart sank. Midlife crisis, rebound, crazy fling—whatever we called it, I couldn't deny that it had been awesome. Damn him for raising the bar!

Cursing under my breath, I looked out at the town again, trying to mentally pull the shore closer so we could get off this boat sooner. Then, once I'd made my escape, I could go drive for a few hours and ask the open road why the hell this hurt so much.

Hurts? It was sex. What the fuck?

After what seemed like days, Paul parked the boat in the slip and turned off the engine. Once the lines were secured, we faced each other.

"Well." He swallowed. "I, uh..."

"I should go," I whispered.

He nodded. So did I.

My feet wouldn't move, though. And I couldn't make myself look away from him. I had to leave, and this had to be the last time we saw each other, and it probably wasn't a good idea to spend even one second making sure I had him committed to memory. What the hell was the point of tracing every last line of his face, or noticing for the first time that he had slightly more gray on his left temple than the right?

I shook myself and stared down at the deck beneath our feet. That was probably less likely to drive me insane than drinking in the way his snug blue T-shirt sat on his shoulders or the way the muscles in his forearm moved when he drummed his long fingers on the railing.

You're an idiot. You know that, right?

My stomach tried to fold in on itself. "Isn't much else to say, is there?"

He sighed, shaking his head. "No."

I gnawed the inside of my cheek. "I should, uh... I really should go, then. No point in dragging this out."

"No, there isn't."

Our eyes locked. We had every reason to get the fuck out of here and stay the fuck away from each other, but neither of us was moving.

Why are we still here?

His eyes didn't offer mine an answer. Not a good one, anyway. Or if they did, I was too busy getting drunk off his beautiful blue—

I really need to go.

I moistened my dry lips. "Do you want me to go?"

Paul shifted his weight. "I'm pretty sure you know the answer to that."

"Humor me."

Another shift, and his gaze darted to the deck between us. "What I need you to do is go. But what I want is... I really want you to..."

Heart in my throat, I took a step closer.

Paul straightened. His Adam's apple jumped, and his eyes flicked up to meet mine.

"That what you want?" I asked.

Slowly, he nodded. "Definitely on the right track, yeah."

My heart slammed against my ribs, and even though I should've been heading for the door, I took another step. "You know this isn't a good idea, right?"

"It's not a good idea." He closed the last bit of distance and put his hands on my sides. "Probably a really bad idea, actually."

"Mm-hmm." I leaned in and let my hips brush his. "Definitely a bad idea."

His fingers curled just enough to coax me toward him. "I mean, if someone were to find out..."

"The consequences would be..."

"Unpleasant."

"Yeah."

Oh God. His lips were almost touching mine now. *Kiss me.*

We hovered there, not kissing yet but close enough we could have. My heart pounded. The thought of not touching him again didn't compute, and the prospect of touching him and getting carried away was equal parts tempting and terrifying. We couldn't. We had to walk away from this now.

But Jesus Christ, I want—

Paul abruptly stepped back. He said something I couldn't hear—cursing, no doubt—and scrubbed a hand over his face.

I exhaled with relief that he'd been the bigger man, and disappointment that I hadn't moved in for that kiss when I'd had the chance. And now that he'd given me enough breathing room to come to my senses, I needed to get the hell out of here before we both found an excuse to get close again.

I cleared my throat. "I should—"

"Yeah." He avoided my eyes. "I'll, uh, take care of everything here." He made a sweeping gesture around the boat.

"Okay. Cool. Um. Thanks for the..." I hesitated. "I should go."

He nodded, but didn't speak.

Without another word, I left the boat, hurried off the marina, and got into my car. I burned rubber on the way out of the parking lot, heading for the highway like the whole town was on fire. As soon as I was on that long stretch of blacktop, I gunned the engine.

I didn't have a destination in mind. I needed to get out of there for a while, so I tried not to think about everything Paul and I had done in this car, and drove.

Hours later, I was still thinking about Paul, but I was also almost to California. I topped off my gas tank and headed back toward Anchor Point.

All the way home, with the radio blasting as if that would help drown out the silence of my car, I couldn't believe I'd been so stupid. I'd known he was an officer. Whenever I'd dropped him off on base, the sentries had saluted him. He had a tattoo from the Academy, for God's sake. I couldn't exactly write him off as an ensign or a lieutenant, not when he was obviously well past his twenties. What the fuck had I expected?

I raked a hand through my hair and then slammed my palm onto the steering wheel. Truth was, I'd shut out everything military when it came to Paul. He'd never volunteered any information about his job or his rank, and I hadn't asked because, goddamn it, I'd already had enough conversations about the Navy to sink a metaphorical battleship. If I never spent another night in bed with someone who thought the intricacies of avionics made good pillow talk, it would be too soon. So when Paul hadn't offered up any shop talk, I hadn't pressed, because fuck that.

Maybe deep down, I'd known there was some reason we shouldn't see each other, so I'd deliberately ignored all the signs. Or maybe I'd been so caught up in the amazing sex, I really hadn't noticed. I couldn't remember what I'd been thinking at that point because all I could think now was *I've been fucking my dad's commanding officer.*

If we'd been caught, God only knew what would have happened. I was a little hazy on the regs when it came to stuff like this, but I was pretty sure there was something in there about fraternization or carnal knowledge or whatever they called it when people hooked up with the wrong people. I doubted his superiors would look kindly on fraternization of the naked variety with a dependent of someone under his command.

It was over, though. No one had to know. Paul's career wouldn't be damaged. My dad didn't need to find out, and since Paul didn't know who my dad was, nothing would change between them at work. Everything would move forward as if nothing had ever happened.

As if I had never picked up Paul at that motel. Never fucked him over the back of my car or in a shady motel bed. Never known what it was like to be kissed and feel like nothing else existed in the world. Never looked at him and wondered how we hadn't known each other our whole lives.

I sighed, pressing back against the seat and focusing on the white lines in front of me. I'd get over him like I'd gotten over every man I'd ever had to give up—or who'd given me up—because of the Navy. At some point, just like every time before, this would stop hurting.

And maybe at some point, I'd figure out why it hurt so bad at all.

I thought we were just having sex. Why does—

Oh right. Because our relationship—whatever it was— had become another casualty of my father's career, and I was one hundred percent over the mess that the Navy had routinely made of my personal life. It wasn't that I'd had feelings for Paul beyond what he could do in bed—I was tired of the Navy basically confiscating every goddamned thing that made me happy.

Right?

When I parked at the curb in front of the house, Dad's truck was in the driveway. My gut lurched. No big deal. All I had to do was play it cool and he wouldn't suspect a thing. Hopefully. Right? Shit.

Poker face. I can do this. Poker face.

I headed inside. Dad wasn't in the kitchen, but he was on his way down the stairs, so I schooled my expression —*Poker face, come on!*—while I fished a bottle of water out of the fridge.

"Oh." He stopped and did a double take. "I thought you were Julie."

"Nope." I smiled despite the ball of lead in my gut. "Sorry. Just the resident freeloader."

Dad rolled his eyes and laughed. "Yeah, okay. Not that you've been around enough to do much freeloading."

"Aside from the rent and insurance, right?"

"True. Haven't seen much of you lately, though." He arched an eyebrow like he was searching for something. "Work keeping you busy?"

I swallowed. "And school, yeah."

"Must be having class outdoors these days."

"Out— What?"

He gestured at me. "Got a bit of a sunburn."

I glanced at my arm, and my blood turned cold. I had turned a little pink today, hadn't I? Oh God. Did I smell like sunscreen? Did I have a tan line from my sunglasses? And now the sting under my shirt made itself known. From when I'd had my shirt off. On the boat. While I was going down on Paul before we'd gone down into the cabin. Fuck. Fuck. *Fuck.*

I had to keep up the lie, though. If Dad saw through me, Paul was fucked even though our relationship was over. Jesus, that hurt to think about. It really was over, wasn't it?

Of course. It had to be. Neither of us could justify staying together if the consequences got too real. Kind of like swimming in a place where sharks were sometimes sighted—only an idiot jumped back in the water after having their toes nibbled.

And my dad was still staring at me, waiting for a response to his comment about my sunburn.

I cleared my throat. "Oh, I was down at the pier today." *I sound casual, right? Like I'm not bullshitting?* "Figured I'd take advantage of some nice weather."

He grunted quietly. "Maybe take some sunscreen next time?"

"I did. Not enough apparently."

Dad chuckled. "You have Irish roots, kid. You can never use too much sunscreen."

"True!" I laughed. *Too obvious. Rein it in.* Clearing my throat, I shifted my weight. "Guess I should get some of the SPF 80 next time."

"Planning to go back down there? I thought you didn't like the crowds on the pier."

I shrugged. "Better than sitting at home watching TV."

"Okay, I'll give you that." He studied me, and I was sure he was going to see right through the lie. I'd said it with a straight face, and didn't think I'd tipped my hand at all, but still.

My heart pounded. My stomach knotted tighter with every second. I was a split second away from coming clean when he shrugged.

"All right, well, glad you had a good time. You watching TV with us tonight? I've got *Unhappy Hour* queued up on Netflix."

It took everything I had not to breathe an incriminating sigh of relief. "Yeah. Sure. I'm going to grab a shower first."

"Okay." He smiled. "We'll put it on when Julie gets home."

"Sounds great. I'll just... um..."

"Shower?"

"Yeah. That." I started to leave.

"Oh," he called after me, "one more thing."

I froze. Slowly, I turned around. "Yeah?"

He nodded toward some papers on the counter. "Need you to fill those in for your tuition assistance. It's due next week."

"Oh." My mouth had gone dry, and I cleared my throat. "Sure. Yeah. I'll get them done tonight."

"Good. Thanks." He paused, rocking from his heels to the balls of his feet like there was still something he wanted to say. Or, worse, ask.

I prayed to anyone who'd listen that he didn't. I wasn't sure I could keep up the "nope, nope, nothing to see here" much longer.

"All right. Well." He shrugged. "I'd better get started making some popcorn. Julie is on her way."

"Yeah. And I still need—" What was I doing? Shower. Right. "I'll be down in a few minutes."

I turned to go, and he didn't stop me this time.

Upstairs in my bedroom, I sagged against the door and released a long breath. As far as I could tell, he didn't suspect a thing. Or if he did, I'd convinced him to let it go.

I'd done it. I'd lied through my teeth to my dad about the relationship I'd had up until a few hours ago with his commanding officer.

And I had no idea how to feel about that.

CHAPTER 12

PAUL

TWO WEEKS after Sean left my sight for the last time, I couldn't feel him anymore. All the aches and twinges were gone. The last bruise—a faint one on my shoulder from an enthusiastic bite—had disappeared. When I ran on the treadmill or along the paths on base, my hips didn't protest. Sitting in meetings or at my desk, there was no lingering soreness from being fucked to within an inch of my life. My chronic injuries were present and accounted for, but Sean? No.

And I was going to lose my mind.

The icing on the cake was how badly I needed a cigarette. Even more than I'd wanted one the night Jayson and I split up. Probably because I didn't run the risk of bumping into Jayson on base. And no one in Jayson's family had any ammunition to try to fuck over my career.

Just one cigarette. One. I'll even smoke it slowly so it lasts longer.

I had this conversation with myself over and over and over again. The only thing keeping me from calling Sean was the consequences, and the only thing keeping me from swinging into the Exchange and buying a pack of Marlboros was the memory of how hellish it had been to quit. It was awful. All four times.

The third time had been during a deployment, way back when I was a lieutenant commander. For ten days, I hadn't touched a cigarette. Most of that period was a blur—an excruciatingly miserable blur—right up to the moment when the XO had taken me out to the smoke deck and *ordered* me to light up.

"You're not going back in until I've watched you smoke two," he'd growled at me. "Don't even think about quitting again until we're back on land and you aren't my problem anymore. Am I clear?"

"Yes, sir," I'd said around my cigarette.

The fourth time, I'd been so desperate to quit, I'd taken twenty-one days of leave so I could knuckle through the withdrawal without it interfering with my work. Three months and twenty pounds later, I'd almost relapsed, but the miserable memories were still vivid enough to keep me on the wagon.

And even now, eight years down the line, I still had to talk myself off that ledge whenever something had me wound up. Quitting Jayson and Sean in short order meant talking myself off it again.

And smoking again means quitting again, and quitting again means going through hell and getting every fucking uniform retailored, so how about manning up and dealing with it?

Intellectually, I knew what was happening here. Sean was a distraction from Jayson. A reason not to think about my breakup.

Except everything with Sean was so much better than it had ever been with Jayson. I never felt like I was walking on eggshells or putting on a façade to keep him from seeing who I really was. He was funny and fun to be around, and despite me being convinced I couldn't possibly have anything in common with someone half my age, we never ran out of things to talk about.

The sex, of course, was nothing to sneeze at. Even during our early days, back when we'd fucked every chance we had, Jayson had never had the kind of enthusiasm that Sean did. He'd always been in it for the orgasm—his orgasm —and didn't really care about the rest. Sean, though. Christ. He was so attentive. And generous. And just... *into* it.

Okay, so maybe he wasn't a distraction from Jayson. He was a distraction from everything, and right or wrong, I wanted that back just like I'd wanted the nicotine high back when the withdrawal had been at its worst.

Was that all I wanted, though? A fix to tide me over until the next craving?

I thought back to the afternoon we'd spent on my boat. *Before* everything had gone to shit, anyway. Yeah, the sex was hot, but the more I thought about it, the more I missed that companionship. We'd barely started getting to know each other, had revealed enough cards to realize we couldn't see each other, and already...

You're losing your mind, Richards.

Lying in bed after turning off my alarm for the forty-fifth time, I rubbed my eyes. Smoking wasn't going to help anything, but maybe a good hard run would clear my head. At least then I could be functional at work today. I needed to run anyway. As it was, I'd started avoiding the gym, preferring to run outdoors instead of risking being there at the same time as Sean again.

That plan had worked for a day or two, but this being coastal Oregon, there'd been quite a bit of rain lately. The

Physical Readiness Test was coming up, and I would be damned if I couldn't keep up with the younger guys, so skipping my workouts was not an option.

I made myself sit up and swing my legs over the side of the bed. Okay. Upright. All I had to do now was grab a shower and get my ass to the gym.

What time does Sean work out?

I cringed. Despite my best efforts, I'd run into him there a few days ago. Almost two weeks after our last night together, I'd walked into the gym just in time to see Sean position himself on a weight bench under a loaded barbell. I'd frozen. I'd stared. And then I'd turned around and walked right back out because I was a goddamn coward and an idiot who was losing his mind over someone he'd fooled around with for a little while.

Sean be damned, though, I needed to get to the gym.

Except it was kind of a moot point now. I'd spent so long trying to talk myself into getting out of bed, I had barely enough time to get my shit together and get to the office. The rear admiral was coming today, and he had an annoying habit of showing up bright and early, so I needed to be put together and mainlining coffee on time.

I'd run later. For now—shower, dress, go to work, and deal with everything like the grown-ass adult I was.

My neck and back smarted as I stood and stretched. No surprise, there—stress aggravated my ancient injuries like it did my latent nicotine addiction. Good thing I had a crapload of ibuprofen in my desk. I was gonna need it.

The shower didn't help. Big shock. Something about being naked and letting water slide all over me like hot, eager hands brought Sean to the front of my mind. As if he'd been very far from it to begin with.

Now that I have your attention, my body seemed to say

as my cock hardened, *you still haven't relieved some of this tension.*

I let the shower spray rush over my face and down the back of my neck. For the last several nights, I'd fought the urge to jerk off to thoughts of Sean, but today, there was no avoiding it. My mind was completely preoccupied with him —his talented mouth, his strong, lean body, his strained voice when he was getting close—and if I was going to be remotely useful during the admiral's visit, I needed to clear my head. And since I didn't have time to run, I gave in. I closed my eyes, and I let myself imagine my hand was Sean's.

In no time, I was there, coming quick and hard after resisting for too long. I hadn't even had a chance to fantasize or enjoy it—a few strokes, and it was all over.

Panting, I rested my head against my forearm. Nope, this hadn't helped. The hard-on was taken care of, and the orgasm's delicious relief was still coursing through my veins, but clearing my head? Restoring my ability to concentrate so I didn't make an ass of myself with the admiral who could decide whether or not I ever got my own ship? Not so much.

I'll get over this.

I got over the nicotine (sort of). I'm over Jayson (kind of). Why should Sean be any different?

All the way to my office, and through my various meetings, and as I waded through my overstuffed email inbox, my mind refused to let go of Sean. It didn't help that Senior Chief Wright went through the building a couple of times on his way in and out of meetings, and every time I saw him, I saw another hint of the resemblance between father and son. I had no idea how I'd failed to notice it before. All he needed was longer hair and a few blue highlights, and—

Don't ogle the senior chief, idiot. That will not help.

The admiral must've thought I was a complete moron. Though I was usually pretty damn good at faking it, he still had to repeat himself a few times after my brain checked out at inopportune moments. That would definitely earn me some points toward taking command of a carrier. The Navy was reluctant to give me a boat anyway—my injuries *just* toed the line of rendering me unfit for sea duty—and being a space case in front of this guy of all people wouldn't help. Fuck.

The next afternoon, I pulled myself together enough to fool him into thinking I really was a consummate professional who'd just had an off day, and I stayed that way until the helicopter lifted off and took him away from NAS Adams. He'd barely cleared the airfield before I texted my secretary to let her know I wouldn't be back to the office. Cutting out early wasn't a privilege I abused on a regular basis, so I decided I could get away with it this one time.

I went for a run to clear my head, but did it do a damn bit of good? Not even a little. I ran five fucking miles, showered, dressed, went home, and *still* had a mind full of hot cab driver.

Since I didn't have any better ideas, I ignored the fact that I had to work tomorrow, and drove out to a bar at the north end of Anchor Point. It was a total dive bar, which I'd expected. Probably not another gay man within ten blocks, and probably not a place where a gay man should be waving a rainbow flag or subtly checking out an ass in tight jeans.

Fine. I wasn't looking for a piece of ass. I wasn't even looking to get drunk. I just needed to spend some time in a place that didn't remind me of Sean, assuming a place like that existed. I probably could go to the base chapel and still find a reason to think about him and feel guilty about it.

The bar was dim, lit mostly by neon signs and the fake Tiffany lamps hanging over three pool tables. The air had probably been thick and gray before Oregon's indoor-smoking ban. Even now it seemed weirdly hazy, like there'd been enough smokers through here to keep it smoky for years to come. I could almost taste the tobacco, though it was undoubtedly just my brain trying to trick me into caving to that subtle, persistent hankering.

Not tonight. No sex. No smoking. Just a beer or twelve and some time away from the house.

There were a few familiar faces hunched over beers or shooting pool. No surprise in a town this small. None of them approached me, though, and I didn't approach them. Hopefully they didn't think I thought I was above them or some bullshit like that—some of the enlisted guys, especially in the lower ranks, had been conditioned to be afraid of the top end of their chain of command. I had the utmost respect for them, and didn't want a reputation as an officer who wouldn't give his enlisted guys the time of day, so I hoped they'd forgive me for not being social tonight.

I found a seat near the end of the bar, opened a tab, and ordered a beer. Before I was halfway through that one, I ordered another. Alternately fucking off on my phone and staring into space, I drank. Only the presence of some guys from the base kept me from pouring beer down my throat as fast as my system could take it. The last thing I needed to do was get fall-down, blackout drunk in front of people who answered to me. Especially since alcohol was one hell of a truth serum, and it wouldn't look good to start rambling about how I'd found an awesome guy who was an amazing lay, only to realize he was the son of Senior Chief Wright.

"Uh-huh, Senior Chief Wright's kid. You know him? I sure do. In the Biblical sense. God, that guy is hot..."

Yeah. No. Didn't need to get that drunk.

After a dozen rounds of some dumb game on my phone, I went to take a drink, but realized the bottle was empty. I pushed it away, and a moment later, the bartender materialized.

She shot me a smile as she took my empty beer bottle. "Another one, sweetie?"

"Um." Hadn't I already had quite a few? Shit. I had. In pretty rapid succession, I'd thrown back three. Not nearly enough to fuck me up, but if I wanted to drive myself home, I'd have to wait a couple of hours until I was out of the DUI danger zone.

"No. Thanks." I forced a smile.

The bartender nodded and continued down the bar.

Another beer was tempting, but not if I wanted to leave here anytime soon.

And go where, Paul? Home to masturbate in the shower?

I sighed, pressing my elbow onto the bar and rubbing my forehead. One more drink meant staying here longer. Skipping that drink meant I could get out of here sooner and go... where? Maybe down to Flatstick for a roll in the hay that already sounded like way too much effort for not a lot of payoff?

Alternatively, I could find another way home.

I took Sean's card out of my wallet. Heart in my throat, I ran my thumb back and forth across his name and cell number.

I'd deleted him from my phone, but still had this. There were a million reasons why I had no business even keeping it. And actually making the call? Meeting him somewhere? Doing something about all this frustration?

Stupid.

Stupid. Stupid. *Stupid.*

Career-damaging stupid.

And so, so tempting. I was the kind of person who could convince myself there was a good reason to backslide and smoke a cigarette—that was why it had taken me so long to quit. Only the memory of the painful withdrawal kept me from going there again. Not the potential for lung cancer or any of the other illnesses. Not the cost, the smell, the yellow stain on everything. No, the single effective barrier was that hellish period after my last cigarette.

In theory, the last couple of weeks should have had the same effect as that withdrawal. Hooking up with Sean again would only mean inevitably going through that pain again. So maybe that meant in another week or two, when the worst was over and I was moving on like I should've been doing now, it'd be easy. Well, easier.

Or not. Especially since I also remembered all too well that nothing ever tasted as good as that first cigarette after an attempt at quitting. If a Marlboro could put me on the edge of ecstasy, I could only imagine what hooking up with Sean again would be like right now.

I shivered, goose bumps prickling under my shirt.

Who the hell was I kidding? I sucked at staying away from things I didn't need to be anywhere near, and Sean was no exception. So why fight a losing battle? Sure, this might fuck up my career, but I couldn't imagine it would do more damage than being a space case like I'd been lately.

Feeling equal parts jittery, guilty, and excited as hell, I flagged down the bartender and ordered another beer.

And while she popped the cap on the bottle, I texted Sean.

Are you driving tonight?

CHAPTER 13

SEAN

I STARED AT THE MESSAGE. I had just dropped off a passenger by the Navy Exchange, and not thirty seconds later, my phone had buzzed. I'd looked at it fully expecting another request for a pickup.

It was a request for a pickup all right—didn't take a genius to read between those lines—but I was pretty damn sure that wasn't some random person. Even though I'd deleted his contact info, I still recognized Paul's number.

Fuck. Just reading that message was playing with fire. Responding to it? Bad idea. Bad. Idea.

I looked around, hoping there was somebody trying to get my attention. There had to be somebody who wanted to go out partying tonight. Right?

And I was kidding precisely no one if I said I didn't want to burn rubber and get to wherever Paul was right now. My concentration had been shot since we'd parted ways for the last time.

My toes curled in my shoes. We couldn't go back to what we'd been doing before, but damn if it wasn't tempting as hell.

One more glance around the parking lot. Still nobody looking for a cab. Dispatch was silent. It had been a quiet night so far anyway, and aside from that unanswered text on my phone, nobody was asking me for a ride. I could either sit here all night, or...

The screen on my phone had gone dark, so I tapped it and brought up the text again. A smart guy would've deleted the text, blocked the number, and gone downtown to see if anyone was stumbling out of a bar in search of a designated driver.

Tonight, I didn't feel like being a smart guy.

Yeah, I wrote back. *Need a lift?*

After the message was sent, and he'd seen it, I held my breath as I stared at the screen. I should've ignored him. I still could, I supposed. If he wrote back, I could insist that someone else had just gotten into my car and asked for a lift to Portland or Eugene or like New York or something. *Sorry, maybe another night!*

Then his response came through, and every excuse I had evaporated:

Need you.

Oh. Jesus.

I chewed my lip. My pounding heart and queasy stomach were trying to talk me out of picking him up. At the same time, the subtle ache in my elbow reminded me that it would be nice to let someone else get me off tonight. I'd been fantasizing about Paul every night and some mornings anyway. Might as well indulge in the real thing.

Except it's a bad idea because—

My phone vibrated.

Paul had texted me an address, and it was one I recognized. It was a bar close to the hotel where I'd picked him up the first time.

Mouth dry and fingers unsteady, I wrote back, *Be there soon.*

I couldn't even say he'd caught me during a weak moment. Most of my good sense had gone out the window the night I'd met him, and I'd been running on fumes ever since, ready to give in and hurry back into bed with him at the drop of a hat. And now that I had the opportunity...

I shifted into drive and headed toward that address. All the way, my heart kept right on pounding. The wheel was slick in my sweaty hands, so I gripped it tighter. I focused on the road, the lines, the cars, the signs—I didn't dare let my concentration wander, because I'd probably wind up in a ditch or crashing through a storefront. I'd been distracted for the last couple of weeks, but it'd be my luck that I'd wreck tonight while Paul was waiting for me with God only knew what dirty intentions.

Somehow, I didn't crash. As the seedy bar came into view, blood pounded in my ears. I made one last attempt to talk myself out of this, but that didn't last long—Paul was waiting outside, watching me as I pulled up to the curb.

There were a million questions on the tip of my tongue —mostly along the lines of "What changed your mind?" and "Are you insane?"—but one look at him erased every word in my vocabulary.

As he got into the backseat like a normal customer, I somehow managed to choke out, "Any place in particular?"

"No."

"So..." I swallowed, meeting his eyes in the rearview. "Just drive?"

Paul nodded.

The night we'd met, the request had annoyed me. Tonight, it had an effect I couldn't quite define. Made me nervous? Excited? Fuck. I didn't know.

But what I did do was drive.

Stomach fluttering, palms sweatier than they'd been on the way here, I left the bar's parking lot.

With Paul.

Right there.

In my car.

What the hell were we doing? And if we'd met up for the reasons I thought we had, why were we just driving around instead of finding some condoms and a flat surface?

We were near the north edge of town, and it wasn't long before we were outside of Anchor Point proper. Much farther than this, and we'd be on that highway that didn't have any places to pull over or turn around for miles at a stretch.

So I found an empty side road, turned, and pulled over. I shifted into park, but left the engine idling. "All right. We need to talk." I twisted around so I could look Paul in the eye. "What are we doing?"

"I'm not sure. I just needed to see you."

"See me?" I asked. "Or—"

The click of his seat belt shut me up. Eyes locked on mine, he slid closer, probably to the edge of the backseat. God, he was almost close enough to touch. Then he leaned a little farther forward, and all my good sense went out the window when he whispered, "I know we shouldn't." He touched my arm, sending electricity all the way down to my toes. "I can't help it."

"Neither can I." I reached for his face. "Or I wouldn't have picked you up."

Paul swallowed. Then he came all the way forward and kissed me over the back of the seats.

Relief and arousal and a million other feelings rushed through me. I grabbed the back of his neck. His fingers raked through my hair. If the seats hadn't been in the way, and I hadn't been twisted around like I was, we'd have been wrapped up in each other and losing our minds by now. Still, this was better than the last two weeks of nothing at all. This might've been a huge mistake, but it didn't feel like one right then, so I ignored good sense and let his kiss turn me inside out.

When he broke away, his forehead was feverish against mine. "Christ..."

Breathing hard, I pulled back enough to meet his gaze. "I guess I'm not driving anywhere tonight?"

"You've been driving me crazy for two weeks."

I groaned. "Did you spend the whole time thinking of that line?"

"Had to do something." He drew me back in. "Otherwise, all I've been good for is—"

I kissed him because it had already been too long, and I knew exactly what he was talking about anyway. I'd barely been able to drive, sleep, study—all I'd wanted the past couple of weeks was this. Him.

"We shouldn't do this," I murmured between kisses. "But I have a feeling we're going to do it anyway."

"I know. And I should be the responsible one and say we can't..."

"I'm as responsible for it as you are. I'm young, but I'm no kid."

"No, but you're not going to hurt your career."

"I might hurt your career and my dad's."

"Fair." He pulled back a little. "We keep doing this *here*, though, you're going to fuck up your neck."

The muscles were getting kind of stiff. I surreptitiously stretched, tilting my head to one side, then the other. "Maybe I should get in the backseat with you."

"I have a better idea." He gestured at the dark, empty road behind us. "Let's get a room."

I blinked a few times. That idea was insane. Get a room? With a bed? That was completely insane and the worst idea ever and... and...

Exactly what I needed.

"Okay. A room." I swallowed. "Good idea."

He grinned, and the lust gleamed even hotter in his eyes. He leaned across the seats again and kissed me once more, and then we both returned to our places. I made a U-turn, burning rubber on the unmarked pavement, and hit the gas. Heart still going ninety miles an hour, stomach still queasy and fluttery at the same time, I drove like a bat out of hell.

In minutes, we were back in Anchor Point, and I pulled into the parking lot of the first shady-looking place with *Vacancy* in the window.

"I'll go check us in." His seat belt clicked before I'd even come to a stop. As soon as the car halted, he was out and headed for the office, and I gripped the wheel and took a few deep breaths to calm myself down. If I was going to bail and get the hell out of here, now was the time, but I barely entertained those thoughts. This was happening and that was final. After tonight? We'd figure that out later. Tonight? I was coming in Paul.

My dick was already getting hard. My skin itched with goose bumps, and I could barely sit still. It was like my heart was pumping liquid restlessness through my veins, and *How the fuck long does it take to get a goddamn motel room?*

As if on cue, he stepped out of the office, card key in hand.

Fuck. *Yes.*

He climbed into the passenger seat. "Entrance is around the side of the building."

"First floor?"

"Mm-hmm."

Thank God for that. I wasn't going up any stairs—not very quickly, anyway—until one of us did something about this hard-on.

I drove around to the side of the small building and took a spot close to the door. Neither of us said a word as we got out, but halfway down the hall to the room, I hesitated.

He raised his eyebrows. "What's wrong?"

You and I both know what's wrong and why we shouldn't be here.

I gulped. "Did you bring... um..."

He patted his jacket pocket. "Swung into the convenience store while I was waiting for you."

"Oh." Well, then. No reason at all to hesitate now. We had everything we needed. One swipe of that key card, and we'd have a bed, towels, and privacy.

He inclined his head. "You okay?"

I nodded. "Yeah. Yeah." I continued toward the door. "Just, uh... making sure..."

At the door, he touched my shoulder, and when I met his gaze, his expression was completely serious. Brow pinched, lips pressed together—a look of nothing but genuine concern in his eyes. His gorgeous blue eyes. "It's not too late, you know. If you don't want to do this, say so."

"It's not a matter of if I want to."

His posture straightened a little. The silence was taut between us.

After a few long seconds, he cleared his throat. "So, should we?"

My heart slammed into my ribs. I knew the answer to

that question. So did he. And once he put the key in the reader and unlocked the door, we'd have a clear path to a bed and nakedness and the sex I'd been missing since—

"No."

The word came out so quietly, I didn't even know if he'd heard it, but when I met his gaze...

Yeah. He'd heard me. His eyebrows jumped. Then his shoulders sank a little.

"No," I repeated, and rocked back on my heels to add a tiny sliver of space between us. "I want to, but..."

He broke eye contact and sighed, staring down at the key card in his hand. Part of me wanted him to argue. I wanted him to ask if I was sure, or maybe give me a nudge. Right then, the tiniest bit of persuasion would have been enough. I wanted him. I wanted him so bad I was standing there with a relentless hard-on and a brain full of fantasies that needed to be lived out. My resolve to do the right thing —or at least not do the wrong thing—would've held up like a spiderweb would've stopped a fighter jet.

"You're right." He rubbed the back of his neck and slumped against the unopened door. Absently turning the key over and over in his free hand, he swore under his breath as he stared up at the ceiling. "This was a terrible idea."

Disappointment and relief butted heads inside my brain, and almost canceled each other out. My body had apparently gotten the message, and the tightness in the front of my jeans eased as my dick softened.

"I'm sorry." Paul moistened his lips, then looked at me. "We can't do this. I know. I shouldn't have texted you. I—"

"I know," I whispered. "I've thought about getting in touch a few times too. We can't, but I won't say it isn't tempting."

He nodded.

The silence was excruciating, and that temptation hadn't exactly faded. The longer we stood there, the more uncomfortable it would be, and the more tantalizing the alternative would get.

I cleared my throat. "I'm, uh, gonna go." I paused. "Except I'm your ride, I guess." Beat. "Your taxi, I mean. Your cab ride."

Paul laughed dryly. "I know what you meant. Actually, I think I might..." He glanced at the door. "I've already got the room. Might watch a movie or something until I've sobered up."

He didn't even seem that drunk to me. A little buzzed, maybe? And for that matter, I was about to remind him he didn't need to be sober to call a cab—a different cab—but I wondered if he planned to do more than watch a movie. Probably the same thing I had every intention of doing as soon as I got home. Not that jacking off would make this situation any less frustrating, but why the hell not? And in this case, it saved us from the painful awkwardness of spending time in the car. Coming back to shore on his boat had been brutal enough.

"Okay. Well." I coughed again and gestured down the hall. "I'm gonna go."

He nodded, avoiding my eyes.

There was nothing left to say. I didn't dare touch him—not a kiss, not a handshake—because then I'd want to touch him more.

So without another word, I left.

I was halfway down the hall when I heard the beep and click of the room door unlocking, and I looked over my shoulder in time to see Paul disappear inside. The door shut again, and I halted, just staring for a minute.

He was probably lying back on the bed we'd planned to share. He probably had his eyes closed and his dick in his hand, and I wondered if he was thinking of me, or anyone *but* me.

And if I went back now and knocked on the door, I wondered if he'd let me take over and finish the job for him.

With that thought, I turned on my heel and continued toward the parking lot. I walked so fast I damn near broke into a run, and my hand shook so much I could barely get the key into the ignition. It finally went in, though, and I started the engine, threw the car in reverse, and got the hell out of there.

All the way home, I tried to think of anyone but him.

CHAPTER 14

PAUL

LYING BACK on the hard motel bed, I stared up at the ceiling.

Hopefully Sean was on his way to a club in Flatstick, or looking through Grindr, or texting a reliable booty call. He deserved a night of stress-free sex with someone who didn't alternate between reckless and indecisive.

I closed my eyes and pushed out a breath.

I didn't even try to convince myself I would've come to my senses before we'd gone too far. We'd gone too far the moment we'd made contact again, and if Sean hadn't put a stop to things, I damn sure wouldn't have. Should've, yes. Would've? Not a chance. Didn't matter how much was on the line or how fucking stupid it was for us to be anywhere near each other—one look at Sean, and all my rational thinking went out the window.

Well, at least one of us was levelheaded. Ironically, he was exactly the kind of person I needed—someone who balanced out my impulsiveness. Even if he was also exactly the kind of irresistible temptation that was my Achilles' heel. *He* might have been levelheaded and rational, but he was also just... so... *hot*.

I stared up at the ceiling again. If he'd stayed, we'd probably be done by now. The first round, anyway. It was always fast and furious, especially if we'd been apart for more than a couple of days. So we'd probably be lying here, sweaty and out of breath, debating if we could stand long enough for a shower or if we should just wait until after we'd inevitably fucked again.

Goose bumps prickled my skin. That man. My God.

At least with the sex, I knew what I was missing by letting him go. What drove me out of my mind was the unknown. Even if we couldn't sleep together, I wanted to get to know him more. What was he studying? What did he want to do after he graduated? Where had he been? Where did he want to go?

But we couldn't. Period. It didn't matter that I'd started to realize Sean was everything I wanted in a man. I had no business getting involved with him—staying involved with him—unless I really wanted to kiss admiral good-bye and go to court-martial instead.

My career was everything to me. I'd given the Navy over half my life, lost some of my best years, and had some scars of both the mental and physical variety to show for it. This career was not something I had ever taken lightly.

Yet one look at Sean...

I wiped my hand over my face and swore aloud. I was obsessed. That was all it was. I'd been dumped, and needed a rebound, and gotten myself in too deep. Fortunately, Sean had done the right thing.

In my mind, I replayed the moment Sean had backed off. Though he'd kept a pretty stoic face, even now I could see the tension in his features and the obvious struggle in his eyes. He hadn't wanted to leave any more than I had—he just had the wherewithal to put a stop to things. I couldn't imagine how he felt now. If he was kicking himself for leaving, or berating himself for even getting into that situation. He might've been pissed at me or—worse—hurt. One way or the other, he undoubtedly felt like shit. Because of me.

I sat up and exhaled. If I couldn't get my shit together over my career, I could stop myself from putting him in that position again. The last thing I wanted was to hurt him or cause him stress like that.

Time to go home and move on, and maybe find someone my own age who wasn't a military dependent. Or be single for a little while. At least that wouldn't get me or anyone else into trouble.

So, determined to *not* be an idiot from here on out, I left the room. I dropped my key at the checkout desk, called a cab from another company, and headed home.

And silently wished Sean the best.

CHAPTER 15

SEAN

IN THE WEEKS after I'd walked away from Paul at the motel, I threw myself into work. Schoolwork when I had it, and hours behind the wheel the rest of the time. On the one hand, my grades were impeccable and my bank account was happy. On the other, I was still distracted as hell by the man who wasn't texting me with motel room information anymore.

A few times, I thought I should bite the bullet and go get laid. There was that club down in Flatstick that had always been a winner. And of course some phone apps. But the thought of hooking up with someone else didn't have much appeal right now. I couldn't even jack off without thinking about Paul, and I had definitely tried.

With sex apparently off the table for now, I still needed to blow off steam, so I finally took my dad up on his constant nagging to come to the gym with him. It helped—couldn't rub one out to thoughts of Paul when I couldn't get it up or move my arm enough. After a week, I was more focused on my aching muscles than anything.

The next week, I wasn't hurting as much, but my workouts gave me something to think about besides Paul. He sure as hell wasn't far from my mind, but it was getting better. Little by little, it was getting better. I'd found something to focus on besides Paul.

For a while.

At ass-thirty on a Wednesday morning, I mustered super-human effort to get myself to the gym. I was still sore from a brutal set of dead lifts the day before, and was one hundred percent *not* motivated… but I dragged myself out of bed, across town, and onto the base anyway because I didn't want to listen to my dad later if I didn't show up. That was part of our deal: either of us flaked out, the other got to give him shit until the following day. Amnesty was only granted for true sickness or work-related delays. Hangovers? Laziness? Up too late masturbating to thoughts about someone's boss? No excuses.

Not only did I make it to the gym, though, I beat my dad. So there was that. On the way in from the parking lot, I texted him to make sure he was still coming, and then continued inside.

As I shuffled across the locker room in search of a bay that wasn't occupied by other guys, I got a text back from Dad.

On my way in.

Cool. I was thumbing a response when someone stepped out in front of me. We nearly collided, but I stopped in my tracks.

And so did Paul.

For a couple of seconds, we stared at each other.

I shouldn't have been shocked. Of course he worked out at the base gym. He was obviously fit, and God knew the place was convenient as hell since he worked on base. If anything, I was surprised we hadn't seen each other here before. It was bound to happen sooner or later, and here we were.

"Um..." I said.

Dad's text message flashed through my mind. Shit!

I cleared my throat. So did Paul. Then, without a word, we both kept walking in opposite directions. I didn't dare look back, not even as I stepped into an empty bay of lockers.

The locker room door squeaked on its hinges.

"Morning, sir," Dad said.

"Morning, Senior Chief," Paul replied. Footsteps continued. The door banged shut.

A second later, Dad appeared, gym bag slung over his shoulder. "Hey. What do you think—leg day?"

My entire lower body ached in protest. I shook my head. "Back and shoulders. My knee's still pissed off about that run the other day."

Dad shrugged. "Sounds good. I'll meet you out there." He went to another bay of lockers while I stood there with an uncomfortable ball of lead forming in the pit of my stomach. As much as work, school, and exercise had pulled my focus away from pining after Paul, all it had taken was one brief encounter to remind me how hard it had been to let him go. And hearing that quick exchange between him and my dad had been salt in the wound. Like the universe had said, *Here's the man you wish you had, and here's a reminder of why you can't have him.*

Fuck my life.

I sat on the bench to put on my shoes. As I slipped them on, I glanced at the door Paul had gone through.

Suddenly I felt conspicuous in the locker room. As if seeing him had tipped my hand. And as if running into each other once somehow meant that now he'd be here every time I came to work out.

And so what if he was? I'd long ago mastered the art of being around naked, half-naked, and on-the-way-to-naked men without giving away that I found men attractive. I never ogled anyway because it was obnoxious, and I pretty much kept my eyes down out of fear that if I let my guard down and made eye contact with someone, it would be one of those gigantic meatheads who was also a raging homophobe.

Now I had yet another thing to avoid—the guy I wished I was still fucking. There were a lot of nooks and crannies in this locker room. If Paul and I ever came in here late at night, and temptation got the best of us, we could always—

Baseball. Think of baseball.

I adjusted the front of my shorts and leaned down—uncomfortably—to tie my shoes.

Today's workout was going to be one long...

It was going to be one hard...

Fuck it. This workout was going to suck.

It wasn't as terrible as I'd anticipated. I didn't see much of Paul. A glance now and then, but he was mostly on the cardio side while Dad and I were lifting at the other end of the gym. Good thing that despite being a small base, NAS Adams had a decent sized gym—at some of the other bases, we'd have been tripping over each other.

Still, it was a hell of a relief when my workout was over and Dad and I retreated to the locker room. Dad went to take a shower while I dropped onto the bench by my locker. Tired and sweaty, I toed off my shoes. I'd grab a shower at home before I went to class—much less chance of accidentally looking at someone the wrong way.

I took my bag out of my locker and put my shoes in it. Right as I was about to peel off my shirt, my neck prickled.

I turned around.

And for the second time today, there we were in the locker room together. At least neither of us had been in the middle of undressing or something. Not that it was much better when he was sweaty and flushed because hello, I loved the way he looked like that. Reminded me so much of—

Things I couldn't have. And desperately wanted. And would have sold my soul to drag into the shower and fuck.

"Hey." I smiled nervously. "Good workout?"

"Yeah." His smile was equally nervous, and like me, he glanced around as if to make sure no one saw us talking. "You?"

"Mm-hmm." I had no idea what to say. We'd always been able to talk until we were blue in the face when we were alone, but now? Surrounded by guys who answered to him? With my damn dad nearby? Shit.

Paul took a swig from his water bottle. "Well, um. I should get back to work."

"Yeah. I need to get to class."

He nodded. "Okay."

Our eyes locked. He couldn't possible have imagined how badly I wanted to say something benign like *Text you later*, but I didn't dare. We couldn't text each other or hook up or anything, and I knew it, but standing with him, it still seemed so casual and normal to act like things hadn't changed.

With a couple of subtle nods and a grunted "Later," he kept walking and I focused on getting my stuff together.

I quickly changed clothes and hurried out of that locker room like it was a house on fire. As soon as I stepped from the stuffy, sweaty room into the air-conditioned, sweaty hallway, I released a breath. There was no rational reason it should make any difference that I was out here, but it did. It felt safer with a door between us.

Except I hadn't done anything unsafe. Paul and I had been perfectly civil and polite like two normal guys in a locker room. Nothing to see here. Nothing going on between us.

My shoulders sank and so did my stomach. I missed him. No two ways about it. I missed being able to text randomly with him. I missed talking to him. I missed his playful smile and subtly smoky laugh.

And I can't have him, so I need to get over him.

This was stupid. I needed to go out and get laid and forget him. Of course, the last time I'd hooked up with someone on the fly, I'd wound up in this situation.

Fuck. Why was I so hung up on him? Probably because I missed getting laid on a regular basis. Maybe it *was* time to go find another bored, horny dude for a night.

Well, I haven't been to Backdoor Bob in a while...

CHAPTER 16

PAUL

SEAN WAS right about Backdoor Bob—they mixed the drinks good and strong.

Apparently not strong enough, though, because two rum and Cokes into the night, I was still thinking about Sean. Exactly the opposite of what I'd come here to do. Leaning against the bar, I pressed the ice-cold glass to my forehead and cursed. I'd been doing so well, too! Okay, maybe not great, but better. Enough I'd started to convince myself I could move on... right up until we'd crossed paths at the gym.

After our brief encounter this afternoon, there'd been no doubt in my mind that it was past time to use my tried-and-true method of getting over breakups. Sean had gotten my mind off Jayson, after all. I clearly needed to hook up with someone else to get my mind off Sean.

I'd considered the internet, and swiped around on Grindr, but it all felt too businesslike.

Hello, Bear71. You look reasonably attractive. I'll meet you at this address at 7 p.m. for sex in a variety of positions. Please bring personal lubricant and prophylactics.

No.

So I'd opted for Backdoor Bob. If I didn't find anyone promising, at least I wouldn't have to spend too much on drinks to console myself because goddamn—my head was already light.

I sipped my drink as I scanned the room. No one I recognized from the base, and no one sporting a high-and-tight haircut, so that was promising. Though on second glance, I was pretty sure the bald guy sipping a longneck over by the other bar was a civilian contractor who worked down on the flight line. He didn't seem to recognize me, so I ignored him.

There was definitely a good mix of men. A couple of gray-bearded guys who looked like truckers or lumberjacks. Some hipsters in ball-suffocating pants who'd probably made the trip from Portland or something. And... *Oh what have we here?*

The man was jaw-droppingly sexy. Clean cut, dark-haired, a hint of a tan that might or might not have been a trick of the club's dim lighting. He had shoulders for days, and something about him made me think he might've been a cop or a firefighter. He had that look about him, though I couldn't put my finger on why.

Well, there was only one way to find out if my hunch was accurate. I took a quick sip of my rum and Coke for a little bit of liquid courage, and started to step away from the bar. I searched for the best route through the crowd, and—

My drink nearly slipped out of my hand.

You've got to be kidding me.

No fucking way.

Sean?

Of all the clubs—

Of course he'd come to this one. He'd recommended the damn place to me.

The firefighter-cop-whatever was suddenly gone. All my thoughts and senses zoomed in on the man I'd come here to forget.

He looked good tonight. Really good. Like a man on the prowl. The black shirt was snug in all the right places, and the club's lighting was just right to pick out those trademark blue highlights in his hair. He was talking to someone, and when he laughed...

I had to pull my gaze away to collect my thoughts. Fuck. I'd come here to get him out of my head, not ogle him while he was dressed to kill.

I cautiously looked his way again.

He was gone.

My stomach knotted. I searched the crowd for him, nervous now that I couldn't find him. It was like seeing a tiger in the jungle, and then *not* seeing it. It was still there somewhere, but without a visual lock, I couldn't be sure I was keeping enough space between myself and the threat. Sean wasn't dangerous, but the temptation sure as hell was. As long as we kept a crowd of dancing drunk dudes between us, we couldn't touch.

But where the hell was he?

A second later, I found him. He was still talking to the other guy, but they'd moved toward one of the chest-high tables along the wall.

I gulped, my mouth suddenly dry. I was about to turn back to the bar when Sean shifted his position and looked right at me.

He froze. So did I. His lips parted, and I begged the ground under my feet to do the same and swallow me up. It didn't, of course, so I searched for the next best thing—an escape route.

Naturally, Sean was between me and the exit, and I knew damn well if I headed in that direction, I wouldn't make it to the door.

Instead, I turned around and hurried toward the men's room. I just needed some space. Some doors between us. A breather while I worked out a game plan.

The men's room was empty, thank God. Or close to it. Some heavy breathing and moaning came from behind a closed stall door, but I ignored it. I'd made out—and more—in my fair share of bathroom stalls.

At the other end of the dimly lit men's room, I rested my hands on the sink and stared at myself in the mirror. For a long moment, I watched the door's reflection, sure it was going to swing open. But it didn't. Sean didn't come in after me. Smart man. At least one of us had his head screwed on.

I released my breath and let my head fall forward. This was stupid. Sean had as much right to be here as I did, and he'd clearly already gotten the attention of some other guy. With any luck, they'd be headed out of the club in no time flat, and that was *not* jealousy twisting around in my gut.

I closed my eyes. Fuck, I was losing my mind. I really should've stuck with the impersonal approach of hookup apps. At least then I could go straight for my target—like, say, the hot cop-firefighter guy—without being thrown off course by another hotter, less resistible man. One I'd already been in bed with enough times to know there was no chance of being disappointed by a sloppy kisser, a malfunctioning penis, or a lack of understanding of basic hygiene.

Rubbing my hand over my face, I sighed. Then I straightened and looked my reflection in the eyes. I was being stupid. Which wasn't exactly a new thing, but I was going to drive myself crazy if I didn't change course.

All I had to do was go back out into the club and work up the courage to approach the guy I'd been staring at before I'd noticed Sean. Simple. Maybe not easy, but simple. I could do this. If I couldn't, well, I could take my ass over to another club and try my luck there.

Deep breath. I had this.

Nervous but determined, I left the men's room.

Went around the corner.

And stopped dead.

Music still thumped in the background. My heart still pounded in my ears.

From several feet away, Sean stood there like he'd been waiting for me, leaning against the wall with his hip cocked as if he wanted me to think he was casual and relaxed. Eyes narrow and lips quirked, he looked back at me like we were the only people in the building.

We locked eyes for the longest time, just staring at each other. I could almost feel the telepathic dares volleying back and forth between us.

Say something.

No, you say something.

Do something.

I dare you.

Finally, Sean moved. He came toward me. And he didn't stop.

One second, we were facing each other from across the narrow hall.

The next, my back was against the wall and Sean's lips were against mine, and *God, I missed you.*

I wrapped my arms around him and grabbed a handful of his hair. He moaned into my kiss, so I held his hair tighter, and when he shivered, so did I. Damn it, wasn't this what I'd come to the club to forget?

Oh to hell with it. He was there, I was there, and if his kiss was anything to go by, he wasn't backing away this time. I sure as fuck wasn't the rational one, so... yes, please. I kissed him deeper and held him closer, and he had me pinned so hard against the wall I could barely breathe. Didn't even care. Oxygen was... whatever.

"I know we shouldn't do this," he said. "There's... so many reasons... and I..." He gripped the front of my shirt and kissed me again, then broke that kiss just enough to murmur, "I need you tonight."

"You have no idea." I slid a hand into his back pocket and pulled him closer so he couldn't possibly miss how fucking hard I was.

Sean whimpered softly and ground his own erection against mine. Holy shit—if this didn't end in both of us naked and panting, I was physically incapable of the amount of jerking off it would take to make up for it.

What are you doing, Paul? This is Sean. It's Sean, for God's sake.

He held the back of my neck and slid the tip of his tongue under mine.

Yeah, it's definitely Sean. Sweet Jesus...

I was out of breath when I broke the kiss. "This wasn't what I had in mind when I came here tonight."

Sean nipped at my lower lip. "You came here to get laid, didn't you?"

"Didn't come here for the drinks."

He laughed, and when our eyes met, the gleam in his weakened my knees. "So we both came here for the same thing."

"Yeah." I hooked my fingers in his belt loops. "Definitely here for the same thing."

Except not with you. Anyone but you.

He swept his tongue across his lips.

Holy shit, I need you.

"Let's get out of here," he whispered. "Or I'm going to end up fucking you right—"

"Let's go."

CHAPTER 17

SEAN

"YOU KNOW we shouldn't do this, right?"

"Of course," I said as we stopped in front of the motel room door. "But I think we both know we're going to."

He glanced down, and I followed his gaze to the key card in his hand. Then we looked at each other again in the low light of the cheap hotel's hallway.

Now was the time for one of us to put on the brakes. We could still back out. Go downstairs. Turn in the key. Go our separate ways. We'd made it this far before and backed away.

I didn't say anything. Paul didn't say anything.

I was too fucking restless to just stand there, so I plucked the key card from his hand and put it into the slot. It took me a couple of tries, but it finally went in, and the green light came on.

No turning back now. Not when I was in the same room as Paul and a bed.

I tossed the key card on the table by the TV. Paul kicked the door shut behind us, pushed me up against the wall, and kissed me hard, and I thought I was going to melt right then and there.

If that wasn't enough, he started down my neck, and his chin was stubbled and rough against my skin, and I decided there was nothing I wouldn't do for him tonight if he kept doing that.

I closed my eyes and tilted my head. "You know hooking up now is going to make it that much harder to not hook up in the future, right?"

"Uh-huh." He kissed his way up the side of my neck. "There's a lot on the line, but goddamn, I can*not* resist you."

I sucked in a breath, gripping his shoulders tighter. "Guess we might as well give in, right?"

"That's what I'm thinking." He lifted his head and met my eyes. "I sure as hell don't want to stop."

"Then why are we stopping?"

Paul grinned, then kissed me, and we definitely weren't stopping.

Okay, so even with my head spinning and my dick hard, I knew that was all crazy talk. Once we'd both satisfied these erections and could think for a minute or two, we'd realize how stupid this was. We'd catch our breaths, we'd get dressed, and we'd agree to go our separate ways again. But for now, with his body against mine and his lips exploring every inch of my neck, it seemed like a pretty good idea.

Clothes started coming off. My shirt tangled in our feet and nearly tripped us both, but we recovered. I was pretty sure we ripped a seam on Paul's shirt, but he didn't seem to care, so I didn't either.

The smart thing to do—besides not doing it at all— would be to have a quickie, be done with it, and get out of there.

Nope. Feet planted, we held each other close and kissed like we had all night, and tomorrow night, and the one after that. Any other night, I'd have been balls-deep in him by now, but I hadn't even kicked off my shoes. Fine by me. If this was going to be the last time I was in bed with him, then hell yes I was going to savor every minute.

Paul slid his hands into my back pockets—I fucking loved when he did that—and pulled me close, rubbing his erection against mine. "I'm sweaty from that damn club. Could go for a shower."

"Yeah?"

"Mm-hmm. Want to join me?"

I grinned against his lips. "How is that even a question?"

Paul laughed. He kissed me once more, then took my hand and led me to the bathroom.

A lifetime of trying to do the right thing and toe the line of being a Navy dependent should've stopped me, but none of that held a candle to how much I wanted and needed Paul. Doing the right thing could wait a little longer.

I glanced up at him, meeting his eyes, which were gleaming with lust. My mouth watered.

Why did I think this was a bad idea again?

Oh right. Commanding officer and... stuff. Something. Whatever.

I tugged at his belt.

We stepped into the shower together, and yeah, doing the right thing could *definitely* wait. Really, how much more hot water would we get into by making out under this hot water? Nobody had to know.

I sent up a little prayer that the motel had one of those water heaters that would last forever, because I loved this. Everything about it. His hands in my hair and on my skin.

The friction of his hip rubbing against my erection. His thick cock in my hand. And holy fuck—his kiss. It was hard to comprehend that there was anything wrong with letting Paul taste and touch and kiss like we had all night.

I loved that we weren't in a rush. There was a different flavor of urgency this time. It wasn't an orgasm I was after. I wanted tonight to be burned into both our memories. If this was the last time I was going to touch him—and God knew it needed to be—I wanted to remember everything.

I ran my hands all over him, taking in every contour of his muscles and the curve of his spine. The edges of some of his tattoos were raised slightly, and I traced them with my fingertips, following all the lines and curves and corners. Now and then, I stroked him or teased his balls to keep him on his toes and turned on, but he sure didn't seem to be losing interest. Not when his cock was that hard and his breath was coming in rapid, uneven gasps like mine.

His hands were all over the place too. For the first time, I actually regretted not having a tattoo, because it meant I didn't have some design for him to trace like I was doing with his. On the other hand, I couldn't complain about smooth, warm palms and talented fingers roaming all over my body. Sometimes he combed them through my hair. Sometimes he cradled my neck or my face. Every now and then, both hands drifted down over my ass, like they did when he was sliding them into my pockets as he pulled me against him and his very, very hard cock.

Kneading my ass cheeks with his strong fingers, he dipped his head and kissed my neck. "Not getting cold, are you?"

Cold? It took a second for me to remember where we were. That we were still standing in the shower with water pouring over us.

"No. Not cold." I bit my lip as his stubble scraped the front of my throat. "Not at all. You?"

"No. But..." He lifted his head. "I think that's enough showering for one night." He reached past me and shut off the water. "Let's go in the bedroom so we can fool around without slipping and busting our asses."

"Oh, I like that idea." *Why did I sound drunk? Why did I feel drunk?* I opened my eyes and looked him up and down. *Probably because I'm standing here naked with a gorgeous, soaking-wet man whose cock definitely needs some immediate attention.*

We stepped out of the shower, dried off enough that the sheets wouldn't wind up wet, and then moved toward the waiting bed.

Just before we reached it, Paul stopped me and pulled me into a kiss, and a moment later, he broke that kiss and went to his knees. I couldn't breathe even before his mouth was around my dick. I combed my fingers through his graying hair, my knees wobbling because I was so fucking turned on. Anything I could do to myself with my hand was nothing compared to the things Paul could do with his hand, lips, and tongue. Or maybe I was just that horny. Or maybe both. Whatever.

He held on to my hips and went to town on me, deep-throating and licking and squeezing with his lips. He moaned around my cock, and I shuddered. Too late, I realized I'd forced myself deeper into his mouth, but he didn't seem to mind. He didn't gag, and kept right on teasing me.

Then he got up and gestured for me to lie down. I did, and he got on the bed, but didn't lie beside me. My way-too-aroused-for-thinking brain couldn't understand why we weren't wrapped up in each other's arms and making out. Why he was moving away from me, turning—

He settled on his side, his very erect cock inches from my face, and took my cock between his lips.

Oh. God. Yes. Message received.

As much as I usually loved sixty-nining—Jesus fuck, I loved sixty-nining—it was actually a little frustrating with Paul. His mouth was unbelievable, and I couldn't concentrate on what I was doing to him when he was turning me on like this. I kept losing myself in the things he did with his lips and tongue. Kept forgetting what I was supposed to be doing with mine.

"You're so good at that," I breathed.

"Likewise."

"I would be if you weren't so distracting."

He laughed, then ran his tongue around the head of my cock.

Still stroking him, I let my head fall back. "Fuck..."

He gave a quiet moan—maybe even laughed—but didn't stop what he was doing. I went down on him again. The second my lips touched his dick, he groaned, his voice thrumming against my skin, and my concentration was shot all over again.

"You are so..." I squeezed my eyes shut as he made another circle with his tongue. "*Distracting.*"

Paul chuckled. "Sounds like a compliment."

"Uh-huh. But it... makes it kind of hard to..." *Fuck, how do you do that?* "I want to... Oh God." I shivered. "You're gonna... make me come."

He stopped abruptly and looked up at me, grinning as he kept stroking. "Can't have that, can we?" Paul shifted back around so we were facing the same direction again, and frustration kicked in for a couple of seconds, but didn't last long. Not when he was gazing at me with that gleam in his eyes. He kissed me, and I didn't protest because my God his talented mouth wasn't only good for sucking dick. The way he kissed drove me wild even more than the way he went down on me. Jesus, but I was going to miss this. I'd been with a few guys who loved kissing, but no one who liked it as much or was as good at it as Paul.

Guess I should've been dating older guys before. Something to be said for experience.

I broke the kiss and swept my tongue across my lips. "I want to fuck you."

He shivered and nodded. "Yes, please." He was so out of breath, and even that made my head spin, especially when he panted, "Nobody fucks like you do."

I squirmed in his arms. "Condoms?"

"Plenty." He kissed me quickly and added, "Should I get one?"

"*Oh* yeah."

He was on his feet so fast, I almost didn't see him move. Chuckling, I joined him, and by the time I was off the bed, he'd fished the condoms and a small lube bottle from his jeans.

He started to lie back on the bed, but I stopped him.

"No. Stay standing." I tore the wrapper with my teeth. "And bend over the bed."

"I like where this is going."

"Figured you would."

He did as he was told, and I poured some lube in my hand. After I'd smoothed plenty onto the condom, I put some on him too. He swore under his breath as I pressed two fingers into his hole.

"What's wrong?"

"Just..." He rolled his shoulders and shifted his weight. "God, Sean, I don't want your fingers."

"What?" I added a third. As I fucked him slowly with my hand, I said, "Have to make sure you're ready and—"

"Goddamn it."

"Eager, are we?"

He grumbled something as he spread his legs wider. Then, clearer, "Just *fuck* me already."

My spine tingled with pure arousal. Even if it made me a selfish bastard or a complete idiot—probably both—I couldn't deny that knowing who Paul was made this even hotter. Everyone on base stood up straight and saluted him, and I had him bent over and begging for my dick.

I slid my fingers free and put some more lube on the condom. Then I positioned myself behind him. He didn't move while I guided myself in, but as soon as the head of my cock slid into him, his whole body responded. His back arched and his shoulders bunched as if he could contain that shudder. He groaned softly, rocking back against me as his fingers curled around handfuls of sheets.

Any other night I might've tried to regain control. Maybe held his hips, fucked him slowly, teased him for the hell of it.

Tonight? Forget it. I fell into sync with him, and drank in the sight of his powerful body and my dick sliding in and out of him. Didn't matter how much I'd jerked off recently —fucking him now, for real, was overwhelming as hell.

Pressing my lips together, I held my breath because I didn't want to come too fast. I didn't know why I bothered, though—I could already feel my orgasm building, building, building. I was either going to come fast or pass out, so to hell with it.

I put my hands on his shoulders and dragged my nails downward, leaving eight red lines and making him release whispered profanity like only a career Navy man could string together. God, yes—I loved turning him on.

I wanted to make this last, but couldn't resist picking up more speed. The temptation was too much, especially when I knew how he'd moan and arch when I dug my fingers into his hips, released my breath, and fucked him good and hard. He didn't disappoint. His head fell forward. His shoulders tensed and rippled. A heavy breath. A soft curse. A low, throaty groan. This might not last long, but I'd sure as hell remember it.

"Fuck," I breathed. My head spun. I forced myself into him so hard he dropped onto his forearm. I lost my balance too, and had just enough presence of mind left to plant a hand on the bed beside him. That kept me from falling farther, so my brain went right back to the most important thing—getting as deep into Paul as I could before I came.

Much too fast, I was there—shuddering, groaning, burying myself as deep as he could take me and riding the release of so, so much need and frustration.

It's only been like two weeks. Why the fuck does it feel like it's been years?

Didn't matter. It did. And finally, I'd had him again, and I'd come in him again, and now maybe I could breathe again.

Except he hadn't come yet. Had to do something about that. Stat.

I pulled out, and my voice was shaky as hell when I said, "On your back."

He wasn't so steady either, but managed to turn onto his back. I leaned down for a brief kiss, and temptation almost got the best of me—I wanted to lie there and kiss him until sunrise—but I whispered, "Back in a sec. Don't move."

He didn't move. When I came back from disposing of

the condom, he was watching me with heavy-lidded eyes, slowly stroking himself as he waited for me to join him again. My God, that man was sexy. Dark hair sprinkled over smooth planes and lean muscles, and his tattoos seemed to glow against the flush of his sweaty skin.

And that look in his eyes?

Oh yes. Consequences be damned, I want you.

I joined him on the bed and started toward his cock with every intention of sucking him off, but he stopped me with a hand on my shoulder. Beckoning to me, he whispered, "C-come here."

I did as he asked. As I leaned down to kiss him, he slid a hand around the back of my neck. Okay, I could work with this. Not like I was going to object to making out with him, especially when he was aroused to the point of shaking.

So I went for the next best thing and closed my fingers around his cock.

"Oh God," he breathed, squeezing his eyes shut.

"Like that?"

"What kind of question is that?"

One he wasn't going to answer, apparently—he kissed me and didn't let up. I stroked him, and my pulse pounded as he rocked his hips in time with my hand, pushing himself into my grip.

His cock was getting even harder in my hand, and his kiss was getting more frantic. Sharp, hot breaths rushed past my skin. His fingers twitched on the back of my neck. God, this was even better than making him come by fucking him. Feeling him fall to pieces, kissing him while he writhed and shook—it was all insanely hot.

And I resisted you for this long... how?

Better make up for lost time.

I tightened my grip and kissed him even harder, and he

rewarded me with a full-body tremor and a soft, helpless whimper. Hot semen landed on my hand and forearm, and he thrust into my fist a few times before he broke the kiss and dropped onto the pillows.

"Jesus," he moaned.

"Nope. Not Jesus." I leaned down to kiss the side of his neck. "Just me."

"Just you?" He laughed, sounding kind of drunk. "No such thing, Sean. No such thing."

I lifted my head. We exchanged blissed-out smiles, and I pressed my lips to his again for another long, languid kiss.

After a while, he murmured, "Another shower?"

"Another shower."

If the motel room's shower had been a little bit bigger with a little more water pressure, we probably would've spent half the night in there. I loved showering with him, and I'd missed it like crazy.

Unfortunately, the tepid, half-assed spray wasn't nearly as nice as it could have been, so we got out, dried off, and sank onto the hard bed together.

Paul turned on his side, facing me, and cupped my cheek. "I still can't believe we're here."

"Probably shouldn't be." *Probably?* No, there was no *probably* about it and no point in convincing myself there was. I lowered my gaze.

"I know we shouldn't. But..." He traced my cheekbone with his thumb. "We are."

I swallowed. "Yeah."

He laughed, sounding a little sleepy or maybe a little drunk. "For what it's worth, you are not easy to forget."

I chuckled as I shifted onto my side. "Neither are you." I draped my arm over him. "I think you might've spoiled me."

"Mm-hmm. Ditto." He ran his fingers through my hair.

I watched my hand run up and down his arm, and my heart sank. The earlier novelty of having the base CO beg me to fuck him was wearing off fast. In its place, guilt crept in. Shit. What was I doing?

It wasn't out of spite toward my dad or the Navy or anything. When I was with Paul, the Navy was the last thing on my mind.

With Paul, I felt attractive and wanted, not just convenient. In fact, I was the opposite of convenient for Paul now, and he *still* wanted me. There were plenty of hot, single gay men in Flatstick, and even in Anchor Point, and he wouldn't have to be nearly as discreet with them as he would with me. He could get busted naked with the entire defensive line of a college football team, and there wouldn't be nearly as many consequences as if he were caught so much as talking to me.

"Sean?" Twin creases formed between his eyebrows. "You're quiet."

"Yeah, I..." I traced his cheekbone with the pad of my thumb. "You're taking a huge chance with me. Why?"

Paul swallowed, avoiding my eyes for a moment. My gut clenched—he was going to see reason and this was over. I just knew it.

But then he clasped my hand, kissed my palm, and met my gaze. "I don't have an answer. I really don't. Definitely not one that will suddenly make it all okay."

"Then why—"

"Because I want you. It's that simple." He leaned in and kissed me softly, letting it linger for a few long seconds. "I haven't been able to stop thinking about you. I'm sure this is crazy and stupid, and I know it's an enormous risk." Another kiss, longer this time. "But I can't get you out of my head."

"Neither can I."

For a while, neither of us said anything. This was dumb and dangerous—if I lay like this for much longer, I was going to fall asleep—but I couldn't resist. I'd already accepted that I was addicted to Paul, and knowing this was the last time... well, it didn't make me all that eager to leave.

My eyelids started drooping. My whole body was relaxed and heavy, and every now and then, I'd catch myself sliding into a dream before pulling myself back into reality. Reality, where I was in bed with Paul even though I had absolutely no business here.

Sighing, I rubbed a hand over my face. "I should go."

"I know." He traced my cheekbone with his thumb. "I shouldn't have kept you here this long."

"You weren't exactly holding me against my will."

A small smile played at his lips. "No, but..."

Our eyes locked. He didn't need to say it. We both knew why I was here and why I shouldn't have been. I had a feeling he wasn't in a hurry to kick me out, just like I wasn't exactly rushing for the door. And now that I was looking at him, falling asleep wasn't as much of a concern.

Heart thumping, I said, "That wasn't the last of the condoms, was it?"

Paul shook his head. "No."

"Good."

CHAPTER 18

PAUL

SEAN and I pulled up the covers and cuddled close beneath them. Aside from our wet hair, we were still hot from the long shower we'd shared, but not hot enough to stay apart. Thank God for that—I loved the way our bodies fit together even when we weren't having sex. He'd lie on his side and mold himself to me, and I'd drape my arm around his shoulders. Even with his hair wet, I liked his head on my chest.

I'd been single or in long-distance relationships for way too long—I'd missed being with another person like this. Living alone was fine, and anonymous sex was fine, and even being single for long stretches was fine. Lack of human contact? That got old.

We lay like that for a while, soaking up the warmth of being next to each other. Eventually, though, my arm started to fall asleep, so we moved around, settling onto the pillows and facing each other.

"Ugh. Hair's still wet." He lifted his head and eyed the pillowcase. "Uh, I have dyed hair, so hopefully I don't ruin the sheets or anything."

I shrugged. "It's a motel. They've seen worse. I take it this"—I ran my fingers through his damp black-blue hair —"isn't a new thing for you?"

"Nope. Been coloring it for years. I change it up every so often, but it's usually black and... something."

I smiled. "It looks good on you."

"Thanks." He combed his hand through my short hair. "Somehow I don't think you'd get away with the same color."

"Uh, no." I sighed dramatically. "I don't get away with a lot of things in this line of work, believe me."

He laughed halfheartedly. "I believe you."

I took a breath to mention that, yeah, he probably understood exactly how strict the military was, but that line of conversation wouldn't do much for the mood.

You're being an idiot. You know you're playing with fire.

I ignored those thoughts and kept my mouth shut.

Sean pushed himself up onto his elbow. "I'm guessing you've been in a long time."

"You could say that."

"Is this the career you wanted?"

I nodded. "I wanted to command an aircraft carrier, but a base is okay too. Overall, yeah, it's what I wanted. It's not an easy life, but it's been a good one." I paused. "Mostly."

"Mostly?"

"Well, you know how it is. The military life isn't without sacrifices. And I admit, there are times when I wonder if the sacrifices are worth it."

Silence wedged itself between us, and stayed there for a long time until Sean whispered, "Are they?"

"Are they, what?"

"The sacrifices. Are they worth it?"

I didn't answer right away. Absently running my hand up and down his arm, I stared at the ceiling for a while. Then, "Ask me again when I retire."

"When do you plan to retire?"

"Depends on if I have a shot at making admiral."

"Think you do?"

I shrugged. "It's hard to say. Not many captains make it, but I'm going to bust my ass until I know if I made the cut."

"So, how do you make the cut?"

"Well, I need to command a ship before they'll even consider it, so hopefully that's where I'll go after Anchor Point." I scowled. "I've been trying to get them to give me a boat for a while now, but..."

"They don't want you in charge of a ship?"

"Imagine that, right?" I laughed bitterly. "But I'm not giving up until they break down and put me on a ship." I paused. "Making admiral also means knowing the right people. I've got a few friends in high places, but I've also pissed off a few people in high places. So we'll see who retires and who's left in Congress after the next election."

"Fingers crossed." He held up his hand, index finger crossed behind the middle.

"Thanks." I laughed again, but it didn't last long. We both sighed and sank back onto the pillows. "We're idiots, aren't we?"

"Yep." He blew out a breath. "But we're here. Might as well enjoy it until we leave."

Which we should do. Like now.

Neither of us moved, though.

The room stayed completely quiet until Sean's stomach grumbled.

"If it's not obvious," he said, "I could go for some food."

"We might have to order something. I don't think it's a good idea to go out together."

He scowled, but nodded. "Pizza?"

"Sounds good to me."

We hunted down a pizza menu, and Sean ordered. While we waited, we put on some pants so we'd be decent when the delivery guy arrived, and lay back on the rumpled bed.

Sean shifted onto his side. "Too bad we can't go out. There are some great restaurants in this town."

"Yeah?"

He nodded.

"Well." I smirked. "They'll either look at us askance because they think I'm robbing the cradle, or they'll think you're my son."

Sean laughed. "Oh come on. We're both of age." A playful grin formed on his lips. "Even if some of us have more years of experience than others with being 'of age.'"

I rolled my eyes. "As long as you don't mind the fact that I've literally been in the Navy your *entire* life."

Sean burst out laughing. "Are you serious?"

"Yes. I've been in twenty-four years."

He whistled. "Wow."

"Yeah. Wow." I chuckled. "It sounds even crazier now that we've said it out loud."

"It is, but crazy is fun, so..."

"I won't argue with that."

Our eyes met, and my heart sped up. This was the point when we should've addressed the aircraft carrier in the living room. Now that we had a few orgasms out of our systems, and we'd started talking about things like the Navy and this enormous age gap between us, I didn't see how we could keep avoiding it.

But he didn't bring it up. I didn't bring it up.

We just sank into another long kiss, and as Sean slid a hand over my ass, he murmured, "Pizza should be here in half an hour. Think we have time?"

I rolled him onto his back. "*Plenty* of time."

I stared out my office window. It was gray and rainy today because this was the Oregon coast, and the weather underscored my shitty mood.

I'd have felt a lot better if Friday night had been awful. But it hadn't been. It had been amazing. With Sean involved, it was impossible for an evening to *not* be amazing.

This morning, however...

I rubbed my eyes with my thumb and forefinger. Hooking up with him had been like binge drinking after a long dry spell. Sure, it was fun for a while, but the aftermath was the opposite of fun. And right about now, I'd have been happy to be hungover and heaving my guts out, because the way I really felt was a hell of a lot worse.

Over and over, I heard our parting words on Saturday morning...

"*We can't do this again.*"

"*We shouldn't have done it this time.*"

"*I know. But doing it again will just make things worse.*"

Then he'd left, and I'd left, and now it was Monday morning and I was at the office with no idea what to do with myself. Good thing none of my superiors were around. I didn't need *distracted idiot—not admiral material* showing up when it came time for a possible promotion.

Except I was starting to think maybe that was true. What kind of admiral did stupid shit like going back again and again to the wrong person? For that matter, I wanted to believe that if Sean called or texted, I'd wisely ignore him or tell him no, but that was bullshit. I was hooked on him in ways I'd never been hooked on nicotine or anything else.

Yeah. Admiral was *definitely* in the cards for me at this rate.

I needed some words of wisdom—more like a verbal kick in the ass—so I picked up the phone and called Travis's extension.

"Hey," he said. Our office had caller ID, so he didn't bother with formality when I called.

"Hey, you got a few minutes to come by my office?"

"I need to dash off an email, but I can be there in ten."

"Great. Thanks."

Exactly ten minutes later, Travis stepped into my office. Our eyes met, and he nudged the door shut behind him. Apparently my "help me, I'm losing my shit" face was more conspicuous than I'd hoped.

He eased himself into a chair, wincing slightly. "So what's up?"

"Well..." A mix of guilt and shame wound itself around my stomach. "Remember when I told you I was seeing someone younger than me?"

He nodded. "I thought you'd moved on. You hadn't mentioned him in a while."

"I..." I let my head fall against the chair back. "I was trying to move on, but man, he is not easy to quit."

"So what happened?" Travis inclined his head. "Why *are* you trying to quit him?"

"Because... the thing is..." I hesitated, glancing at the door, and lowered my voice. "Nothing leaves this office, all right?"

"Of course." Travis sat up a little, eyes wide. "What's up?"

"Well, it turns out he's someone's dependent."

Travis blinked. "Oh. Shit."

"Yeah."

"Someone in this command, I assume?"

"Yep. So now you can see why I've been trying to stay away from him?"

"Oh yeah. Definitely." His eyebrow arched. "Question is, why would you be talking to me and saying *trying* unless you've been backsliding? You're playing with fire, dipshit."

My cheeks burned. "I know. Believe me. The thing is, we'd been seeing each other for a while before we realized his dad works for me. If it had come out right from the start, it wouldn't have bothered me."

"But you had a chance to get attached to him."

"So much." My chest ached at the thought of how I felt when I was with Sean. And when I was away from him. What had I gotten myself into? "It's a small town. We quit seeing each other, but then we ran into each other at a club, and it caught us both off guard, and..." I made a rolling motion with my hand. "You get the idea."

"Sounds to me like this is more than hooking up. I mean, even if the physical stuff is great, I know you—you're not going to be an idiot just because a guy is good at sucking dick."

"Exactly. But what difference does it make?" I tapped my nail on my armrest. "Regs are regs. I mean, it's one thing when it's my career. But this could fuck up his dad's career too. I can't... I can't do that."

Travis scowled. "Jesus. I don't even know what to suggest."

"There isn't anything to suggest." I rubbed my stiff

neck. "The only thing I can do is get over him." I paused, then exhaled hard. "Which I've been trying like hell to do, and it's not working."

Releasing a long breath, Travis leaned back in his chair. "Man. That is a mess."

"You don't say." I swallowed. "The truth is, right or wrong, I have never felt like this for someone. But it doesn't matter because we can't..." I waved my hand.

He said nothing for a moment, then shook his head. "I wish I had some advice, but I've got nothing."

"Aside from 'stay the fuck away from him'?"

"Well. The Navy says to stay the fuck away from him." Travis smiled a little, but something in his eyes told me he was completely serious as he said, "I'll do a lot of things for my friends, but tell them to stay away from someone they love? Forget it."

"Exactly what I need—an enabler."

"I'm not enabling anything." He shrugged. "But I know you. And I know you're not stupid when it comes to your career. If there's something about this kid that keeps pulling you back to him even when you know damn well it's a bad idea... well, who the hell am I to tell you to stay away from that?"

"My best friend who doesn't want to see me torpedo my career?"

"I want to see you happy, Paul. You know that."

God. Right in the balls, Travis. Right in the balls.

I lowered my gaze. "The regs are pretty clear on this shit."

"I know. And I'm sorry. I was really hoping you'd struck gold with this kid."

I did. You have no idea.

After Travis had gone, I stared out the window again,

watching a few streaks of rain slide down the glass in front of a blurry gray backdrop.

The regs were what they were. Circumstances couldn't be changed.

And even though I knew it was stupid, that I was risking everything I had ever worked for, I hoped Sean would call.

CHAPTER 19

SEAN

SCHOOLWORK WASN'T HAPPENING because that required more than three brain cells devoted to something other than Paul. Workouts weren't a helpful distraction anymore, because I kept expecting to see him at the gym. Driving? I could barely concentrate enough to start the car, let alone drive anyone anywhere.

I was losing my fucking mind.

And finally, I couldn't take anymore. This morning had been too much. We'd crossed paths at the gym for the umpteenth time, and I'd spent my workout alternating between surreptitiously drooling over his physique and fighting back tears. At least my dad had taken my watery eyes to be a sign that I was pushing myself during my lifts, but I was rattled.

So I'd given in.

I'd texted Paul.

I'd driven to a crappy little motel outside of Anchor Point.

And now we were lying together in bed, satisfied and grinning. My guilty conscience was eating at me, but not as much as usual. This was stupid and wrong, but damn it, cuddling up with Paul and kissing and touching... it all felt too right to be wrong.

I'll deal with my conscience tomorrow. Tonight, I need you.

Right. Because that had worked well in the past.

Oblivious to my brain doing somersaults around all the reasons we shouldn't have been here, Paul smoothed my hair. "You mind if I ask you something personal?"

"While I'm naked in a seedy motel bed after fucking you senseless?"

Paul chuckled. "I'll take that as a yes." His expression turned more serious, and he rested a hand on my waist. "You've been a Navy brat your whole life, I assume."

I nodded.

"How... I mean, how has that been? That had to be rough."

"It's the only life I've ever known." I shrugged. "I think the completely civilian life would be a bit weird for me now."

"Well, yeah. But still. It's hard on me, and I'm the one getting a paycheck. It's hard to imagine what it's like to be in it your entire life."

"It has its really, really shitty moments," I said quietly. "Obviously there's..." I gestured at him and me, and he grimaced as he nodded. I went on, "But it's got its perks too. The health insurance is nice. Having my tuition paid. I've gotten to live in some cool places. Most of the time, the military has been good to me."

"Glad to hear it." He paused. "Your dad must be close to retiring by now."

I laughed humorlessly. "Dad? Retire? Not until he makes master chief at least. I heard him tell his girlfriend he thinks he could become Master Chief Petty Officer of the Navy."

"Ambitious."

"Uh-huh. And it would mean moving to DC." I wrinkled my nose. "No, thanks."

Paul grimaced. "Yeah. That's not a great place to be stationed. What about your mom? Is she military too?"

I shook my head. "No. And I kind of liked the idea of one of my parents staying in the same place, but living with her didn't work out."

He lifted his eyebrows a little, like he wanted to ask what happened but wasn't sure if he should.

I shifted a bit. "The whole reason I live with my dad is my mom couldn't support me. They split up when I was fourteen, and I was supposed to go live with her once she got settled in. But between the economy and her résumé, she couldn't get any decent work."

Paul nodded slowly. "My ex-wife had the same problem. We'd moved around so much, she couldn't hold down a job for very long, so her résumé had too many gaps and not enough long-term employment."

"Yeah, exactly. And it's not like I want to rip on the Navy. It's obviously been a good career for you and—" I hesitated. "It's a good career, you know? But man, it's hard too. The whole military life? And it isn't like it's shitty for me and sunshine and roses for my dad. I mean, he and his girlfriend have had it pretty rough too. They've only been together a year, and they're already talking about getting married because once he gets orders somewhere else..."

Paul frowned. "It's either leave her behind or have a long-distance relationship."

"Yep. And he doesn't really want to get married, but she really doesn't want to do the long-distance thing. So it's been hard." I paused and met his gaze. "Is it weird to bring up my dad? When we're... uh..."

"No. He's part of your life, same as the Navy."

"I know, but..." *We shouldn't be here and we both know it, and talking about this is talking about exactly why we're being fucking morons.*

"I get it." He kissed my temple. "And yeah, when you think about it, this whole thing is kind of weird. But it is what it is. I'm curious about you, and he's part of your life."

"Even—"

"Yes. Even if we shouldn't be here." He stroked my hair. "That doesn't make a difference to me, by the way. I mean, I know it should. Professionally, it should. But here?" He cupped my cheek. "It doesn't even register. You're just you, not the kid of someone under my command."

I flinched, but then pressed against his palm. "Same here. I have to stop and think about it to remember you're his CO." *Because I'm stupid.* "All I think about is you."

Paul nodded. "Me too." He sighed before continuing. "You know, I wouldn't trade my career for the world, but I won't pretend it's been easy either. Isn't easy for dependents either."

I sighed. "Yeah."

"Both of my ex-wives struggled like hell with it, believe me." Paul released a long breath. "Well, that's not entirely fair. The Navy didn't make my marriages *easy*, but it wasn't what ended them."

I watched him for a moment, not sure if I should prod. Though we'd been getting to know each other more and more lately, and he wouldn't have brought it up if it was off-limits, so I quietly asked, "What happened?"

He looked up at the ceiling, absently running his fingers up and down my arm. "If you'd asked us at the time, we'd have told you they didn't realize the Navy came first, and I was stupid enough to *put* it first."

I didn't say anything. It was hard to imagine Paul being like that.

"The reality was..." He closed his eyes. "It was my fault. Not the Navy's. Mine. We..." He was quiet for a moment. "Okay, in a way, it was because of the Navy. DADT was in effect, and every officer I knew drilled it into my head that no one made it past lieutenant without a wife and kids. A good-looking wife and well-behaved kids, of course."

"I've heard that," I said.

"Yeah. And I believed it. I also thought if I got married, no one would ever suspect I was gay."

"Except you."

"Except me." He sighed. "Because back then, becoming a pilot and eventually becoming an admiral seemed like they were worth giving up anything. Including having sex or falling in love with people I was actually wired to have those feelings for."

I shifted a little. "So wait, are you gay or bi?"

"Gay. One hundred percent gay." He rubbed his eyes, then sighed as he dropped his hand to his side. "But if I'm trying to stay married and preserve my career, I can fake it like you wouldn't believe." He grimaced. "At the expense of both my ex-wives. I doubt they'll ever completely forgive me for it, and I don't blame them one bit." He turned to me. "That was a long time ago. I promise I'm not the asshole I was back then."

I smiled and ran my fingers through his damp hair. "I know. I wouldn't be here if you were."

His lips pulled into a faint smile as he lifted his head to kiss me softly. Lying back again, probably hoping I didn't notice that slight wince, he rubbed his neck and continued.

"My second marriage was a disaster from the get-go. Tina and I, we got married... I don't know, a year or so after my first marriage ended. To this day, I couldn't tell you why."

"What do you mean?"

"We didn't get along at all. About the only thing we did right was fuck, and even that..." He shrugged tightly. "Like I said, I'm gay. There's only so much I can fake, you know?"

I nodded. "What about your first marriage?"

"The first..." He released a long breath. "If I take one regret to my grave, it'll be my first marriage."

"You didn't get along with her either?"

"Quite the opposite," he said, almost whispering. "Mary Ann and I were close friends for a long time. Since middle school. She kind of hinted about wanting to date, and we did go to things like prom and homecoming together, but I never wanted to take it further than that. Which I think she kind of liked too—I didn't push her for sex like all the guys who did date her. So she kept gravitating back to me."

"Even though you weren't into her?"

He nodded. "Like I said, I didn't push her. And I was still figuring out who I was. I had some, you know, thoughts about guys, but didn't think much of it." He swallowed. "Then I went to the Academy, and a few months into it, I fooled around with another cadet and started realizing I was definitely gay. But I was terrified of anyone finding out. I'd worked my ass off to get into the Academy, and to graduate almost at the top of my class. If I came out, or if someone outed me, I'd lose all of that. For a while, I flew below the radar as much as I could. But then I almost got caught one night, and decided I was playing with fire, so it was better to get married and kill all the rumors. So... Mary Ann and I started dating, and then we got married."

"Did she know about you? That you're gay?"

"No." He said it so softly, I almost didn't hear him. "She had no idea. Close as we were, I was afraid to tell her or anybody else I was gay. In fact, she'd had a crush on me for a long time. People thought we were high school sweethearts, and no one was surprised when we got married, because they all knew we'd end up together. And I mean, I loved her. God, I loved that woman. But I wasn't in love with her. She was my closest, most trusted friend, and I always felt safe with her."

"But not safe enough to come out?"

Scowling, he shook his head. "By the time I realized what I really was, we had started dating, and I didn't want to hurt her. Plus I stupidly figured I could make myself straight and be happily married to her. I mean, we were friends, so..." He went quiet for a minute, then went on. "She deserved so much better. I did the best I could, and tried to be a good husband, but I wasn't what she needed any more than she was what I needed. Maybe if we'd been in one place, and I'd had a normal job without all the stress of deployments and combat, we could've at least brought it down gently and moved on as friends. But..."

"But that stress takes its toll," I said quietly. "That's what happened to my parents too."

"Damn, that's rough."

"It is. And that was even without things like DADT."

Paul winced. "Yeah. Nobody needed that shit." He paused. "You know what's really shitty? When we divorced, I thought the worst part was that I wouldn't be able to hide being gay anymore. Which... I mean, that's exactly why I can't blame her for leaving—I was more concerned about me and about my career than I was with her. It was all about my image, my career, my future. She was a trophy wife and a beard." He closed his eyes again and exhaled. "I hurt her *so* badly, and it took way, *way* too long for me to realize the worst thing about the divorce was losing my best friend."

"So it didn't end well?"

Eyes open but unfocused, Paul nodded. "It was pretty nasty. We saw each other at our high school reunion a few years ago, and managed to be cordial, but..." He sighed. "That's probably as good as it'll ever be again."

"Wow. Sorry to hear it."

"Me too." He scrubbed a hand over his face. "At least she found somebody better. She got married around the time my second wife and I were divorcing, and last I heard, they're perfectly happy together."

"That's good."

"Yep. I wish them both the best too." He rubbed his neck and stared up at the ceiling. "They definitely deserve it."

Neither of us said anything for a long time. Finally, I cautiously broke the silence. "So are you out now? As gay?"

Paul nodded again, still looking up. "When DADT was repealed, I stayed closeted at first for political reasons. But then when I realized the younger guys were scared to come out because they expected repercussions from the upper chain of command, I decided I owed it to them to set the example. So, I brought my boyfriend to the Navy Ball and the Christmas party, and that was that. I was out."

"That's pretty admirable. Especially if there were political reasons."

He laughed quietly. "Well, I'm pretty sure it kept me a commander for an extra year or two, but there wasn't as much backlash as I expected."

"Wow." I whistled. "Hard to imagine having to come out as an adult."

He arched an eyebrow. "When *did* you come out?"

"To my friends, when I was thirteen. Parents, fifteen. It seems kind of stupid now, but I was afraid my parents would kick me out or something."

"Stupid?" He shook his head. "Seems like a reasonable thing to be afraid of, given what's happened to a lot of people."

"Yeah, but I knew my parents better than that. When I told them, my dad didn't even blink." I laughed, rolling my eyes at the memory. "He said he'd known since I was like six, and I said, 'Well why didn't you tell *me*?'"

Paul chuckled. "Wow."

"Yeah. He said he didn't tell me because he knows I hate spoilers."

Paul blinked. "He... seriously?"

"Yeah. Guess he knows me."

"Still. Wow. I can't even imagine being able to come out like that."

"Your family doesn't know you're gay?"

"Oh, they do now. It's taken a good ten years for my dad to come to grips with it, and my mom still asks me from time to time if I'm *sure* it's not just because of my divorces, but I've brought a couple of boyfriends home." He met my gaze. "At the risk of sounding like an old man, we're from two different generations. I envy yours because there's so much more support and openness now. When I was a teenager, my God—the AIDS crisis was in full swing, and we had those preachers screaming on TV that it was divine punishment, and... believe me when I say things were very, very different."

"Back in the olden—"

"Watch it." He laughed as he lifted his head to kiss me. "Respect your elders. Or something."

"I'll get right on that."

We laughed, but then sobered a bit. We both turned onto our sides, facing each other, and I rested my hand on his waist. "Okay, I'm curious about something."

Paul held my gaze. "Shoot."

"If you knew you couldn't be out, why did you join the Navy?"

He pulled in a long breath. "Well, I was still kind of in denial at that point, but I also had some goals that could only happen through the Navy."

"Which were...?"

"I wanted to fly, and I wanted to be an admiral."

"Oh. Would you still be flying now if... that landing...?"

"No, no. Pilots usually have to hang up their wings when they start getting into the higher ranks. You can't be a pilot and a CO." He released a long breath. "My RIO didn't stay in after the accident. He couldn't deal with being grounded even after we'd both lost some friends and had enough close calls to be well aware of our own mortality. I made peace with it, though. I mean, I *did* get to fly. It's what I wanted. So I hung it up and focused on making admiral."

I lifted myself up on my elbow. "So, when you do, what then?"

"What do you mean?"

"I mean, once you make admiral, are you going to retire?"

Paul shrugged. "Well, I mean, I actually have to serve as an admiral for a few years. And then it's a matter of whether I want to try for that second star, or retire with one."

"What are you going to do after that?"

"What do you mean?"

"Like when you retire?"

His eyes lost focus again, and he released a long breath. "I don't even know yet. The Navy has been my whole life for so long, it's hard to imagine what I'll do after. Maybe work as a DOD contractor or something? I have no idea."

"I guess it isn't like you need to make a decision next week. You've got a few years to go."

"Yeah. And my retirement pay will be enough that I won't *need* to get a job, but I sure as shit better find something to do so I don't keel over from boredom."

I laughed. "You don't really seem like the type who could sit on the couch and watch TV all day."

"Not for long, no." He paused and sobered a little. "You want to know what I want more than anything after I retire?"

"Hmm?"

"A dog."

"Really?"

He nodded. "I haven't had one since my ex-wife took ours with her, and can't really justify it because I could still get deployed. But God, I miss having pets. I especially miss having a dog."

"A lot of people have them, don't they? I mean, I see them in base housing all the time."

"They do, but it's not fair to the animals, you know? Moving around is stressful enough, but the deployments... a dog can adapt to a new house, even if there's a road trip or a plane ride involved. When you disappear on them for six months or a year, though?" He shook his head. "I can't do that to a dog."

"No kidding. They don't understand." I paused. "I'm not sure who has it worse, to be honest—the dog who doesn't know what's going on, or the kid who does."

He looked in my eyes. "It must be brutal."

"It sucks." I paused. "Do you think you'll get deployed again?"

He swallowed. "It's a possibility. It's not likely at the moment, but I've been trying to get a ship for a while now. I need to command a boat if I want to get promoted. If that happens, it'll mean deployments."

Nodding, I ran my hand down his arm, over the Super Hornet tattoo. "If it does happen, then... I mean, I guess we'll deal with it when it comes."

He took my hand and kissed my palm. "That's about all we can do. Dating's a risk, and when the military's involved, well..."

"No kidding." I exhaled. "It's so stupid to take a chance like this."

Without a word, Paul drew me back in and kissed me again.

And at least for tonight, the risk didn't matter.

Except it did matter. It always mattered. There was so much on the line if anyone found out!

But... every time I was with him, it was harder and harder to talk myself into leaving and out of meeting up again.

But... this.

Sighing, I closed my eyes and let myself get lost in his kiss. I was pretty sure I wasn't going to put on the brakes. I should've been, though. Even if a relationship with Paul hadn't been forbidden because of his rank and my father's, he was still in—and I still depended on—the military. We lived in a world where everything on a calendar or in an address book was written in pencil because things could change on a dime. Falling in love with someone was a gamble in the same way playing with a piece of unexploded ordnance was dangerous—odds were, it was going to blow up in your face.

Wait.

My heart stopped.
Who said anything about falling in love?
I drew back and met his gaze.
Paul smiled. My heart started beating again.
Oh.
Oh crap.

The motel where we'd hidden out was close to a deserted stretch of shoreline. Since we were miles out of Anchor Point, seemingly a world away from NAS Adams and all its regs, we wandered out onto the beach.

I wasn't sure why we were doing this to ourselves. Meeting up for sex was stupid. Communicating at all was stupid. Pretending there was any reason for us to be strolling along the shell-littered sand like a couple of guys on a date... really, really stupid.

But there we were.

We didn't talk much. Paul might've been alone with his thoughts. Maybe wondering what the hell he was doing, or calculating how much more sex we could squeeze out of tonight before we parted ways for good this time. Just like we were supposed to have done the last time.

Me, I was afraid to open my mouth. Every time I took a breath to speak, I hesitated. Whenever I even thought about saying anything, I had this split second of panic like I was going to blurt out something completely different and not realize what I'd said until it was too late. Especially since the words were there at the tip of my tongue. I knew exactly what wanted to come out, and I was scared shitless I'd say it without thinking about it.

I really want to tell you I love you, but I'm afraid that'll be the moment you realize I'm too young and too dumb.

My cheeks burned with preemptive embarrassment.

And what's the point anyway?

Preemptive embarrassment turned into that all too familiar disappointment.

No matter what I feel, it isn't like I can have you.

So I kept my mouth shut. I enjoyed the rare chance to be with him, and took in the scenery because that kept me from staring at him.

And it really was pretty out here. The sky was completely clear. This wasn't one of those nasty, garbage-covered beaches like I'd seen in other places—here was nothing but sand, driftwood, rocks, and seashells. A hundred yards or so inland, some cabins were tucked into the evergreens that covered the rolling hills. Closer to the water, the odd boat was tied to a barnacle-covered post.

Some crows argued with a seagull over a half-eaten crab, but otherwise, we were completely alone.

After a while, Paul laughed softly.

I looked at him. "What?"

"Nothing." He shook his head. "I guess I was thinking about everything. With us."

"Such as...?"

"How crazy it is. Everything is so... different with you."

Like the part where you shouldn't be *with me?* "In a good way, I hope?"

"Yes." He smiled. "Very. It's crazy, but it's very good."

"It *is* kind of crazy, isn't it?" I said. "It's hard to believe it hasn't been that long since some depressed guy got into my car and bought me a bottle of water."

Paul gazed out at the sand. "Feels like ages ago."

"It does. I guess I kind of understand now what it means

when people say it feels like you've known someone your whole life." My heart pounded. I'd stupidly rambled a little too much and gone a little too far, and now he was probably going to—

"Me too."

"Really?" I asked.

Paul nodded. "I mean, when I think about how people might react if they knew about this, you know the first thing they're going to ask is how the hell we get around the age gap."

Scowling, I looked out at the sand in front of us. "No kidding."

"And the thing is, if they do ask, I don't have an answer."

I shifted my gaze back to Paul and arched an eyebrow. "You don't?"

"No. I guess..." He kept his eyes down for a few steps, then shrugged as he glanced at me. "Answering assumes I've given it any thought. And I haven't. Because with you... there's nothing to think about. I can't tell you why it works because it just *does*."

"I know what you mean." I slid my hands into my pockets. "I guess it's kind of like the way I drive sometimes."

"What do you mean?"

It was getting harder and harder to keep those words tamped down where they belonged, so I was extra careful and deliberate about everything I did say. "No map. No real destination. No idea what's up ahead. I get in the car and..." *Go way too fast in a direction I really, really shouldn't be going.* I shrugged. "Just drive." The words echoed in my mind, and I laughed, shaking my head. Looking out at the water, I muttered, "I didn't realize how crazy that sounded until I said it."

But it's better than what could have come out, so I guess it's okay.

"It doesn't sound stupid."

I turned to him. "It doesn't?"

"No." Paul didn't look at me. "Everything in my life has always been according to a plan. Even when the Navy throws me a curveball and sends me on a deployment or transfers me to some place I've never heard of—"

"Like Anchor Point?"

"Mm-hmm. Even then, it's all been part of the big grand plan to get me up the ranks so I can make admiral before I retire. Be in command of a base now, take command of a ship next, make sure to kiss all the right asses—everything's always been..." He blew out a breath. "Calculated. So maybe this is exactly what I need."

"Something that's improvised?"

Paul nodded. "Yeah. So there's no plan and no pressure."

"Sounds like something we both needed."

A smile spread across his lips, and if we hadn't been out in public, I'd have lifted myself up for a quick kiss.

But that sinking feeling came back. We could talk like this, pretend we really had something between us and that this wasn't going to end with, *We can't see each other again.* All we were doing was making it worse. Every time we gave in and met up, walking away would be infinitely harder. A relationship—sexual, romantic, whatever—wasn't going to get any less off-limits.

If I was smart, I never would have broken down and made contact this time.

If I was smart, I never would have come out here in public with him.

If I was smart, I would turn around right now, walk back down the beach, get in my car, and leave.

But I had, and I was here, and I wasn't leaving, because I was a fucking idiot.

Paul broke eye contact. His features tightened, and I wondered if he was thinking the same thing. Instead of hoping he'd be the voice of reason, I caught myself regretting not taking that opportunity for a kiss. So we were out in public? We were on a beach. There was no one out here. We were miles from Anchor Point, miles from NAS Adams, and if anyone saw us, they wouldn't have any reason to give a damn except that we were two men. No one around here had any idea about all the *other* reasons to get pissed off about us being together.

I held my breath and slipped my hand into his. Paul didn't pull away. He separated his fingers, letting mine slide between them, and clasped them together between us.

Some tension melted out of my shoulders. This was amazing. I would have sold my fucking soul for us to be like this all the time—out in the open, not hiding anything. Not looking over our shoulders in case of homophobes or people from the base. But right now, we had this, and I loved it.

Then our eyes met.

My heart went crazy, especially as he took off his aviators and let me see his vivid blue eyes.

"I know we shouldn't be here," he said softly. "But I'm really glad we are."

My throat ached with way too many emotions. "Me too."

We were both silent. Standing there. Touching. Looking at each other.

I'm going to put my foot in my mouth if you don't say something, so for God's sake, say something.

He cupped my face, and his expression turned my knees to liquid. Every time he smiled at me like that, I should have remembered that I was the last person he had any business with, but instead, he made me feel like the only person in the world. This time was no exception.

He took a breath like he was about to speak, but then hesitated and released it. He looked out at the water. For some reason, I was suddenly afraid he was going to take his hand off my face, so I put mine over it and held it there.

Paul faced me again. There was definitely something on the tip of his tongue. The creases between his eyebrows and the subtle tightness in his lips were unmistakable. My hand was still over his, and he intently watched his thumb tracing the side of mine.

I swallowed. "Something on your mind?"

He jumped a little. "I, um…" He took in another breath and locked eyes with me. My heart sped up. What *was* on his mind?

Tell me we need to walk away.

Please, say it.

Because I can't. And we can't do this.

Say it…

"Paul?"

My tongue stuck to the roof of my mouth.

"I don't care how old you are. I don't care who your father is." He smoothed my hair. "I…" He paused, and when he inhaled, he pushed his shoulders back. Stepping a little closer, he drew me in, and just before our lips met, he whispered, "I love you, Sean."

Then he kissed me.

And everything was… still.

And perfect.

And how the hell was this real?

CHAPTER 20

PAUL

THE WORDS WERE OUT THERE. No going back.

I'd kissed him, partly because I wanted to and partly to keep either of us from speaking right away. I was sure he'd tell me to slow the fuck down and back off.

But Sean wrapped his arms around me, and I didn't think his kiss had ever been so tender and needy at the same time.

After God knew how long, he broke the kiss and touched his forehead to mine. "I love you too."

Relief rushed through me. I laughed a little, even though that seemed insane, but he did too, and then one of us moved back in and we were kissing again. His hand was firmly on the back of my neck, his other arm around my waist, and I loved feeling like he didn't want me to pull away from him. I'd tipped my hand further than I'd meant to, and he was still holding on tight.

He'd overwhelmed me from day one. First with the mind-blowing sex, and now with this. I'd actually fallen for someone who felt the same? Holy shit. Holy shit!

I held him tighter, and he leaned into me. My stomach fluttered. This was amazing. This was *real*.

It took me four and a half goddamned decades to find you, and you'd better believe you were worth the wait.

The kiss came to a gentle, perfect end, and Sean looked in my eyes. "Are we insane, thinking something like this could work?"

I brushed a few strands of blue-black hair out of his face. "Maybe?"

He grinned cautiously. "Is an ex-fighter pilot really the one I should be asking about insane things?"

I laughed again, pulling him closer. "Probably not." I pressed another soft kiss to his lips. "And yeah, maybe we are insane, but I really like this. Everything about what we're doing."

"Especially the part where we're breaking rules?"

"Well, that part does have a certain appeal." We both chuckled, but as I held his gaze, I sobered. So did he. The wind whipped at his hair, and I smoothed it out of his face again. "Circumstances are what they are. Maybe this is insane and reckless. In fact, we both *know* it is. But every time we've tried to pull apart, I keep gravitating back toward you. So, even if it's crazy, I don't want to fight it."

"Neither do I," he whispered. "I keep worrying it'll blow up in our faces, though."

"It still could. But I haven't gotten very far talking myself out of it."

He chuckled and drew me into another kiss.

Back in the motel room, with our clothes on the floor where they belonged, we sank down to the mattress together.

And slowed... right... down.

I lost all track of time. At some point, we'd walked along the beach to get back here, but that felt like hours ago. Days ago. There was no way we'd only been holding each other and kissing for a few minutes. And we could have done it all night for all I cared. As long as he was in my arms even after I'd stupidly blurted out that I loved him, I didn't care what we did.

One thing I was sure of—there'd be definitely something involving orgasms. We were both too hard and frantic for this to end any other way. I just didn't care how we got there. Fucking? Blowjobs? Handjobs? Whatever. One way or another, I'd get him off tonight, and that thought alone nearly got *me* off.

I pressed against him, kissing him harder, and he did the same.

Abruptly, he jerked back, and looked right in my eyes as he panted, "Need a condom. *Now.*" The fierce hunger in his expression gave me goose bumps.

I nodded toward the nightstand. "Same place we left them."

The corners of his mouth turned up. He kissed me once more, lightly this time, and lunged for the nightstand.

With the condom and lube in hand, he sat back on his heels, and...

Paused.

Swallowing hard, he turned the square packet over and over between his fingers. Some of the hunger in his eyes faded in favor of something I couldn't quite read. Nerves? Here? In bed?

I touched his thigh. "What's wrong?"

"Nothing. But I..." He closed his hand around the

condom and met my gaze. "Maybe we don't need this tonight."

My heart sped up, and I slid my palm over his thigh. "It's up to you."

Sean thumbed the wrapper. "We've seen each other's test results. I haven't touched anyone but you since we met."

"Neither have I. I'm happy with whatever makes you comfortable."

Sean took a deep breath. Then he tossed the condom back on the nightstand, wrapped his arms around me, and kissed me again.

"I'll take that as a yes," I murmured between kisses.

"Turn around. I can't wait."

"Neither can I, but just like this. I want to be able to kiss you."

Sean exhaled and let his lips graze mine. "Love the way you think." We both sat up, and he opened the lube bottle. In between playfully kissing, we put some lube on both of us. Then I lay back, spread my legs, and tried like hell not to come unglued from watching him.

And then...

Oh God.

The slick, blunt pressure of his dick sliding into me was hot enough. The way Sean closed his eyes and let his head fall back? Whoa. He exhaled and looked down again, and his features tightened with intense concentration as he eased himself deeper. A whispered "Fuck..." slipped off his tongue. Or maybe mine. With or without a condom felt more or less the same to me, but the difference for him was written across his face. As he rocked his hips, picking up a smooth, steady rhythm, his eyes lost focus and his lips moved soundlessly.

I ran a hand up his abs and teased his nipple with my

thumbnail, grinning when he sucked in a sharp hiss of breath.

"F-fuck," he moaned.

"You've never done this before, have you?" *When did I run out of breath?*

Sean clasped my hand against his chest. He swept his tongue across his lips as his eyes flicked up to meet mine. "No. Never."

"Like it?"

He nodded slowly, eyelids drooping. "Yeah. A lot."

"Thought you would." I pulled our clasped hands. He got the message and came down to me, and now... holy shit, *now* it was perfect. I wrapped my arms around him, and didn't care if I came too soon or not at all.

Sean dipped his head and started on my neck. Oh, sweet Jesus, yes. I tilted my head so he had more access, and he took full advantage. As he kissed his way up and down the side of my throat, he rocked his hips just enough to take my breath away. He wasn't thrusting—he was barely moving at all—but it was amazing.

He kissed under my jaw and moaned again as he slowly pushed back in. "My God..." He lifted himself up and looked down at me, blinking a few times as if it was a struggle to focus his eyes. Then he dropped a soft kiss on my lips before he pulled out. "Turn over."

Well, I wasn't going to argue with that. We shifted around, and in seconds, he was inside me again. I couldn't see him or kiss him, but he felt so good right then, I didn't care.

With his body weight, he guided me down, all the way down, and I relaxed onto the mattress. He paused, adjusting his position slightly, and then he started moving again. Faster. Harder. Oh fuck. I closed my eyes, pressing my forehead onto the mattress. Being fucked was amazing enough, but the added friction of my dick rubbing against the sheet was unreal.

I clasped our fingers together and held our joined hands against my chest, keeping him as close to me as possible. Sean's stubbled chin burned against my shoulder, and he groaned as he forced himself as deep as I could take him. His thrusts knocked the breath out of me, and if I could've, I would've rocked my hips to encourage him to fuck me even harder. Maybe it was just as well—if this got any more intense, I'd probably turn to ash.

Sean touched his forehead to the back of my neck. "Oh God..." He gripped my hand tighter as he pounded me even harder. "I'm gonna come."

I moved my hips a little, and that must've been exactly what he needed, because he sucked in a breath and shuddered. The way he gasped and shook, how his rhythm fell apart like he was just too overwhelmed to maintain it, was sexy as fuck.

He buried his face against my neck and sighed as he relaxed on top of me. "Jesus."

"Feel good?"

"So good," he murmured. "If I'd known what I was missing, we'd have done this a long time ago."

I laughed. Tonight was the perfect time. He was ready for it. Any other night, he might've been edgy and uncertain, and it wouldn't have been this good.

"Still have to make you come." He kissed the side of my neck as he pulled out. "Back on your back."

Sean barely gave me a chance to turn over before he descended on my cock. Jesus. Yes. His lips were *magic*. I kneaded his scalp and closed my eyes as he took me deeper in his mouth.

He wasn't done, though—he put his weight on one arm, and my heart sped up when I realized he now had a free hand.

Oh yes.

He nudged my thigh, encouraging me to spread my legs.

Oh yes. Yes, please.

Two fingers slid into my well-lubricated hole, and before I'd finished shivering from that, he fluttered his tongue around the head of my cock.

"Fuck," I moaned. "Oh Jesus." I was afraid I'd get too enthusiastic and push his head down on my cock—fucking *hated* it when guys did that—so I moved my hands to the sheets instead.

His fingers crooked inside me, and I gripped the sheets tighter. My spine arched off the bed and the darkness behind my eyelids turned white and everything was spinning, spinning, spinning, and he didn't stop. His lips and tongue, his fingers—he just did not let up, not until I started to come back down and everything was suddenly too intense, and I pleaded, "S-stop."

Sean wiped his mouth with the back of his hand, and as soon as he was within reach, I grabbed him and kissed him. My heart was going wild, my whole body still shaky and tingly, but my lips knew what to do with his. Kissing him was as easy as breathing—didn't require any focus at all.

After a moment, I broke the kiss and met his gaze. "Don't know if I ever mentioned this," I said, struggling to enunciate, "but your mouth is amazing."

"You seemed like you were enjoying it." He grinned and added, "So you think we should stay here all night?"

"Absolutely." I kissed the tip of his nose. "I'll have to bust out of here by about seven, though."

"Work?"

"Tee time."

Sean laughed. "Of course."

"But I'll make sure to wake you up before I go." I winked. "Nothing kicks off a round of golf like some morning sex."

"If you can still play eighteen holes of golf after I've fucked you, I'm doing something wrong."

I laughed. "You're more than welcome to try."

"I will."

"Promise?"

"You bet." He grinned. "For now... shower?"

"Shower."

Under the hot shower, I wrapped my arms around Sean and kissed him. His body was warm and slick against mine, his kiss lazy and gentle. We'd soaped and rinsed, but surprise, surprise—neither of us was in any hurry to get out of the shower. Typical.

Eventually, though, every shower had to end, and we finally made our way back to the bed. There, we faced each other under the sheets.

Sean laughed softly.

"What?" I asked.

"How *are* we going to make this work?"

I shook my head. "I have no idea."

I'm still wondering if it's even possible.

"We still can't tell anyone."

"No, definitely not." My stomach tightened. Secret relationships were a recipe for disaster. Now that we'd taken a pretty significant step forward, I couldn't help wondering if the inevitable was right around the corner.

But Sean just kissed me again and smiled. "Well, don't know *how* this is going to work. All I know is I want it to. So, we'll find a way."

You have no idea how much I want that to be true.

"That's enough for me." I kissed him gently.

"I love you."

"I love you too."

We settled in to go to sleep. Sean turned on his side, and I molded myself to him. In no time, he was out cold.

Me? Not so much. I was exhausted, but I couldn't sleep. Lying there in the dark motel room, trailing my fingers up and down his arm and listening to him breathing, I was wide-awake.

Somehow, today had gone from *I need to see you* to *I love you*. It made sense, but it still blew my mind.

And for that matter, made me wonder if I was being a complete fucking idiot.

What am I doing?

I liked to believe I wasn't stupid, but I wouldn't deny I could be fucking reckless. Being reckless with a billion dollar aircraft was one thing. With a twenty-plus-year career? Two twenty-plus-year careers? Not to mention Sean's emotions?

This had gone beyond reckless. There was no more pretending this was something to do until the Navy inevitably torpedoed it. No, we'd gone and gotten ourselves a lot deeper than we should've.

But... *how* had we gotten in this deep? We shouldn't have had this kind of connection. He was too young. I was too old. There were too many professional reasons I didn't have any business being close to him, let alone this close to him.

I couldn't have stopped it if I'd wanted to, though. It

didn't matter how or why he'd gotten under my skin—he had. Whatever this was, it was nothing like any of my previous relationships.

Well, of course this was nothing like my previous relationships. Those had all been based on things that should've had no place between two people. Marriages to keep the gay rumors down. Boyfriends who looked at my rank and saw dollar signs, or who were willing to be paraded around as a political statement until that novelty wore off. If all of my relationships had one thing in common, it was the bullshit. There was always some ulterior motive. Smokescreens. Statements.

There was none of that with Sean, though. If this came out, my career was fucked and so was his relationship with his father.

And we'd already let things get too deep. The longer we let it go on, the deeper it would get, and there'd just be more and more opportunities for someone to find out.

But lying here with Sean against me, my head still light from the day we'd had and the sex we'd had, I couldn't justify walking away. I wanted to see where this could go. Consequences be damned, I wanted to know what it was like to be in love with someone for no other reason than, well, being in love with him.

This connection—it was terrifying, and amazing, and addictive, and if I had a brain left in my head, I'd walk away. But I knew damn well I wouldn't.

Jesus. No wonder we both kept forgetting about our age gap—he was wise beyond his years, and I was the idiot who wouldn't man up and be the voice of reason. It should've been me saying, *Look, there's too much on the line*, or, *As much as I'd love to do this...* But whatever angel of maturity sat on my left shoulder was muffled by the devil on my right who kept reminding me how much I'd been missing someone like Sean in my life.

I held Sean a little tighter and kissed the side of his neck. He murmured in his sleep and pressed back against me, but didn't wake up.

I didn't know how in the world we'd make this work.

I just knew we had to.

CHAPTER 21

SEAN

ALL THE WAY home from the motel the next morning, I felt like shit.

I should have been grinning like crazy, giddy over knowing Paul loved me. Not to mention spacing out as my mind replayed all that incredible sex we'd had last night and this morning.

But no, I felt like shit.

We were leading each other on, and I knew it. He had to know it too. It didn't matter if we were in love, or if he could make me come harder than any man on the planet, or that sleeping next to him was the most perfect thing ever. He was still my dad's commanding officer, and this was still something that couldn't happen. Or... well... *keep* happening.

I shook myself, gripping the wheel as I followed the familiar roads on autopilot.

Now what?

Now we...

Fuck, I didn't know. I knew what we should do, but what we were going to do? Anyone's guess, since apparently "the thing we're supposed to do" wasn't always the thing we did.

I pulled up in front of the house to my usual parking spot, and my throat tightened. Dad was still home. Shit.

He wouldn't question me for being out all night. It wasn't the first time and wouldn't be the last. But my guilty conscience was wide-awake and nagging at me now, reminding me with every little twinge that I'd been in bed with Dad's CO last night.

You knew better. What the fuck were you thinking?

Dad had no way of knowing, but that sure didn't stop me from worrying that he'd suddenly catch on. It took all the concentration I had to nonchalantly pour myself a bowl of cereal and eat it while acting like nothing had happened last night that would cause anyone any problems if someone found out. Christ, I hadn't even been this nervous the first time my dad had picked me up from base security when I was twelve. Or the third time, when they'd been threatening me and a friend with felony charges for smoking weed in base housing.

I managed to play it cool, though, and finally, I was finished with my breakfast. After I'd rinsed my bowl, I headed for the stairs. I was home free. Thank—

"Hey, Sean?"

I stopped.

Be cool. Play it cool.

I turned around. "Yeah?"

Dad tilted his head slightly and motioned for me to come back into the kitchen. "Can I talk to you for a second?"

I joined him, and gulped. "Sure. What about?"

He pressed his hip against the counter and folded his

arms loosely across his chest. "You've been seeing someone, haven't you?"

Funny you should ask.

"Uh, yeah." I fought the urge to fidget nervously and give myself away. "Why?"

He studied me, letting the silence linger to the point of excruciatingly uncomfortable before he finally spoke. "Listen, your personal life is your business. I'm not asking you to bring him over so I can meet him until you're ready for that."

I shuddered at the thought, and instantly regretted it when Dad's forehead creased.

"I'm serious," he said. "But you've been acting weird, and I'm worried." He chewed his lip. "The guy you're with —is he treating you all right? I mean, is there something you need to talk about?"

I dropped my gaze. That was probably incriminating as hell too, but I couldn't look him in the eye. And my conscience didn't need anything else to bitch at me about, but now I got to add "Dad's worried sick and thinks your guy is abusing you" to that hot mess.

He pushed himself off the counter and stepped a little closer. "Sean, you're an adult, but I'm still your dad, and I know when something is wrong. Talk to me. What's going on?"

I forced back the emotions trying to rise in my throat. Being reckless with careers was bad enough. Making my dad feel like this? Fuck. "I'm not with anyone who's hurting me, okay?"

"Then what's wrong? Because you haven't been yourself."

"Nothing's... nothing is..." God, I sounded pathetic. "It's just a little... I mean, things are kind of..."

"Sean." He put a heavy hand on my shoulder. "Look at me."

It took some effort, but I did, and the palpable worry in his eyes cut me right to the core.

"Talk to me," he said. "Please. You're scaring me."

Jesus. This was a man who'd seen boots-on-the-ground combat. He'd listened to mortars falling without knowing where they'd land and which of his people—himself included—might die. He knew what fear really was—he still had the nightmares and flashbacks to prove it had never fully gone away—and now he was scared for me. Because I'd been acting weird, because I was involved with someone I never should have touched.

Before I could stop myself, I blurted out, "He's your CO."

Dad froze. "Come again?"

I slouched against the counter and exhaled. "He's... I'm seeing your CO. Sort of."

"'Sort of'?" He took his hand off my shoulder. "What the hell does that mean?"

"I mean, we..." Oh, there was no explanation of our relationship that wouldn't take all day, and Dad definitely wouldn't have the patience or time. So I just sighed and shook my head. "I'm seeing him. I'm seeing your CO."

He stared at me for a long moment. Jaw slack, eyes wide, he watched me as if he were waiting for the punch line. When I didn't deliver it, he threw up his hands. "For fuck's sake! Are you kidding me? Do you have any idea what could happen if something like this comes out?"

Resentment simmered under my skin. Yeah, I knew. Yeah, I'd done it anyway. And yeah, I was kind of fucking tired of reining in my personal life because of the Navy. "Dad, I—"

"What happens if I make master chief this year, huh? Captain Richards *signs my fit reps*. You don't think anyone might wonder when a guy makes rank while his kid is dating the CO? You don't think that'll look like a favor handed down for—"

"I get it."

"Do you?" He exhaled hard. "I have never interfered with your love life. Never. You're a grown man, and who you date is none of my business. But this time—" He shook his head. "For God's sake, what are you thinking?"

That Paul pushes all my buttons and checks all my boxes in ways no other man ever has?

"Look, I'm—"

"It doesn't even matter, honestly," Dad said through his teeth. "This is the kind of thing that could cost him his career and screw me out of making master chief. Stay away from him, Sean." He paused, tightening his jaw. "Does he know who you are?"

I narrowed my eyes. "You mean, does he know who *you* are?"

He glared at me. "You can split hairs all you want. The fact is, he's my commanding officer."

"I know. I know and—"

"Jesus Christ, Sean." He pinched the bridge of his nose, then dropped his arms to his sides again. "There aren't enough guys in this town? You have to find one who's on the goddamned base, and in my chain of command? At the *top* of my chain of command?"

"So now I can't date military guys?"

Dad scowled. "If you do, you can't exactly be surprised when it causes problems."

"Oh, I'm not surprised." I glared at him. "Well, at least when I do date military, I'm already used to the bullshit. I know what can come my way. If he goes off on a combat deployment, I've got *plenty* of practice with losing sleep and avoiding the news." Those memories sent a queasy chill through me, but I refused to let it show. "The only difference is I won't be a kid wondering if his dad's going to come home alive—I'll be a grown-ass man wondering if his boyfriend will."

Dad drew back a little. "I'm..." His Adam's apple jumped.

"I'm sorry." I lowered my gaze. Jesus. That was so out of line. What was wrong with me? I was pissed at the Navy, not at him. He didn't deserve me lashing out, never mind throwing *that* in his face. "Sorry. I didn't mean... It's..."

"I know," he said quietly. "And it's not that I would ever oppose you dating someone who's military, but he's my CO. And it's not only my career. It's his too. What do you think will happen if anyone finds out he's dating my son?"

I looked at him again. "How would they find out?"

He said nothing.

Fresh anger tightened my chest. "Are you threatening to have him strung up for this?"

Dad's eyes narrowed. "What would you like me to do?"

I tongued my back teeth, letting that center me and pull my concentration away from how close I was to snapping at him or breaking something. Didn't help me come up with a solid answer, though. There wasn't one. We both knew there wasn't one. Pissed off as I was, I couldn't pretend Dad was wrong. Or that I was surprised this had finally blown up in my face.

"Sean..." He exhaled hard. "Look, you need to really think about this. It isn't just about what I would do or what I would put first. If your relationship with him does come out, do you really think Captain Richards is going to give up a career like his over something that's a few weeks old? You're half his age. He's an Academy grad. He wants to make admiral. That's not a man who takes his career lightly. Mark my words, Sean—the first sign of trouble, he's going to let you go before he risks tarnishing his career."

My stomach dropped into my feet. I hadn't thought about that, and now that it was out there, I... couldn't argue.

"I'm sorry," he said.

"I'm sure," I snapped.

Dad sighed. "For God's sake. You know I'm not doing this for kicks. You're my son. Of course I care about *you*."

"More than you care about your fucking career?" As soon as the words were out, I regretted them. Tonguing my teeth some more, I rubbed a hand over my face and laughed bitterly, because it was either that or break down crying. "I guess I should've known the Navy would eventually end this too. God knows it fucks everything else up in my life."

Dad's shoulders sank. "I'm—"

"Don't." I put up my hands. "Please. Don't say you're sorry again."

He held my gaze but didn't speak.

I swallowed and pushed myself away from the counter. "I need to go out for a bit."

"Are you going to see—"

"I just need to think."

He called after me, but I didn't catch what he said because I was already hurrying for the door. Without stopping or looking back, I went to my car, got in, and got the fuck out of there.

At least Dad didn't try to stop me. He was probably rolling his eyes, shaking his head, and telling Julie I'd be back once I cooled down. Which was true. As I drove out of the neighborhood, gripping the wheel like my life depended on it, even I knew damn well I'd be back to finish this once I'd blown off some steam. Apparently that was something I'd inherited from my mom, and it kept things from getting entirely out of hand when Dad and I butted heads.

As I drove, I couldn't calm down. I couldn't relax. I didn't even know where I wanted to go or which highway would be the best place to focus on some bends and curves. The road noise didn't do a damned thing. What the hell?

Shit.

Of course it didn't help. How the fuck was I supposed to drive around and blow off steam when I was literally driving around *inside the place Paul and I had met*? I'd been sitting right here when he'd gotten in the first time and told me to just drive. This was where he'd kissed me the first time. In the rearview, I could see the backseat where he'd gone down on me the first time. Hell, the first time I'd fucked him had been right over the back of this car.

I made the mistake of glancing in the rearview, and swore I could see the phantom reflection of Paul bent over the trunk while I'd railed him from behind.

And now he was the reason Dad and I were fighting, and the reason I was achy and exhausted and felt like the world's biggest jackass, and...

My heart sank. My hands loosened a little on the wheel.

The confrontation had left me jittery. My heart raced and my knees shook, like that panicked feeling after a near miss on the road. Dad and I never fought. Okay, we'd argued plenty of times when I was a teenager, but most of the time, it was smooth sailing. Even when I did fuck up, he was chill and reasonable.

Right up until I slept with his CO.

I cursed into the silence. I wanted to hate my father for interfering, but what could I do? He was right, and I knew he was right, but I also resented the hell out of the Navy for constantly throwing monkey wrenches into my life. Everything in my world came back to the Navy. To my dad's career. Couldn't behave certain ways online because it might reflect on him. Getting caught smoking weed when I was sixteen was enough to get me grounded, but getting caught in base housing by base security had created a shitstorm that may or may not have affected my dad's promotion that year. All I knew was he hadn't made rank, and he hadn't talked to me for three days after the results came out.

And now, like everything else, my sex life suddenly fell under Navy jurisdiction, and my choice of partners didn't fly because of my dad's fucking career. Especially now that he was in the senior enlisted ranks, he couldn't afford for me to be involved with his CO. And Paul definitely couldn't afford for people to find out he was involved with a subordinate's kid. The next rank for him was admiral, and making admiral was a one-in-a-hundred shot that almost *literally* required an act of Congress. Political games might be bullshit to me, but they were mission critical for Dad and Paul, and whatever Paul and I were doing... well, it wasn't going to help either of them.

No matter how much I let myself fall for him, the truth was still there—if someone found out about us, Paul wasn't going to choose his twentysomething boyfriend over his career. I couldn't ask him to, and even if I did, there was no way he would.

Which meant there was only one thing I could do.

CHAPTER 22

PAUL

IF THERE WAS one thing I did *not* sign up for when I decided to join the Navy, it was the goddamned meetings. I'd wanted to fly, and the polar opposite of flying was sitting in a chair and trying to stay awake while other people—sometimes above my rank, sometimes below it—rambled on about shit that could've been condensed into an email. Screw ergonomic chairs, I wanted one fitted with an ejection system.

But some Congressional committee had a bug up its ass about closing down one base and moving its squadron to NAS Adams, so meetings had to happen to make sure we were all briefed and prepared for next week's meeting with the commodore and a couple of apparently bored senators. That was probably my least favorite part about being a commanding officer. I'd known that once I reached this level, there'd be politics and ass-kissing, but I hadn't anticipated how much I'd hate it. Good thing I liked the rest of my job. Maybe when I was an admiral, they could all kiss *my* ass.

For now, though, I had to make nice with them because

they could make or break my chance at a promotion. Assuming I *had* a chance, which I wouldn't until the Navy gave me a goddamned ship, but maybe firmly lodging my nose between a senator's ass cheeks would help speed *that* process along. The right phone call from the right senator to the right person on high could do the trick, after all, and at this point I wasn't above anything that might put me at the helm of an aircraft carrier.

Finally, the meeting was over. After shaking hands with everyone, I headed out of the conference room. As I started down the hall toward my office, I reached into my pocket for my phone, but before I could check the screen, a voice stopped me.

"Sir, could I speak to you for a minute?"

I turned to see Senior Chief Wright standing by my office, cover tucked under his arm. Something tightened in my gut, and I pocketed my phone. "I've got some time. What can I do for you, Senior Chief?"

He set his jaw and shifted his weight. "Is there any chance we could do this in private?"

"Uh, yeah. Sure." I motioned for him to follow me. "This way."

We stepped into my office, and Wright closed the door behind us.

I took a seat at my desk, gesturing at the two chairs in front of it. "Sit down, Senior Chief."

"Actually..." He cleared his throat and put his hands behind his back, stiffening slightly and almost assuming a parade rest stance. "I'd rather not, sir."

"I see." I folded my hands on the desk. "So what can I do for you?"

"It's about my son."

My blood turned to ice.

Oh shit. He knows.

"All right." I inclined my head, hoping he took it as the casual *go on* of someone without a reason to be guilty.

He stood even straighter. "My son's name is Sean Wright."

I gulped. "Sean Wright?"

Wright narrowed his eyes. "You're familiar with him, then?"

"Uh..." *How the fuck had he found out?*

"Black hair? Cab driver? Hasn't even been alive as long as you've been in the Navy?"

I gritted my teeth. Normally, I didn't tolerate subordinates talking to me like this, but normally I wasn't involved with their adult children. I was lucky he was being this calm.

"When we met," I said, "I wasn't aware he was your son. I didn't know until recently."

"But you know now."

"Yes."

"And before that, you must've been aware he's half your age, *sir*," he spat.

"He's an adult."

"Barely!" Wright blew out a breath. "With all due respect—"

"No." I shook my head. "Let's drop the professional pretenses and discuss this man-to-man."

"No, sir, I disagree," he said coldly. "I think you need to remember who you are, who I am, and who it is you're fucking."

I flinched, and so did he, as if he hadn't intended to verbally acknowledge exactly what was happening between Sean and me.

I folded my hands on the desk and started to speak, but Wright beat me to it.

"With all due respect, sir, I couldn't care less about my son being involved with a man. Even a much *older* man." His lip curled with a hint of disgust. "But I draw the line here. Sir, you and I both know there's a lot at stake if this gets out."

Pursing my lips, I nodded. "I know. And I'll speak to him."

"And this won't... it won't continue?" There was a hint of menace in his voice. A thinly veiled threat. An unspoken... *or should I stop at the JAG office on my way out?*

"It won't, Senior Chief."

Wright slowly released a breath. "Thank you, sir."

I gave a slight nod.

He shifted, glancing toward the door. "I, uh, should get back to..."

"Right. Yeah. Uh, dismissed." Did I even need to dismiss him? He'd been confronting me. And rightfully so. What was the protocol? Well, whatever. I'd dismissed him.

Wright hesitated as if he had something else to add—maybe one last warning to stay the hell away from his son, or maybe he was also confused about the protocol for ending this kind of conversation. Then he adjusted his cover, which was still tucked under his arm. With a curt nod, he said, "Sir."

I returned the nod. "Senior Chief."

Thank God, he turned to go, and he didn't stop.

After he'd closed the door, I leaned forward in my chair and rubbed my temples. Well, shit. How exactly Senior Chief Wright had figured things out, I didn't know, but it didn't matter. I'd known I was playing with fire, and I'd gone back for more. Now it was time for some damage control before one of us got burned.

And whether I liked it or not, damage control meant ending things with Sean for good this time.

Sighing, I pulled out my phone. When I turned it on, there was already a text waiting for me.

We need to talk ASAP.

CHAPTER 23

SEAN

WE AGREED to meet in a motel room.

That was dangerous, but necessary. We couldn't do this out in public, and I didn't feel right doing it over the phone. Tempting or not, I owed it to him to face him, in person, and do what we should have done ages ago.

When he let himself into the room where I was waiting, the sight of him had never hurt so fucking bad. A mix of pain and rage churned in my gut.

Why did I let myself fall for you?

Why would you tell me you love me when you knew damn well this would never work?

Why the fuck can't I find a way to make *this work?*

He shifted his weight. "So your dad knows."

I winced. Apparently Dad had beaten me to the punch. "Yeah."

Paul chewed his lip. "How did he find out?"

"I told him."

"What? Are you insane?"

"No." I avoided his eyes, and hated the way my voice

shook. "But if there's one thing I can't do, it's lie to my father. He confronted me because I've been acting weird, and I—"

"It really doesn't matter." Paul's voice was gentler now. "It's out. And it..."

"Yeah." Well, shit. I'd spent the whole drive working up the nerve to get here, I hadn't bothered rehearsing what to say. "So I guess there isn't much to talk about. We have to stop doing this. For real, this time."

"I know." He sighed. "We shouldn't have let it get this far."

"No shit. Besides, even if no one had found out, we both know the Navy would've ended it for us sooner or later." The words came out with a lot more bitterness than I'd intended, and judging by the way he eyed me, Paul hadn't missed it.

"What... what does that mean?"

I blew out a breath. "You know it's only a matter of time. You and Dad are both lifers. I know what your careers mean to both of you, and I can't be why they're damaged, especially this close to the end." I swallowed hard, wondering how long I could keep this lump from rising in my throat. "I also can't stick around knowing I'll be jettisoned the second anything happens."

"What? No!" Paul stared at me like I'd smacked him across the face. "I wouldn't... Sean, that's—"

"Paul." I shook my head. "You've been working on your career longer than I've been alive. Can you really tell me honestly that you'd give that up for me?"

He opened his mouth like he was about to speak, but stopped.

"See?" I dropped my gaze. "The thing is, I'm exhausted. I'm tired of always coming in second to someone else's career. And I get it, you know? Your career's important to you, and my dad's career is important to him. I know things can reflect badly, and you can wind up in deep shit for this, and..." I waved my hand. "I get all of it. But I also get that I've been dragged all over the place by the Navy for as long as I can remember. I haven't lived within two thousand miles of my mom in ten years. I went to three high schools. Everyone I've ever known..." I paused to collect myself. "I'm sorry. I can't keep doing this."

Paul swallowed. "I can't fix this, or I would."

"I know. And I didn't say it was your fault. It is what it is." I shrugged as much as I could with my shoulders feeling so damned heavy. "I can't handle it anymore."

"There has to be a way," he said, barely whispering. "We're—"

"Don't." I shook my head. "I mean, think about it. Everything we've done has been fun, but how long is that really going to last? I mean, I'm twenty years younger than you. You've devoted your life to building this career. If the Navy put you on the spot and told you to choose between it and me, we both know what you'd pick."

Paul's eyes flicked downward, and his lips pulled tight.

I swallowed the lump in my throat. I'd known damn well I was right, but the silent confirmation stung more than I'd thought it would. So that was what people meant when they said the truth hurt. On the other hand, maybe this meant I could walk away for good this time.

"What do you want me to say?" he whispered, meeting my gaze again. "I love you. You know I do. But I—"

"There's nothing you can say. There's nothing anyone can say." I shrugged, which took way more work than it should have. "We need to accept it and move on."

"There's…" He shook his head. "There has to be some way we can—"

"There isn't. You know there isn't. And I can't."

He watched me, brow pinched and eyes wide.

"I'm sorry, Paul." I shook my head and took a half step toward the door. "I have to go."

I didn't feel right walking away from him like I had with my father. Dad was used to me storming out when my temper got the best of me. Paul and I had never done this before. And I wasn't angry at him. At our situation, yes, but mostly, I hurt. I didn't want to be anywhere except right here with him.

But the longer I stayed here, the more likely he'd come up with something to say that would keep me from leaving.

So without another word, I turned and walked out.

And he didn't try to stop me.

Teeth grinding, I left Anchor Point in the dust as fast as I could.

I was done. Completely and utterly done. I was done with this godforsaken town. I was done with its airbase. No, with the Navy. It wouldn't be any different near any other base. Truth was, I should've known better from the start. I should have asked Paul what he did in the military. I should've screened him through the filter of Dad's career, and nipped this in the bud before it had a chance to become something painful to leave behind.

If I'd been out of my dad's house and out from under his dependent status, it wouldn't have changed anything with Paul. Dad was still under his command, and dating me still would've had Paul hemmed up for fraternization or whatever they called it when a CO did something like this.

I was exhausted. I understood the Navy's rules, but I resented them. I hadn't chosen the Navy life.

I needed to get away from the Navy. It was time to live my own life. Somehow, I was getting the fuck out of here and going someplace where I didn't have to check a guy for a military ID before I banged him. I didn't know where I would end up or how I'd get there, but somehow, I needed to find a place that had never seen a ship before.

I'd figure it out. For now, I needed to be alone. I needed my car and my thoughts and the radio and the road noise. I needed a bendy, winding highway to nowhere in particular.

So I headed south.

Got on the highway.

And drove.

It was almost three in the morning when I parked on the curb in front of Dad and Julie's house. Just the sight of his truck in the driveway made my teeth grind.

Happy, Dad? It's done. It's over. Nothing's going to happen to your goddamned career.

Swearing under my breath even though no one was around to hear me, I thumped the wheel with my fist. I couldn't even be mad at him. I wanted to be, but...

I sighed. It was what it was. And it was my own fault, too. I'd been the one to let myself get hooked on the wrong guy.

Dad wasn't lying—he'd never interfered with my love life before. In hindsight, I was pretty sure he'd *wanted* to a few times. I would have bet money Dad had literally bitten his tongue over some of the guys I'd brought home. He'd never said a word, though. He'd quietly waited for the inevitable, and always been there for me when the time came to pick up the pieces. No "I told you so." No "You can't be surprised he turned out to be a douche bag."

Tonight, as I sat in the car and dreaded going inside, I wished he had been more of an asshole about my past boyfriends. I wished he'd interfered, voiced his disapproval, forbidden me from seeing people. Then I'd have a reason to be pissed at him for stepping in between me and Paul.

But I'd been lucky as hell to have a dad who let me make my own mistakes, and so I had absolutely zero leverage to be angry at him now, the one time he spoke up about my choice.

Well, idiot. What did you think was going to happen?

I cursed again, yanked my keys out of the ignition, and got out of the car.

One of the downstairs lights was on, but that wasn't unusual—they always left a light on for me when I was out late.

It wasn't just a light, though. In the kitchen, Dad was waiting. Neither of us said a word as I hung up my keys, but I knew better than to assume I was free to walk out.

Fine. Fine. Let's do this and be done with it.

Jaw clenched, I turned to him.

He was leaning against the counter, arms folded across his T-shirt. "Where have you been?"

I narrowed my eyes. "Does it matter?"

"Kind of, yeah." He tightened his arms and glared back at me. "Were you with Captain Richards?"

"I went to talk to him, if that's all right." Through my teeth, I added, "Apparently you already did, though."

"Yeah. I did. I—"

"You couldn't even give me a chance to handle it?" I snapped. "You had to go—"

"What did you want me to do? Believe it or not, you're not the only one affected by this."

"You could have at least let me talk to him and call it off."

"Did you?"

"Yes!" I exhaled hard. "I told you I would, so I did."

"Good. And I hope this is the last time we—"

"Dad." I put up my hands. "Don't. Please. Just... don't."

His expression hardened. "I think I have a vested interest in—"

"We're not seeing each other anymore, okay? I get it. And I get why." I rolled my shoulders, wondering when they'd started getting so tense. "Can we leave it alone?"

He scowled, but then shrugged. "Fine. But so help me, God, if I hear even a rumor about the two of you—"

"You won't. It's done." My voice threatened to break, but whatever. "It's done, okay?"

He watched me for a moment. Finally, he gave a slight nod. "All right."

Good enough. I broke eye contact and walked out, and Dad didn't try to stop me.

Upstairs, I lay back on my bed and stared up at the ceiling.

It was so weird how my dad treated me like an adult most of the time, but the second we butted heads over something, I was suddenly a child and he was suddenly *Dad* again. And it didn't matter that I knew he was right this time. That I'd known before he did that I shouldn't have been involved with Paul.

He was mad, he was right, I felt two inches tall, and the humiliation was excruciating.

"I can't see you because of my dad. Sorry."

I groaned, scrubbing my hands over my face.

The humiliation wasn't even the worst part. Turned out walking away didn't get any easier. One thing was for sure—Paul was going to be one tough act to follow.

But we had to stop. Not because we were incompatible. Not because of our age gap.

Because of the Navy.

Always because of the fucking Navy.

CHAPTER 24

PAUL

THE ICE in my drink had mostly melted. The glass was sweating, condensation pooling at its base on the coffee table.

I hadn't touched it.

I wasn't even sure why I'd made it. Or how. Sometime after Sean had left, after the sound of his car had faded into the distance, I'd checked out of the motel and driven back to my big, empty house on base. Walked in the door, opened up a bottle of bourbon, and poured it over some ice. Was the bottle still out on the counter? Probably. I didn't bother looking. I just sat there on the couch and stared at the glass and the ice and the tiny puddle.

The frozen peas had long since thawed. They were in a heap next to my drink because I couldn't muster up the energy to take them back into the kitchen and toss them in the freezer. They hadn't done a bit of good, either. The stiffness in my neck had grabbed on to my shoulder, and I didn't need a crystal ball to know this was going to be a miserable night.

It would've been miserable even without a stiff neck,

though. The booze wasn't helping. The frozen peas weren't helping. The triple dose of Motrin wasn't helping.

What I needed was Sean, and he wasn't here, and I didn't know what the fuck to do with myself.

I could keep a cool head under pressure. Sure, I might've done some shaky chain-smoking in the aftermath, especially after a firefight or a shipboard crisis. I'd spent plenty of nights lying awake and replaying every command and every decision, searching for any mistakes I might've made. But in the moment, when the bullets were flying or the shit was hitting the fan, I had it together. Always did.

Relationships, though—that was where I always fucked up. The one place where I let emotions take over and made rational thought sleep on the couch, and it always bit me in the ass. Always. Why had I thought this would be any different? Hell, I'd known this would blow up in my face sooner or later. I just hadn't expected it to hurt this much.

I picked up the drink and took a watered-down swig of bourbon. It still didn't do a damned bit of good. I hadn't expected it to. And the cigarette I was craving would help like water would help a drowning man, but that didn't stop me from eyeballing my keys and wondering if I should give up and go get a pack of Marlboros. The Exchange was closed by now, but the Shopette was open. Five minutes down the road, and I could have a cigarette.

I shook my head, banishing that thought. Drinking, smoking, feeling sorry for myself: none of it was going to bring Sean back. That reality, though—realizing he was gone and there was nothing I could do about it—only made me want to dive as deep as I could into a bottle, a pack of Marlboros, and a goddamned pity party.

It was probably a good thing I didn't fly anymore. Most of my "What the fuck were you doing up there, Richards?"

moments in my CO's offices had appeared to be nothing more than a hothead pilot and his RIO doing stupid reckless shit in a billion-dollar toy. No one but me needed to know that nearly all of those incidents had been hot on the heels of a bitter breakup or a nasty fight. It was a miracle I didn't get grounded during my second marriage—every time Tina and I fought, I'd taken it out on my jet, usually in some way that pushed the sound barrier and challenged the laws of physics.

These days, I didn't have access to Super Hornet therapy at Mach 1, so it was a choice between chemicals that would be as helpful as ejecting before takeoff.

Losing Jayson had been hard. If anything, I'd felt defeated. We'd tried to make it work, and we'd failed, and we'd thrown in the towel long after we should have. It was a relief and a disappointment at the same time.

But nothing about walking away from Jayson had hurt like watching Sean walk out tonight. This was all wrong. There'd been none of the fighting, bitterness, name-calling, door-slamming, and cold-shouldering that led up to every breakup I'd ever had. People didn't just... *leave*.

Except he couldn't stay. When he said he had to go, I didn't stop him because he was absolutely right. We'd both known it from the moment we realized his father worked for me, and no amount of flying under the radar was going to change anything. The best-case scenario was one or both of us getting tired of the secrecy. The worst case... well, it didn't get much worse than twenty-four years of work down the shitter.

So Sean had wisely called time. I could be angry with him all I wanted for calling this thing off, but the truth was he hadn't had a choice. If anyone deserved to be angry, it was him. Especially since I'd poured salt in the wound before we'd even reached this point. Knowing full well this would blow up in our faces eventually, I'd told him I loved him. I'd meant it. I still did. How much harder had that made it for him to leave tonight? I could only imagine.

But he'd still done it. I exhaled, staring up at the ceiling. One thing was for sure—Sean was a hell of a lot stronger than I was.

I leaned forward, rubbing my neck and shoulder. I dug my fingers in until my eyes watered. At first, I told myself I was trying to loosen up the tension, but I gave up on that before long. I focused *hard* on the pain. I concentrated on it. Obsessed over every twinge and spasm. If I could've counted the affected muscle fibers, I would have. Anything to keep my mind off Sean.

It figured that this one time, the pain wasn't enough to hold my attention. Normally, I couldn't concentrate on anything else. This time... well, I wasn't surprised. Sean hurt a hell of a lot more than an ancient career-derailing injury.

I didn't even want a cigarette. Smoking meant breathing, and even that hurt right now.

What did you think would happen?

He's a senior chief's son. He's half your age. He's...

Amazing. Sweet. Fun.

Gone.

He's gone.

I covered my face with both hands. I'd said good-bye to too many people in my life to be this lost right now. Did this happen every time, and I only remembered it with less intensity? Did it always seem so much worse in the moment than in hindsight?

No, I distinctly remembered walking away from Jayson.

Especially since I'd walked out of his room and right into Sean's car. And besides, that had been a necessary breakup.

So is this one.

My eyes stung. It was a necessary breakup, but that didn't make it easier to swallow.

And wallowing in this wasn't going to bring him back. Nothing would. It was over because it had to be. But I was allowed one night of self-pity, wasn't I? Self-pity wouldn't change anything, but neither would stoicism.

It hurt, so I let it.

There was nothing else I could do, so I gave in.

I let myself break.

And cried.

CHAPTER 25

SEAN

MY DAD'S footsteps in the hallway raised my hackles. As I shoved a few T-shirts into my bag, I telepathically begged him to keep walking.

He didn't.

He stopped, and my neck prickled. Neither of us made a sound, but I knew he was there. My stomach somersaulted. I had hoped to get my shit together and get out quietly, but he'd gotten home a little while ago. He'd talked to Julie for a few minutes. Then he'd come up here.

Now, he was in the open doorway of my bedroom, and nothing made me feel more like a kid than my dad lurking outside the door with an uncomfortable topic hanging in the air. He'd already put me in my place once today.

Just let me leave, okay?

I can't breathe. I can't live my own life because of what you need to live yours.

Just... let me go. Please?

Dad finally spoke. "Where are you going?"

"I called a friend from class." I grabbed wallet and keys

off the nightstand and put them next to my bag. "He's going to let me crash on his couch until I figure it out."

Dad was quiet for a while. "Do you need anything?"

I froze, then turned around. He was still in his uniform, gold anchors gleaming on the blue camouflage lapels. His feet were right at the seam between the hallway carpet and my bedroom, something he'd always done when I was a teenager and he wanted to talk without invading my space. I couldn't even explain why, but that infuriated me this time.

I hooked my thumbs in my pockets. "What?"

He moistened his lips. "Do you need anything? Money? Or—"

"I'm fine. I've got some money from work." Never mind that I had a car payment due and insurance coming up, or that even with Dad's GI Bill, I still had to cough up some money for school. And if I had to work enough hours that I couldn't go to school full-time, then I was fucked out of military healthcare, which meant I'd need to get on the ACA, which would mean even *more* money.

Still, I didn't want his money. It probably wasn't my most mature moment, but I couldn't stomach the idea of taking anything more from him. Relying on him into my twenties was what had put me in this mess. If I'd been on my own two feet and out from under dependent status, Paul and I could have...

No, we couldn't have.

Well, it didn't matter. I wasn't and we couldn't and we weren't.

"Are you in a hurry?" Dad asked.

Like you wouldn't believe.

I swallowed hard and met his eyes. "Why?"

He folded his arms loosely across his chest and pressed

his shoulder against the doorframe. "Can we talk for a minute?"

I played with the zipper on my bag. "What about?"

"You and Captain Richards."

I squeezed my eyes shut and forced out a breath. "His name is Paul."

"Okay." The doorframe creaked a little, so he must've been shifting his weight. "You and... you and Paul."

"What is there to talk about? It's over."

"I think we both know you don't want it to be."

"Of course I don't." I shook my head. "But that doesn't change anything."

"It doesn't mean you can't—"

"Just stop, okay?" I faced him again, looked him in the eye, but it was hard. "There's nothing to talk about. Can we not?"

His lips pulled tight.

"Look," I said. "I get it. I know why I can't see him. But the thing is, I've lived my entire life according to the rules of your career. And I can't do that anymore." He opened his mouth to speak, but I was afraid anything he said might break me down, so I kept going. "I don't have a single long-term friendship because we were never in one place long enough. I've known literally all of my friends through social media longer than I've known any of them in real life. Any relationship I've ever had that didn't fizzle out on its own ended because we moved." I swallowed, forcing back the lump in my throat. "I just can't do it anymore. I'm tired of giving up everyone and everything that makes me happy because of your career. I need to figure out how to live my own life."

That was all I had, so I stopped. Sooner or later, I was going to have to let him say his piece, so I waited, and tried like hell not to let him see that my hands were shaking.

Dad stared at me. I thought he might lash out—in a weird way, I kind of hoped he would—but he didn't. He didn't do or say anything for the longest time.

Why aren't you getting pissed?

And why can't I stop shaking?

Dad let out a long breath. "I'm sorry, Sean. For everything."

In an instant, the pain in my chest turned to pure white fury.

"*Sorry?*" I snapped. "Fuck you, Dad."

He blinked. "I beg your—"

"You're not sorry. This career is what you've always wanted, and you knew I'd be along for the ride. *Sorry* doesn't give me back my childhood, all the friends I've had to leave behind, or my parents' marriage, and it sure as fuck doesn't give me back the first person I've ever felt this way for. You can—"

"I get it, Sean," he said through gritted teeth.

"No, you don't. You think you do, but you don't. All those sacrifices you talk about? The ones we've all had to make as a family. You get something in return. You get your career and all your fucking medals, and what do I get?"

"Besides a roof over your head and healthcare?"

I broke eye contact for a second. "Was the Navy the only way we could've had those things?"

"It's the way we—"

"It really doesn't matter." I picked up my wallet, pulled out my military dependent ID, and tossed it on the bed. "That's why I'm going out and getting those things myself. I'm almost too old to be a dependent anyway, so I might as well get a head start on taking care of myself. I don't need you or the Navy anymore. The Navy's taken enough from me, and it's not getting any more."

"Sean, for God's sake, we—"

"I've heard it all before, Dad, okay?" I swallowed, trying to keep my emotions in check, which was getting harder by the second. "And I know it doesn't seem like it, but I've tried like hell not to screw up your career. I'm done with it, okay? I mean, when I was a kid and I got in trouble, it was always about how it reflected on you. Not about whether I was fucking myself over. Or even if I was doing something dangerous. It always came back to *you* and the fucking Navy."

"I know," he said quietly. "I know it hasn't been easy to—"

"'Hasn't been easy'?" I threw up my hands. "Do you hear yourself?"

Dad avoided my eyes.

"Moving every few years isn't easy," I said, my voice way too shaky. "Giving up someone like Paul..." I clenched my jaw and looked away because I was not going to let my dad see me cry. Not this time.

He pushed himself off the doorframe, but didn't come into the room. "How do you really feel about Paul?"

Okay, if he kept that shit up, I *was* going to cry.

Just let me leave. *Please?*

I swiped at my eyes. "Does it matter?"

"It matters to me."

"But it's not going to change anything."

Dad lowered his gaze. I watched him, not sure what I even felt right then. Except I was damn sure what I felt about Paul. If there was one thing I knew in that moment...

"I love him."

Dad looked at me. "What?"

I cleared my throat. "I love him. Okay? That's how I really feel about him." I couldn't read Dad's expression at all, but I didn't want to hear what I was pretty sure was coming, so I added, "And you were right that I was being selfish. He was risking a lot to be with me, and I... I can't ask him to do that. So I broke things off."

"Oh."

My emotions were threatening to get the best of me—my chest was tight, and the ache tightening in my throat wasn't getting any better—so I picked up the bag I'd packed and slung it onto my shoulder. Without a word, I walked out. Dad moved aside and didn't try to stop me.

CHAPTER 26

PAUL

I NEEDED A GODDAMNED CIGARETTE.

Sitting in my office, drumming my fingers on my desk beside reports I couldn't comprehend, I hadn't itched for a cigarette like this in a long time. Deep down, I knew I didn't really need it, and I didn't really want it, but the craving was a powerful one.

I shook myself and looked at the reports in front of me. I had work to do. Responsibilities. Everything from disciplinary issues that needed review to more bullshit about the squadron that may or may not have been transferring to NAS Adams. I needed to be Captain Richards right then, but God, all I wanted to be was Paul, the idiot who'd gotten himself in over his head with someone he couldn't have, and really, really, *really* needed a cigarette.

Fuck it.

No one needed me for at least another hour. I had meetings all afternoon, but this morning was mercifully quiet. So I muttered an excuse to my secretary and walked out of the office.

I drove over to the Shopette around the corner from the

building and bought a pack of Marlboros. I was halfway to my car before I realized I didn't have a lighter anymore, so sheepishly went back in and bought one of those too.

Outside, I smacked the pack against my wrist a few times, then opened it. I leaned against the car as I freed a cigarette, then froze. The quiet creak of the shocks flooded my mind with memories, and damn it, I couldn't get the smoke into my lungs fast enough.

Hands unsteady, I finally got a cigarette free. It felt weird between my lips. Like something comfortingly familiar and completely alien at the same time.

I cupped my hand around the tip, flicked the lighter, and lit the end. Then I took in a long drag.

Instantly, the smoke burned the back of my throat, and I coughed like I had the first time twelve-year-old me had tried this. My lungs itched and burned, but I took in another drag. On the third try, I didn't cough at all, and slowly released a cloud of smoke into the air. The next drag was slightly more pleasant, but it tasted terrible.

I didn't feel any better. Even the rush of nicotine barely registered. My head spun a little, and my heart sped up, but my mind was still on the reason I'd bought the pack in the first place.

I didn't need a cigarette. I needed Sean. I just wasn't sure which habit was worse.

Didn't matter. Both habits needed to be broken.

With the cigarette dangling between my lips, I fished Sean's business card out of my wallet. I held it up, flicked the lighter under its corner, and watched it curl up into flames. I let it burn to my fingers and dropped it to the pavement. Once it had been reduced to ashes, and there was nothing left that I could possibly use to contact Sean, I smothered the remaining flames with my boot.

Then I finished my smoke and got the fuck out of there.

In my office, I shoved the cigarettes into my desk drawer and told myself I wouldn't touch them again. Yeah right. If that were the case, I'd've thrown them in the trash, just like I should have tossed Sean's card when we'd gone our separate ways the first time.

I leaned back in my chair and rubbed my stiff neck.

I wanted to tell myself these were all unfamiliar thoughts and feelings, but it was the same shit, different day. In fact, it was the DADT era all over again. When I'd married—and hurt—two women because I'd *needed* to be straight. I hadn't set out to hurt them. I'd known it was a risk, and I'd gambled with the possibility that I could fool them and the Navy into believing I was a respectable straight man who could be trusted as a lieutenant, a lieutenant commander, a commander...

I sighed into the silence of my office. It had made sense at the time. I'd desperately been trying to hold on to my career because I couldn't shake the identity that threatened to destroy it, and I'd regret until the day I died how much I had hurt both of those women in the process. I'd even told Sean how much of an idiot I'd been when Mary Ann and I had split up. How it had taken me way too long to realize that the damage to my career and my no-really-I'm-straight façade shouldn't have been more important to me than how she felt, and how much I was losing when she walked out that door.

This time, I was well aware of how much Sean was hurting. Even though he'd been the one to call things off, he wasn't doing it because he wanted to. He had to. For his dad, and for me. And then there had been the added blow of asking me point-blank if I'd choose him or my career, and

I hadn't been able to say I'd choose him. The hurt in his eyes had been palpable. Could I blame him?

But what else could I do? This was two and a half decades of my life. No matter what I felt for Sean, or how much it hurt to lose him, there was simply too much riding on this.

I looked up at the dozens of certificates and plaques on the wall. There was a photo of me shaking hands with the president when he'd visited Yokosuka. An older photo of my RIO and me in front of our bird about six months before the landing that grounded us. A group picture of my squadron on the flight deck before one of our missions into Iraq.

I still had my certificate from crossing the equator—seemed like everyone displayed those until the end of time, even if they'd earned it as a lowly lieutenant like me. There was my diploma from the Academy. A couple of awards for shit that didn't seem to matter now. Tucked into boxes in my garage and my attic, there were dozens more.

When I retired, I'd pack this shit up, move it to wherever I decided to put down roots, and put everything back up on the walls. And... then what? What would all of this mean at the end of the day? All those years of pretending to be straight. All the time and energy wasted on two marriages—one of which had left me broke and bitter, the other broke, bitter, and estranged from a woman who deserved better. All the boyfriends who'd felt temporary, guys it wouldn't hurt as much to say good-bye to.

I rubbed my eyes with my thumb and forefinger. As I thought back on all the time I'd devoted to the Navy, I was tired. Drained from twenty-four years of being everything I'd ever dreamed of except happy, and leaving behind a trail of casualties made out of the people who'd tried to love me.

And what was left? A star if I played my cards right and

finally got command of a ship and the planets aligned perfectly? *Maybe* two if I stayed on for another five, ten, fifteen years? When was it enough? And what was left when it was over? Sure, there was the pride and accomplishment of serving my country and doing it—I thought—pretty damn well. My retirement pay would keep me comfortable for the rest of my life. If I stayed on for six more years, I'd get even more retirement—three-quarters of my salary instead of half.

But was it worth it?

And... did I really *want* to be an admiral anymore?

I'd spent most of my life aiming for that rank. The more the Navy pushed back, the more obstacles I had to get over, the more I wanted that star so bad I could taste it.

But thinking about it now, weighing it against everything I'd sacrificed and would continue to sacrifice to reach that coveted rank, the thought of being an admiral exhausted me. For the first time, it looked less like an ultimate prize after a long career, and more like an extension of all that work. Something that would take what energy and optimism I had left and wring it out of me until I was too gray, hunched, and tired to enjoy my hard-earned retirement.

I leaned forward, elbow pressed on my desk as I massaged the side of my neck. Funny how I'd been feeling that injury more since Sean left than I had while we were having sex every five minutes. Contorting myself to kiss him or go down on him didn't put nearly the strain on my neck as working myself into a stressed-out frenzy over losing him. Being with him had not been for the faint of heart or the weak of body, but it had been amazing. It had been right. And now that he was gone, and the only thing left was to continue on that long career climb, that coveted star had lost its luster.

Is that still who I want to be? Do I want to be anything that isn't with you?

My mind drifted back to the Academy, and one of my mentors there. Commander John Henderson. I'd admired his single-minded ambition. He'd said he wouldn't retire until he was a three-star admiral, and five years ago, he'd done exactly that. He was one of the most decorated officers I'd ever personally met, a fantastic leader, and a legendary pilot.

Less than a month after his retirement, John was wearing those three stars when the casket lid was closed. He'd been healthy and fit as a recruit fresh out of boot camp, and dropped dead of a heart attack while he was out jogging.

I stopped rubbing my neck. With my hand paused where it was, my pulse prodded at my palm.

Was I next?

I flicked my gaze from the reports on my desk to the awards on my wall.

Then I turned to my computer, pulled up my letterhead template, and began typing.

After I was done, I read and reread the words. Jesus. I hadn't sent it up to the admiral yet, and it already felt liberating. There would still be some time yet before I actually retired, especially since another commanding officer would need to be brought onboard, but as soon as I sent that message, the ball would be rolling.

A million emotions knocked into each other and tried to cancel each other out. I didn't feel much of anything right then. That would come later, I guessed. After the admiral had given me the "I'm sorry to see you go" and "I'm disappointed—you had so much potential" talk that I gave most of my personnel when they retired.

Or maybe I wouldn't feel anything other than how I'd walked in this morning. Retiring was fine and good, but I was still sleeping alone.

The phone on my desk rang, startling a few curses out of me.

Of course it was ringing. No rest for the captain who was ready to leave the base and never come back.

When I answered, my secretary said, "Sir, Senior Chief Wright is here and would like to speak to you. He says it's urgent."

I closed my eyes and bit down on a string of profanity that would've made my Sailors blush. Then, "Thank you. Send him in."

"Yes, sir."

I braced myself and held my breath as the door opened.

He kept his eyes down and shut the door behind him.

"Sir." He gave a slight nod.

"Senior Chief." I gestured at the chairs in front of my desk. "Have a seat."

"Thank you, sir." He took a seat, and as he did, he slid an envelope across my desk. "I wanted to give this to you personally."

"Oh." I picked it up and opened the flap. Neither of us spoke while I unfolded the letter.

Instantly, I zeroed in on one word: *retirement*.

My heart sped up. I read the letter, which sounded eerily like the one I'd just written. Enlisted personnel followed different procedures at this stage, but the letter declared his intention to retire at the end of his current enlistment.

I lowered it and looked at him across the desk. "Looks

like we've both been on the same wavelength this afternoon."

His eyebrows rose. "I beg your pardon?"

"I'm, uh, sending a letter like this—" I held it up, then laid it down beside my keyboard "—to the rear admiral."

Wright stared at me incredulously. "You're... Are you retiring because of Sean?"

"I'm..." I chewed my lip. "I don't have to explain to you how taxing this career is."

"No, you don't."

"So you probably understand what I mean when I say I'm exhausted."

Wright nodded.

I took a breath. "No, retiring is not a hundred percent because of Sean, but he's basically the battleship that broke the camel's back."

"What do you mean?"

"I mean, I've spent the last twenty-four years choosing the Navy over everyone and everything. I was going to make admiral if it killed me. And when I realized there was no way I could have both him and the Navy..." I rubbed the bridge of my nose, then dropped my hand into my lap. It wasn't that simple, but I didn't have the energy to explain it all. "I guess I decided it was too much. One sacrifice too many."

"Does he know about this?" Wright barely whispered the question.

I shook my head. "No." With a soft laugh, I added, "Knowing him, he'd try to talk me out of it."

"Yeah. He would." Wright dropped back against his chair and exhaled hard. "Wow."

"What?"

Wright fixed his gaze on the floor in front of my desk.

"You're..." He met my eyes. "You're willing to walk away from the Navy after all these years. Without a star. For him."

I nodded. "I wouldn't have risked my career if Sean hadn't been worth it. I will happily give up that star if it means I have even a fighting chance of having him back in my life."

The senior chief's lips parted. "I don't even know what to say."

I muffled a cough. "Would you object to me reconnecting with him?"

Without hesitating, he shook his head. "No. An hour ago, yeah, I... I might have. I don't know. But what kind of father would I be if I stopped someone who's willing to do this much for him?" He laughed humorlessly. "Hell, I'm his father, and I wouldn't give up my career for him."

"Before today, you mean."

Wright flinched. "Kind of seems like too little too late at this point."

I wasn't sure how to respond to that. We sat in silence for a moment. I wanted to be relieved to the point of giddy over his blessing to be with Sean again, but would Sean even take me back? Was it too little too late for *us*?

Out of nowhere, Wright broke the silence. "I always knew this life was hard on him. When I started really thinking about it last night, I..." He exhaled hard. "You ever regret your career?"

"No," I said without hesitation. "If I had it to do over, I would. All of it." I leaned back against my chair and sighed. "It's everything outside of work I would have done differently."

The senior chief nodded. "Yeah. Me too. Especially when it comes to Sean." His Adam's apple bobbed. "The last twenty-five years have been one sacrifice after another from him. I mean, when I made chief, we had *just* settled into a new duty station. Sigonella. Sean had been looking forward to living in Sicily ever since I'd gotten my orders. And not three months after we got there, he met this boy in class and hit it off." Wright's shoulders sank, and he pressed his elbow into the armrest as he rubbed his eyes. After a moment, he dropped his hand. "We'd been there six months when I was selected, and six months later, we were on our way back to Norfolk."

"Damn."

"He finally got to go somewhere interesting," Wright went on. "And he met a nice boyfriend. And then he had to give it all up."

"Jesus."

Wright sighed. "It's not the first time or the last time I've made him give shit up for me. And it's not just him." He shifted, eyes losing focus. "I love my girlfriend. We'll probably get married, and we'll be happy. But between you and me, I'm pretty sure Sean's mom was the love of my life. The thing is, the military life..."

"It's hard on people," I said.

Wright nodded. "Some people can handle it. Some can't. Sean's mom... she couldn't. If I'd been a civilian, and we'd stayed in the same town, and..." He shook his head. "I don't think she would've left. I mean, I don't know. Maybe I would've found some other way to screw things up with her, but..."

"I'm pretty sure you're not the only divorcé in the military who can say that." I sighed. "If not for the Navy, I never would've married my first wife. Well, I wouldn't have married either of them. But at least Mary Ann and I might still be friends."

He grimaced. "That's brutal."

"Yeah." I drummed my fingers on the armrest. "There are people in this line of work who stay happily married the whole time. Maybe I should've been asking them their secrets instead of finding mentors to help me get promoted."

He chuckled dryly and nodded. "Yeah. I hear that." He rubbed the back of his neck, then folded his hands in his lap. "Well, you still have a shot at someone."

I raised my eyebrows.

Wright swallowed. "Look, I don't have a clue what you two have in common, or how any of this even works. All I know is, he's happy when he's with you, and now he's miserable." He sat a little straighter. "So, I think you and I should both sit down with Sean."

Returning the smile, I said, "I guess we should give him a call, then, shouldn't we?"

CHAPTER 27

SEAN

COULD you come by the house? We need to talk.

I glared at my dad's text message. What was left to talk about? It wasn't like anything could change the situation, and I really wasn't interested in hearing him apologize again.

Or hell, I thought, maybe he had some more good news for me. Like some orders to God knew where. I'd settled into Anchor Point and knew my way around, so that was the perfect time to uproot everything and send us to Pensacola or San Diego or whatever godforsaken bases were still out there.

Gripping the wheel tight enough to make my hands hurt, I followed the familiar streets, and at the stop sign before the cul-de-sac, I paused. Then didn't move. I stared down the road. From here, I could see the front of Dad and Julie's house. The bumper of Dad's pickup stuck out just beyond the end of the privacy fence.

If he had orders, I'd find out sooner or later. If he wanted to talk, or bitch at me, or "apologize" again... fuck, I did *not* want to hear it. I was done.

What was the point? I'd broken up with Paul. What more did Dad want from me? A confession to the Pope?

Letting the engine idle, I blew out a breath. The fact was, as much as I wanted to hate him for pushing me and Paul apart, he hadn't had a choice. And whether or not I could have Paul—which I obviously couldn't—I didn't want to lose my dad. Regardless of why he'd called me over here, we did need to talk and clear the air.

So I swore under my breath, pulled away from the stop sign, and turned down the cul-de-sac. I parked next to Dad's truck. At least Julie's car wasn't here. This would probably be awkward enough without an audience.

Hands in my pockets, I walked up to the front door, but hesitated. I'd technically moved out even though most of my shit was still here. So was I supposed to knock? Or—

The door opened.

My dad met my gaze across the weathered welcome mat. "Hey."

"Hey." I gulped. "You, um, wanted to talk."

He nodded and stepped aside, gesturing for me to come in. Without a word, we went up the steps and into the living room, and I started toward the couch to sit down, but stopped dead.

I blinked a few times. "Paul?"

He rose slowly from the sofa. "Hi, Sean."

"What are—" I looked at Dad. Then at Paul. Then back at Dad. "Uh, what's going on? And why didn't I see your car outside?"

"He parked in the garage," Dad said.

"Probably best if no one sees that I'm here," Paul added.

I gritted my teeth. "Then why *are* you here?"

"Sit down." Dad gestured at the empty armchair. "I think we all need to talk."

A lump rose in my throat. "Can we not? It's done. What more is there to talk about?"

"Sean." Dad motioned toward the chair again. "Just sit."

I hesitated. This was going to hurt, wasn't it? Did they think I was an idiot? Like I hadn't gotten it far enough into my head, and they both had to sit me down and explain to me why we couldn't—

"Sean," Paul said softly. "Please."

Stomach in knots, I took a seat. "Okay. So, what's going on?"

They glanced at each other, and my stomach knotted even tighter. What the hell had these two been talking about?

Dad finally cleared his throat and turned to me. "Listen, I know the Navy life has been hard on you."

I gritted my teeth. He thought he got it, but he didn't know the half of it.

He went on. "I've done some thinking, and I think it's time you stopped paying dues for my career."

I blinked. "What?"

Dad took a deep breath. "I'm retiring. I have another year and a half left on my contract, but I've notified my chain of command"—his eyes darted toward Paul—"that I'm retiring once that time is up."

I'd barely had time to process the words before Paul chimed in: "And I'm also retiring."

"You're *what*?"

He nodded slowly. "I sent my letter up to the rear admiral this morning."

My jaw dropped. "But... why?"

He looked me right square in the eye. "Why do you think?"

I stared at him for a moment, then stood, raking a hand

through my hair. I paced in front of the fireplace because I suddenly had too much nervous energy to deal with, and my brain reeled from everything they'd said. "This is insane. You're... You can't be retiring because of me."

Paul stood too. "No, what I can't do is choose the Navy over the love of my life."

My heart dropped into my feet. I leaned against the mantel. "But..." I glanced back and forth between them. "Okay, look. The gesture is great, but Paul, what happens in a couple of years when you're tired of me and you resent me because—"

"That isn't going to happen," he said. "The novelty of any relationship is going to wear off, and if we're in it for the long haul, we're going to end up in a comfortable, boring rut like everyone else. But I've already been married to the Navy long enough to know exactly what I'm giving up for the chance to be in that comfortable, boring rut with you."

My throat tightened. "But what if this doesn't work out?"

"Maybe it will. Maybe it won't."

"I don't want you to hold it against me if it doesn't."

Paul shook his head. "That's not going to happen. I'm leaving the Navy because being with you made me realize I was ready to move on. And that... that I'd already given up too much for the Navy. I can't give you up too."

"But... your star..."

"It's not as important to me as it used to be. I can—" He paused, lowering his gaze, then cleared his throat and looked me in the eye. "The thing is, I can either spend the next few years kissing the right asses to make sure the Senate approves my promotion, or I can start enjoying my life and be with you."

"You've been working toward that for years, though. How can you give it up without knowing if we'll even stay together?"

"I'm willing to take the chance. It's a risk, yeah. There's no map. There's no destination." He smiled. "All I want is for us to get in the car and just drive."

My heart fluttered. I'd thought my own little analogy had been kind of stupid and clichéd, but hearing it from him, when he said it like he really meant it and it really was what he wanted...

I exhaled and rubbed a hand over my face. "What if I say no?"

Paul swallowed. "I can't force you. My decision's already made, though. I'm retiring. I'm done. I've given the Navy enough." He moistened his lips. "Being with you reminded me that there *is* life out there besides the military. And I want to start living that life while I still have some of it left."

I lowered my gaze, fighting to keep way too many emotions in check. "I don't... I don't even know what to say."

His hand materialized on my shoulder. "We can make this work. The Navy's out of the way. The only thing left is for you to tell me if you want to stay or go."

"Of course I want to stay." I looked in his eyes, and blinked mine into focus, then swiped at them with a shaky hand. "I never wanted to leave."

Paul smiled.

I glanced at my dad, who also smiled.

And suddenly, it sank in—this was really happening. Paul was here, and my dad wasn't trying to keep us apart, and the Navy *couldn't* keep us apart anymore.

I swallowed. "This isn't a joke, is it? You guys are—"

"We wouldn't joke about this," Dad said. "I want you to be happy." He gestured at Paul. "And you two deserve a shot at making each other happy."

My tongue stuck to the roof of my mouth. I couldn't fit all this into my head. Was this... was this *real*?

"I want to see where we can go together," Paul said. "But... of course, you *can* say no."

"Like hell I would." I stepped closer and threw my arms around him, and squeezed my eyes shut as I held him to me. "God, I love you."

"I love you too."

I loosened my embrace enough to meet his gaze. Heart pounding, knees shaking, I still couldn't even believe this was real.

And then, right there in the living room, with my dad standing a few feet away, Paul cupped my face and kissed me. My knees almost dropped right out from under me, but it didn't matter if they did. Paul was holding me up and melting me at the same time.

Dad cleared his throat. "Well, I think this is settled?"

Paul and I separated, and my face burned.

Dad chuckled as he stood. "I'll leave you kids alone, but..."

Paul and Dad exchanged glances.

Paul straightened. To me, he said, "We'll need to keep things discreet a little longer. Until after I retire."

"How long will that take?" I asked.

Paul shrugged. "A few months, maybe."

"Like I said, it'll be another year and a half or so for me," Dad said. "But I think once Paul's retired, there's no reason you two can't be open about it."

All the air went out of my lungs. "Really?"

He nodded. "Absolutely."

"Whoa." Just the thought of being with Paul, not looking over our shoulders or hiding in motels... "This is insane." I turned to my dad. "Thank you. I..." I blew out a breath. "That's all I can say."

He smiled, then came closer and hugged me tight. "I'm so sorry for everything."

"I know." I struggled to keep my emotions in check. "You didn't have a choice."

"No, but I should have tried harder to keep—"

"Dad." I pulled back and met his gaze. "You did what you could. I know. It's okay." I glanced at Paul, and smiled. To my dad, I said, "Thanks for this."

"Don't mention it." He let me go and turned to Paul, extending his hand. "Good luck."

"Hey!" I laughed. "What's that supposed to mean?"

Dad winked. "It means I know you, kid."

I rolled my eyes as they shook hands. "All right, rule number one? Neither of you calls me 'kid.' Okay?"

They both laughed. Then Dad left, heading downstairs to the man cave, and it was just me and Paul in the living room.

I exhaled. "This was, uh, not what I expected when I came over."

He wrapped his arms around me. "Yeah, we weren't quite sure how to explain it via text."

"You do realize, I almost turned around out there." I gestured toward the end of the cul-de-sac. "I almost didn't show up."

He held me a little tighter. "Well, I'm glad you did."

"Me too." I lifted my chin and kissed him softly. "What do you say we get out of here?"

Paul grinned. "Let's go."

I took out my keys, took his hand, and headed for the front door.

And I still couldn't believe this was real.

CHAPTER 28

PAUL

I DIDN'T CARE where we went. Sean drove, and he drove fast like he knew where we were going, and I just hoped there was a bed on the other end.

Turned out there was—not twenty minutes after leaving his dad's house, we swung into a convenience store for some lube, and ten minutes after that, he'd parked behind a tiny rundown motel outside of Anchor Point. I hated to keep coughing up money at these places, but until I was retired and detached from the Navy, discretion was the name of the game.

Before the motel room door had even clicked shut behind us, I had my hands in Sean's back pockets and he had me pushed up against the wall.

God. Yes. *Finally*.

"Could fuck you right here," he murmured between kisses, "like that time over the back of my car."

"No," I breathed. "Not this time."

"What? Why not?"

I pulled his hair back so I could kiss his neck. "'Cause I want to see your face. When you..." His shiver sent one through me. I found my breath again, and whispered, "When you come."

Sean gripped my shoulders as he bared more of his throat. "That's... gonna be sooner than you think if you keep doing that."

I slid my hand down over his thick erection. "Just means I'll have to make you come twice."

Sean closed his eyes and moaned. "Why are we not in bed yet?"

"Good question."

Moments later, naked, hard, and completely out of breath, we were very much in bed. Now that we were here, though, we slowed down. Sort of. I was horny as hell—it was impossible not to be turned on like this in bed with Sean—but the need for sex and orgasms took a back burner to how much I needed *him*. I couldn't believe he was here —that we'd found a way to be together—and I couldn't keep my hands off him. I traced every slope and angle of his body, every inch of hot skin, memorizing him all over again.

I pushed him onto his back and started kissing down the side of his throat. He moaned. Arched. Swore. I fucking loved the way he loved having his neck kissed.

His nails burned across my shoulders and down my arms. Every time he moved, his hard cock brushed mine, and I went a little crazier. I could feel his heart beat against my lips. Or maybe it was my own pulse pounding beneath my skin. I'd lost track, and it didn't matter—he was turned on, and I was turned on, and none of this was stopping until neither of us could move.

"Lube," he murmured. "Get... Need..."

I pried myself off him and reached for the convenience store bag we'd dropped on the floor. I'd barely come back to him before he grabbed the bottle from me and opened the top.

"I'm gonna stay just like this." He glanced at me as he poured lube in his hand. "You're gonna get on top."

My whole body broke out in goose bumps. Yes, fucking *yes*.

Sean put the bottle aside and stroked the lube onto his cock. My mouth watered. It had been how long since we'd fucked? And I hadn't gone completely insane?

After Sean had lubed himself up, he reached for me, probably to put some on me, but now that I knew what he had in mind, I couldn't wait. I pinned his wrist to the pillow and climbed on top of him.

"Plenty of lube," I said as I positioned myself. "Don't need any more."

"Fine by me." He tugged his arm free.

As he steadied himself, I eased myself down onto his slick cock, Sean bit his lip. Squeezing his eyes shut, he arched his back and ran his free hand up and down my side.

"Like that?" I asked.

"Uh-huh." He swept his tongue across his lips and met my gaze. "You?"

"What do you think?"

He grinned, and we both exhaled as I took him all the way inside me. I started to lift up again, and Sean mouthed something I didn't understand. More curses? No idea. But judging by the way his eyes rolled back and his whole body trembled under me, it was hardly "stop."

Riding him slowly, I stared down at him. I still couldn't believe he was here, that we were back together and soon we wouldn't have to hide it anymore. If I hadn't been so damn turned on right then, I probably would have collapsed into an emotional mess, but I was much too busy being fucked by his thick cock. Everything else could wait until we'd both come, and oh God, it wouldn't have to wait long.

Sean dug his teeth into his lip as he thrust up into me. We fell into perfect sync, and I tried not to think about moving in time with him—if I did, I'd concentrate too hard and fuck it up, and I didn't want to ruin the amazing rhythm we'd found. I didn't have to worry about thinking too hard, though. With his cock slamming into me and his muscles straining with exertion, all I could think about was how good he felt and how amazing he looked and—

"Fuck!" I threw my head back, and my rhythm was gone. Sean didn't miss a beat. He held my hips tighter and fucked me harder, and then his cock was pulsing inside me and I couldn't tell his moans from mine anymore.

All at once, he collapsed back onto the pillows and I slumped over him. We tried to kiss, but... we were both breathing too hard. And I was too dizzy and shaky. And way too distracted by the aftershocks of the powerful orgasm. Holy fuck.

When my arms could hold me up, I lifted myself enough to meet his eyes.

He grinned. "I missed you."

"Missed you too." I dragged my lips across his. "Missed waking up and not being able to move."

Sean laughed. "Yeah. Me too." He glanced down, probably at the sweat and semen on his abs. "We should get a shower."

"Good idea."

After a long shower, we dried off and returned to the hard bed. We pulled the sheets up to our waists, but didn't really need them. Between the hot shower and our body heat, we weren't exactly cold.

Sean rested his hand on my waist. "So how long do you think we'll have to keep this quiet?"

"I'll find out soon." I brushed a drop of water off his temple. "The admiral hasn't gotten back to me yet, and I'll probably work it out so they have time to bring in the new CO. But... not too long. A few months, maybe. At least until the current fit rep cycle is over and I won't be signing your dad's anymore. We won't be in the clear, but it'll be better."

Sean's lips tightened for a second, but then he nodded. "I can handle that. We were discreet before."

"I know. And I'm sorry we'll still have to be for—"

"It's okay." He smiled. "Being discreet for a while beats the hell out of the alternative."

I pushed out a breath. "It really does."

He ran his fingers through my hair. Something in the tension of his lips told me he had something on his mind, so I didn't speak.

Then he lifted his head, kissed me, and pulled me down to him. The tension melted away as we wrapped our arms around each other and let this soft kiss linger for a while. Whatever he'd wanted to say, it didn't seem to matter now. Instead, all that mattered was... this. My favorite thing in the world—lying in bed, skin to skin and limbs tangled up, kissing now and then but mostly just *being* here. And not having to sweat over why we shouldn't be, or how long it would be before someone caught on.

After a while, Sean met my gaze, and that unspoken something was back.

I swallowed as I brushed a few blue-black strands out of his face. "What's on your mind?"

"I..." He watched his fingers trail along my collarbone.

Then his eyes flicked up to meet mine again. "You're really giving up the Navy for me?"

I nodded, then leaned in for another gentle kiss. "I've accomplished enough in the Navy. I'm ready to move on." With a quiet laugh, I added, "Eighteen-year-old me probably wouldn't understand, but he didn't know about you."

Sean smirked. "To be fair, eighteen-year-old you existed before I did."

"Goddamn it."

He snorted, and we both burst out laughing.

I pressed a soft kiss to his forehead. "Either way, eighteen-year-old me will get over it."

"I hope so." He smiled. "And hey, now you'll be able to get a dog."

"You're right. God, finally." I paused. "You like dogs, right?"

"Pfft. What kind of question is that? Of course I like dogs."

"Good." I cupped his face and kissed him again.

"I love you," he whispered.

"I love you too."

Nothing had ever felt more amazing than holding on to Sean and knowing the Navy wouldn't take him away. I wasn't sure what it would be like to be a civilian again, but I was already getting used to the idea of being in love with someone without wondering when the next deployment or set of orders would drop out of the sky.

It reminded me a little of when the landing mishap had grounded me. At first, I'd fought it. I'd refused to give up what I'd worked so hard to achieve.

But then the cracks had started showing. I'd realized how much worse that accident could have been. That there would be ample opportunity for it to happen again. I'd seen several friends badly injured—in a few cases killed—in training accidents, ejections, disastrous landings, and one catastrophic mechanical failure.

Back then, it had been hard as hell to give up flying, but it had been time.

Today, it wasn't easy to give up the Navy, and to let go of the star that I'd set my heart on two decades ago.

But it was time. There was someone in my life who meant more than that star ever would.

I didn't know if this would work out. Neither of us could see the future. There was no telling if we'd fizzle a year from now, or if we'd pull this off. All I knew for sure was that Sean was here now, and this relationship wouldn't be another casualty of my career. I couldn't know what the future held, but I firmly believed this was the beginning of something amazing.

And I couldn't wait to see where we went from here.

EPILOGUE

Sean

ABOUT EIGHTEEN MONTHS Later

"Never thought I'd say this—" Paul tugged at the sleeve of his dress whites. "But it feels really weird to wear a uniform."

"Of course it does." I put my arms around him from behind and kissed above his starched collar. "You've been assimilated into the civilian world."

"Ugh. You ain't kidding." He fussed with the sleeve again. Then he turned around inside my embrace, straightened my tie, and kissed me lightly. "Looks like we're both ready?"

"I've been ready for twenty minutes. Been waiting on you."

He rolled his eyes and kissed me again. "Do we need to let the dogs out?"

I shook my head. "Did that ten minutes ago."

"So what you're saying is, we should go."

I nodded.

Paul kissed me one last time, and we *finally* headed out. We took my car to the base, showed our IDs, and continued toward the complex behind the commissary and Exchange. The building shared a parking lot with the base theater, so at least there were tons of parking spaces.

"One of these days," he said, "I'm going to forget myself and take that spot again out of habit." He gestured at the space that was reserved for the CO.

"I don't know." I pulled into another spot. "She doesn't seem like she'd like you taking her parking space."

Paul laughed. "Probably not." We'd had dinner with the new CO after the change of command ceremony when she'd first arrived. Turned out she'd been two years behind Paul at the Academy, and they'd flown together briefly before he'd been grounded. The world was small and the Navy made it even smaller.

We got out of the car, and Paul put on his cover and paused to fuss with his uniform one more time.

"Ready?" he asked.

"When you are."

On the way in, he offered me his elbow, and I smiled as I took it. This was the first time we'd been able to be together openly while he was in uniform. Now that he was retired, and no longer Dad's commanding officer, we had no reason to hide it anymore.

So we didn't.

Arm in arm, we walked into the room where twenty or thirty people—most of them in uniform—were milling around.

"Captain on deck!" someone barked, and everyone in the room snapped to attention. No one saluted—we were indoors, after all—but all eyes were on Paul. And me. On us.

"At ease," he said, and the whole room relaxed. As we

continued inside, he added under his breath, "I should've worn a suit."

"Oh, admit it—you like it."

He glanced at me, then chuckled. "Okay, so I do. But this isn't my event."

"But it's a military event. How many times will you get to wear your uniform again?"

"Fair point."

My dad and stepmom had already taken their seats in the front row, so we joined them. Paul and Dad shook hands, and we'd barely sat down before the two of them were talking about something that had happened on base recently. My stepmom and I exchanged glances, rolled our eyes, and shook our heads. Paul and Dad could live a hundred years after retirement, and would still be talking shop and telling sea stories.

At least they got along. In fact, these days, it was hard to believe there'd ever been a time when our relationship had caused strife between me and my dad. Once Paul retired, and there wasn't any work-related conflict anymore, they'd started getting to know each other. And they'd started golfing, which meant I had Sunday afternoons to study in peace.

Paul had been retired for just over a year now, and the transition hadn't been completely smooth. He'd struggled to adapt to the civilian world for the first few months—he'd mentioned more than once that he now understood how convicts felt after being paroled—but he'd found his stride after a while. The boredom had been the worst part. His retirement provided more than enough income, so he didn't have to get a job, and there hadn't been a lot of civilian jobs that appealed to him. He had found some places to volunteer around town, though.

And no surprise—two days into volunteering at the animal shelter, we were the proud dads of a six-year-old boxer and three Siamese cats. After that, I'd gently told him we had enough animals, but then the most adorable black lab puppy *ever* came to the shelter, and even I couldn't say no. As Paul and I waited for my dad's retirement ceremony to start, I was pretty sure all five animals were sleeping peacefully on the couch. Seemed only fair to me—I'd said no more pets, and Paul had said no pets on the couch.

At least he wasn't jumping out of bed at six in the morning anymore. And even though he was no longer held to military fitness standards, he didn't slack on his workout regimens. If anything, he went to the gym more often to occupy some of the newfound free time on his hands. I sure wasn't going to complain about the results.

He'd grown his hair out too. Not super long, and he'd never really had a high and tight to begin with—he just looked a bit more... relaxed. The gray was more obvious now too. He hated it, but I liked it. A *lot*.

Someone walked past me, snapping me out of my thoughts. Chief Romero, one of Dad's friends, stepped up to the podium and started the ceremony. Like any military function, it was a lot of pomp and circumstance, and a lot of the same old shit.

I'd been to dozens of retirement ceremonies in my life. A little over a year ago, I'd gone to Paul's. Now, as everyone went through the usual speeches and plaque presentations, I wondered if this would be the last one I attended. That was a weird thought.

Dad and Paul both had friends who were still in, though, so there'd probably be more of these. Still, it was odd to see my dad at his retirement, knowing this would be his last active-duty function. He'd been in the Navy since before I was born. Seeing him walk away from it hit me in the gut. More than I'd thought it would. As much as I'd resented the Navy at times, it had been an enormous part of both our lives. I'd been a Navy brat from the day I was born. Leaving all that behind was... well, it kind of took my breath away.

Paul squeezed my hand. I turned to him, and he lifted his eyebrows in an unspoken *You okay?*

I nodded, squeezing back, and as subtly as I could, wiped my eyes.

The master chief's wife got up to do the spouse part of the ceremony, which included reading a poem about life as a military spouse. As always, there was a certificate and a small award for the retiree's wife. I gritted my teeth through that part of the ceremony. I loved my stepmom, and she'd definitely had to deal with some of the Navy's bullshit, but she'd only joined him for the last three years or so of his career. In a weird way, it seemed like my mom should've been up there getting *something*. After all, she'd been there for the first sixteen years of his career, including all of the deployments, not to mention the early years when he'd been entitled to the shittiest base housing and barely made enough to keep us off welfare.

And, finally, it was Dad's turn to get up and hand out a few things and say a few words. I wondered if he might get emotional, especially when he mentioned some of the guys who'd gone to Afghanistan with him and hadn't come home, but he held it together.

"And of course," Dad said, "no one is in the Navy alone. My wife has been there through the last few years, but I want to give a small gift to the person who's been there the longest, and who's gone through all kinds of hell so that I could get here. Sean?"

Cheeks burning, I rose. Paul squeezed my arm, and we exchanged glances before I walked up to the podium where my dad waited. I'd kind of expected this part, but it was still weird to be in front of everyone. Dad had kept himself from getting emotional—I hoped like hell I could too.

He cleared his throat and looked at me. "I'm going to keep this short because I know you hate stuff like this."

I chuckled, and quiet laughter rippled through the group.

Dad went on, "I could stand up here for a long time and talk about everything you've had to go through because of the demands of my career, but I'm not going to tell you anything you don't know. What I will tell you is this—I may regret that my career forced you to be as strong and resilient as it has, but I will never stop being proud of you for being that strong and resilient."

I smiled, and goddamn it, that whole not-getting-emotional thing was getting tougher by the second. "Thanks, Dad."

"So I've got a plaque for you that I think sums it up nicely..." He handed the small plaque to me.

I read the engraved words: *Sorry for all the bullshit. Love, Dad.*

I burst out laughing, which—thank God—helped me corral my emotions again. "Thank you."

He laughed too, and then he hugged me. Everyone applauded, and there were a few "Awws."

Dad held on a bit longer than I thought he would. "I'm proud of you, Sean. I really am."

I sniffed. "Thanks."

As he let me go, he kept a hand on my shoulder. "I said I'd keep this short, but I *do* have one more thing for you before we're done."

I raised my eyebrows.

Dad smiled. "My very enthusiastic blessing."

"Huh?"

He nodded past me.

I turned around, and my heart stopped. When the hell had Paul joined us?

And what the hell was in his hand?

And why the hell was he getting down on one...

I gulped.

Paul took a breath and held up the small black box. "Sean, I gave most of my life to the Navy, but I want to give the rest of it to you. Will you marry me?"

I stared at him in disbelief. Everyone in the room was dead silent, and I could feel them all watching me. When I looked at my dad, he inclined his head as if to say, *Well?*

My mouth had gone dry, but as I faced Paul again, I managed to whisper, "Of course I will."

Paul laughed with palpable relief as he stood, and when he was on his feet, he pulled me into a kiss.

"What'd he say?" someone called out from the back.

Into the microphone, Dad replied, "He said yes, Petty Officer."

And the room erupted with applause.

Laughing, Paul and I separated. My face was on fire, but my head was spinning and my heart was pounding so fast, I didn't even care if I'd turned twelve shades of red.

Dad reached past me and shook Paul's hand. "Welcome to the family, sir."

Paul laughed. "Thank you, Senior Chief."

Dad clapped my shoulder. "Congratulations, kid."

Ignoring that damn "kid," I just smiled and said, "Thanks."

We took our seats again, and the retirement ceremony went on, but for me, the rest was a bit of a blur. My mind had gone blank and my head still spun from the shock of Paul's proposal. I hadn't seen it coming at all. We'd talked about getting married, but this... Jesus. Mind blown.

When the whole thing was over, everyone moved to the NCO club next door for the retirement party. After we'd congratulated my dad and gotten some drinks, Paul and I hung back by the bar so we could have a minute to ourselves.

Hand on my waist, he grinned. "I get the feeling I caught you off guard."

"You think?" I glanced toward my dad, who was talking to some uniformed guys I didn't know. "He didn't mind us upstaging him, did he?"

Paul laughed and kissed my temple. "This was his idea, actually."

I blinked. "You're kidding."

"Nope. We were out golfing, and I told him I was thinking about proposing." He shrugged. "Between you and me, I think he still feels guilty for how things went because of our careers, so he thought it would be... I don't know..."

"Poetic?"

"Pretty much, yeah."

"Wow. How long have you guys been planning this?"

"A few weeks."

"I didn't suspect a thing."

"I know." He grinned. "That was the idea."

"Mission accomplished, then."

"Very much so."

I checked out the ring he'd put on my finger. It was a simple band, nothing extravagant or flashy. Exactly what I would have wanted, and I still couldn't believe I was wearing it. I couldn't believe he'd asked, or that we'd made it this far after that rocky start. We'd come so close to losing this. But somehow, here we were.

I turned to Paul. "Back when we first met, I asked you if you thought the military was worth it. All the sacrifices, I mean."

"I remember that, yeah. And I seem to recall I said to ask me again after I'd retired."

"Mm-hmm. So, now that you have..." I raised my eyebrows. "Was it?"

He was quiet for a moment, looking out at the sea of uniforms as people congratulated my dad. Then he turned to me, and he smiled. "Considering it brought you into my life?" He kissed my cheek. "Absolutely."

"Aww. You're such a sap."

"That shouldn't be a surprise anymore."

"No, it's not." I wrapped my arm around his waist. "I wouldn't expect any less." I paused, then grinned. "You ever think your father-in-law would be younger than you?"

Paul laughed. "Eh, I got used to the idea about five minutes after I decided I wanted to marry you. And besides, I only have, what, two years on him?"

"Something like that." I rested my hands on his sides. "So where do we go from here?"

"Don't know. We get married. And then..." He shrugged. "See where the road takes us."

I pulled him closer, wrapping my arms around him. "I really, really like that idea."

"Do you?"

"Very much." I scanned our surroundings. All the people and uniforms and decorations. "Maybe not a crazy complicated wedding that requires a lot of planning, though."

"Oh thank God. The simpler the better." He smoothed my hair. "Maybe something on the beach?"

A memory flashed through my mind of the first time he'd told me he loved me, and goose bumps prickled my spine. "The beach sounds perfect." I lifted my chin and kissed him softly. "I'll let you plan everything. That should give you something to do in between adopting every critter that catches your eye."

"Oh, that reminds me. They brought in a really sweet collie yesterday, and—"

"*Paul.*"

"I'm kidding." He kissed the tip of my nose as he pulled me closer. "She was adopted five minutes after she came in the door."

"Not by you?"

"Not by me."

"Good."

He chuckled, then pressed his lips to mine. Barely breaking away, he whispered, "I love you, Sean."

"I love you too."

He kissed me again and let it linger. It didn't matter who saw us now. Anyone who didn't like two guys kissing could look away, but no one could tell us we couldn't do this. Tonight, we'd go home together like we did every night. In a few months, we'd be married. No one had any reason— or authority—to stop us now.

Dad and Paul would be telling sea stories for the rest of their lives, and there would be Navy-related decorations in both houses until the end of time, but as of today, they were both retired. From here on out, it was the civilian life.

For me and Paul, there was nothing standing in our way anymore. The only thing in front of us was an open road.

And all we had to do was drive.

The End.

DON'T MISS THE REST OF
ANCHOR POINT!

THE ANCHOR POINT SERIES

Afraid to Fly
Chief's Mess
Rank & File
Going Overboard
Once Burned
Wash Out
Sink or Swim

Find them all on my website:
http://www.gallagherwitt.com

ABOUT THE AUTHOR

L.A. Witt is a romance and suspense author who has at last given up the exciting nomadic lifestyle of the military spouse (read: her husband finally retired). She now resides in Pittsburgh, where the potholes are determined to eat her car and her cats are endlessly taunted by a disrespectful squirrel named Moose. In her spare time, she can be found painting in her art room or destroying her voice at a Pittsburgh Penguins game.

Website: www.gallagherwitt.com
    Email: gallagherwitt@gmail.com
    Twitter: @GallagherWitt

For more books by L.A. Witt, please visit

http://www.gallagherwitt.com

Romance * Suspense

Contemporary * Historical * Sports * Military

Titles Include

Rookie Mistake (written with Anna Zabo)

Scoreless Game (written with Anna Zabo)

The Hitman vs. Hitman Series (written with Cari Z)

The Bad Behavior Series (written with Cari Z)

The Gentlemen of the Emerald City Series

The Anchor Point Series

The Husband Gambit

Name From a Hat Trick

After December

Brick Walls

The Venetian and the Rum Runner

If The Seas Catch Fire

...and many, many more!